Nowhere to Hide

& OTHER STORIES
by Jim White

 FriesenPress

One Printers Way
Altona, MB R0G 0B0
Canada

www.friesenpress.com

ISBN
978-1-03-914714-0 (Hardcover)
978-1-03-914713-3 (Paperback)
978-1-03-914715-7 (eBook)

1. Fiction, Short Stories (Single Author)

Distributed to the trade by The Ingram Book Company

To Alister,

Live Long
Be Strong

Table of Contents

XXXXXXXXXX

>   <
  >   <
    >   <
      >   <
        >   O   O   <
          >   *   *   <
            >   <
              >   <
                >   %   <
                  >   <
                    >   <
                      >   <
  <
                        >   -----+-----   <
                          >   <
                            >   <
                              >   <
                                >   <
                                  >   <
                                    >   <
                                      >   <
                                        >>><<<

Dedicated to Judi

Purple Sunset

Dedicated to the martyrs

James was standing in the kitchen. Looking out the window over the back forty.

He was destined to die. Only he knew why. The question wasn't why. His name was "Tear in the Eye" but everyone called him James.

James was one hundred & five in dog years. Fifteen for a human being.

James had made his decision-- for the first time in his life-- he was in control.

He'd been planning this for awhile now. He had resolved this--- his final action--- would bring him release.

All his life he'd been pushing the rock uphill. Only to have it fall slowly, agonizingly, back down again & again & again.

James was determined to move on.

This world had been nothing but pain, hurt, deceit & lies for him. Oh how he'd tried to feel. But every time it just flew like feces right back in his face.

James withdrew his gaze & shuffled over to the sliding glass patio doors.

The sun was streaking through the grove of trees growing in the back. Sun not yet set. The western sky all ablaze. James stood gazing through the glass. He hesitated looking down the yard at the tree with the chosen branch, shrouded in glistening leaves. It stood out unique awash in the afternoon sun. No regrets he thought.

James slid the glass patio doors open. Stepping through into a calming prairie breeze. Pausing for reflection, he slipped down into his favorite patio chair. His life flashed in postcards through his head.

*****

It was absolute chaos.

James was two still in diapers. Crusty cloth, dry scratching his skin. To walk hurt. He was standing frozen to the cabin floor. Panic was flashing through his baby mind.

Liquor bottles, Lysol cans cluttering up the room. Dry food crusted on bowls piled in a sink. Sticky dirty linoleum floor. A wood stove glowing bright red in the middle of the room. Throwing sparks-- as if alive-- throughout the gloom. Plastic flowered curtains covering the kitchen window over the sink, bursting in flame. Blazing flaming dancing figures in a greasy black reflection. Demons on display deep in a mirror

James' father was passed out on an old smelly couch. His mother screaming. James was screaming. His older brother rushing over to James. Wrapping James up & throwing him outside. Through the door into the snow.

Mother & brother running all over the place, screaming, yelling, crying, pushing, pulling, piercing sounds, dogs barking. His mother insane. His seven-year-old brother in despair.

Alone, James was standing all alone in the snow. A dreadful fear weeping through his baby bones. His little baby feet covered in oversize rubber boots. A grown up parka wrapped around his tiny shoulders. Standing there by himself in the snow, crying. Sobbing, crying so hard… making himself sick- scared.

His mother running all over the place.

'Wake up''wake up,' Mother screaming in the cabin, at a drunken father on the smoldering couch. Puffs of smoke raising like signals from a pipe.

His Mother was hysterical. The couch now bursting in flames. His father was comatose with drink. She couldn't move him. He was too heavy for her & she was too drunk.

'Leave him, leave him' his brother screamed.

The smoke was surfing from the house in waves. Baby James was afraid. He wanted his Mother so he started to go back in, sniffling furiously. Another scream, His mother-- looking into the kitchen window flickering in flames-- saw baby James walking toward the burning cabin. A burning baby ghost.

She exploded hysterically,

'Stop!'

His brother burst from the house running through sooty snow scooping Baby James up. Throwing him---back further--- into an ash strewn snowy mound. Baby James cried on & never stopped.

+++++

James leaned back on the two legs of his wooden patio chair. Balancing precariously, looking up to the sky. Bare toes rocking the chair too & fro.

+++++

James found out later that his father died in the fire. That really didn't mean much to him then or now. . . really.

The family had been living in a cabin, more like a shack. On the edge of a reserve in Northern Alberta. It had been a tinderbox just waiting for a disaster. Sure enough it happened. It wasn't that unheard of. Considering how cold it got in the winter.

The cabin was a rickety structure with a door that stuck when it closed. A creaky linoleum floor, sticky & dirty. An old porcelain kitchen sink stuffed full of dishes. Beds in the back. Peering through hanging cheap blankets serving as curtains. Giving some privacy for modesty. Outhouse at the end of the path, outback.

Wood stove smack dab in the middle of the cabin floor. Centerpiece for heating & cooking.

One winter, their friend Teegum burnt his new house down.

Teegum got a new house on the other side of the reserve. Beautiful place, two tiered, paneled walls, linoleum floor. Big wide picture windows, looking out into the forest. Off private in the woods. Good location everyone thought. Porcelain toilet that flushed.

Well Teegum-- who was of ancient Dene lineage-- still yearned to live off the land. So he saw all this wood around & figured out how to use it. He figured if he punched out the bay window over the kitchen sink he could cut down a tree & trim it. Push it right through the open window into his potbellied stove sitting in the living room.

So Teegum chopped down a tall birch tree & trimmed it up. He then proceeded to feed it in through his cabins' kitchen window. Right into the waiting potbellied stove. Easier then chopping wood all his friends said. Teegum thought he was pretty smart until his new house burnt down.

The log burned down & fell out of the potbellied stove while the family were all sleeping. The family all—eight-- lucky to get out alive. Plus a couple guys sleeping over dead drunk, survived. Teegum was fortunate he had two sets of twins. Twins tend to look out for one another. When one wakes it disturbs the other. Even though they were only three & five years old their screams managed to wake the house.

Teegum ended up-- after his new house burnt down--back in his old wooden shack just down from James' family. The band wasn't gonna give

Teegum another new home. So Teegum basically moved back to where he had been living before. His name was placed back at the bottom of the accommodation list in the band office.

James' father talked about that story often when he got drunk.

'At least I ain't as stupid as Teegum. He burnt his house down because he was stupid.' He'd say when Teegum wasn't in the room.

But when Teegum was over for drinks James' father was totally supportive. Heartily agreeing it wasn't much of a place anyways & fuck the white man for making us live like this.

James' father—unfortunately-- wasn't as fortunate as his friend Teegum. James' father died obliterated on booze & Lysol in a fire which was inevitable. He wasn't coming out alive. His life had been over many moons ago. A victim of imposed desperation.

The reserve was the poster child for extreme absolute abject poverty to the outside world.

The community was decrepit. Wallowing in its own moral decay & pain--- lamenting a way of life long gone--- prepared only to survive one day at a time.

Death by fire was---for some---seen as a comfortable convenience.

+++++

James settled the chair down on all fours & stood up. Laying his elbows on the deck's wooden rail. Looking out over the backyard of the foster house. It was a beautiful sunny afternoon. Endless blue prairie sky with its sense of forever. Sun settling down—in the west-- its day almost done. Waves of infinite solitude flowing over him.

It was perfect, he'd wait until the sun was going down a bit more. Take his walk slowly to the hanging tree. It'd be like a picture. A bright red prairie sunset would be his last view. That, would be his final act.

James straightened up gazing down the yard. It was a typical Alberta acreage he was looking at. Long beautifully manicured lawn. The perfume of it nestled around him. A grove of trees, leafy green, bordering the back yard. Past that the prairie.

James looked around the patio deck. A good place for barbeques when it wasn't snowing he thought. He had been comfortable here. That wasn't the thing.

He turned his gaze back down the yard.

It would be a beautiful walk he thought. Christ in transit with his cross. Cept James'd be carrying rope over his shoulder.

+++++

After the fire James didn't really recall much. A river of eyes & faces came & went through his life. James finally settling in a foster home. No more mother, no more brother. He wasn't on the reserve anymore, he knew that. But where he was he wasn't quite sure.

James remembered smelling clean, no more diapers. Clean water, clean bed, clean curtains, clean floors, clean rugs, clean glasses, clean plates, clean socks, clean pants, clean hands, clean face, clean ears, clean feet, clean bum, clean dinky, clean food.

He guessed he'd never really been clean before. All around him were very serious that it was very important to be clean.

James' dad mentioned as an afterthought. That he had died in the fire. James didn't know what happened to his brother. His mother came & went, He didn't understand. He did like the cartoons on the T.V. every Saturday morning.

Foster parents hugging him, all the time. Telling him what a good boy he was. How much they loved him. How important he was. How handsome he was. What a good little soldier he was.

It all meant nothing really to James. He was just a little boy, trying to be safe. But he wasn't safe at all. He screamed in the night. Couldn't sleep in the dark. Was scared of his shadow. He didn't know who he was, He didn't know if everything was going to change again tomorrow. He was just a scared little boy.

Why didn't these people know that? Why did they fuss over him so, James thought.

He just wanted his mommy & his big brother. Where were they? Why had they left him here. He just wanted to hear their voices.

+++++

James started to stretch out standing on the deck, arm raised, shading his eyes from the setting sun--- sat back down—this time in the foster dad Ron's special chair. Ron enjoyed his comfort. A deep cushy cushioned seat. James started to relax.

It all made him so mad. Why hadn't anyone just told him what was going on?

+++++

One day it all changed. A car came & his mother took him from the foster home. She picked him up in her arms. Smelling of smoke & put him in the backseat of a yellow cab. She told the driver where to go--- it was over. He was back with his mother.

But what did he know? James was four.

+++++

James settled back in the comfortable cushy chair on the deck. Embracing the warmth of the sun on his face. He stared directly into the scattered rays. He was going to be okay. He felt good.

+++++

James' mother lived in town now.

James never got a chance to say goodbye to those people at the foster home. He did faintly remember some tears being shed & an old lady sniffling. It was almost like a kidnapping.

James' mother told him she missed him & loved him & that they were going to be a family. Away they went in the yellow cab. He on his mother's lap.

The drive was a mist. James could remember watching all the lampposts & trees zooming by. Elbows on the back window. Feet still in mothers lap. The yellow cab finally stopped. When they got out Mother was holding his hand. She took him up a flight of stairs & there at the top-- was his big brother.

This was a happy time. Just his mother, big brother & James. It was a one-bedroom apartment walk up. Kitchen, living room, porcelain toilet. James & his brother slept on a bed in the bedroom. His mother slept on the couch in the living room.

They had a T.V. & even some toys. His brother had a hockey stick. James had a ball. His brother would take shots & James made the saves playing in their room.

Mother always made supper & they had food for breakfast, treats & juice.

They would watch T.V. together at night. Mother would tuck him into bed. Lie with him until he went to sleep. When he woke up in the middle of the night he'd cry out. Mother would come in & rub his head. Tell him,

'it's okay honey, its okay,' her soft breath whispering in his ear.

Why oh why couldn't that have gone on forever. Why did anything have to change--- why don't things just stay the same he thought.

But they don't.

+++++

James stood up out of his cushy seat, stretching his legs. He was almost getting sleepy. The wind was picking up. Soft wind swirling the long black hair off his face.

He breathed deep, deep & hard, again & again. Filling his lungs, facing, challenging the wind. Sucking it up harder & harder. He sat back down squishing into the cushioned seat. The wind wound through him, pushing, pulling, plying, crying.

Entreating . . .

+++++

One night after James had just gone to bed—his life changed again. Mother was up having tea watching T.V. James was almost asleep when he heard a knock on the door.

'Ray 'he heard his mother exclaim.

It was his mothers' cousin Ray from the res.

Cousin Ray needed a place to stay. James heard his mother fatally say, 'Ok, but just for tonight.'

Things started to go bad after that.

The drinking started up that night. Drinking, smoking, always smoke, always loud voices. Broken bottles, cigarettes in overflowing ashtrays, needles on the floor, pipes on the couch. More & more liquor bottles & smoke--- always smoke.

The people-- especially the men-- arguing, laughing, pushing, shoving. His mother laughing, screaming, yelling, breathing, dancing. The music loud--- always loud.

James wasn't safe anymore. It was a party every night. He & his brother scared in bed huddled together.

Landlord banging on the door every night

'Shut up in there,' the landlord shouts & is duly ignored. One night it got especially heated.

'Shut up or I'll call the police,' the landlord screamed through the door.,

'Fuck you,' yells back one of the drunk guests,

'Go ahead you fuck.' shouts back another partying reprobate,

Mother crying hysterically,

'Shut up shut up, shut the hell up, turn down the music--- get the hell out,'

Mother yelling being totally ignored.

The party goers were too far gone to leave. Refusing to tone down their revelry the landlord eventually brought the cops. Mother pleading with the landlord she'll change. Pushing the partiers out. The cops telling everyone to leave or they'll all be arrested. One of the party goers taking a swing at the police. Cops handcuffing the bum & threatening to take in James' mother.

James & his brother standing at the door to their room. Both their pajama bottoms wet with fear. James watching the whole scene like a horror movie.

The cops never arrested Mother. But they gave her a stern warning. Mothers head nodding up & down like a puppet on a string. After that night the party kept on going, it never stopped. It was just more of the same. Just a little quieter. A lot more drugs & a little less booze. Sometimes the party would take a small break to accommodate physical recovery.

He & his brother were looking after themselves now. There never seemed to be enough food, everything was always dirty. The sink always had dirty dishes. Ashtrays were always full of butts. Rug caked in mud & potato chips. The apartment smelled like, urine, stale booze, cigarette butts & sour smoke.

+++++

James could never forget that smell. Relaxing in his cushy patio chair breathing in the west wind it all came back. Everything started to swirl. James got up from his chair & laid down on his back on the deck. Looking up at nothing. Not wanting to be part of this life anymore. He couldn't take that smell. That sickly ugly, putrid smell.

+++++

Things got worse for James & his brother. Eating whatever they could. They would lie in bed awake. Little boy arms wrapped around each other trying to be tough.

Terrified, never knowing what will come.

One night as they lay in bed listening. A man beast crashed through their bedroom door.

'Get out of there,' mother screamed rushing in right behind him.

'What the hell,' slurred back. The man beast talks.

Mother staggering in. Grabbing this shadowy apparition that looked like a Sasquatch. Pushing it from the room. Out the door & pulling it back into the bathroom. Slamming the bedroom door as she left. James & his brother-- shivering clutched together--laying in fear in the darkness that followed.

Soon after that the party was over. The lady in apt 202 right across the hall finally phoned child protection services. Why should this Mother, she thought, get to keep her kids when she herself was stuck here living alone. Her own kids long gone lost to the system.

The Social Workers came & took James away. He didn't know where his mother was. What happened to his brother? He couldn't understand what was going on. It appeared no one did.

James was seven.

*****

Once again, a wall of clean descended on him. But this time it came with a price.

James was placed in another foster home. Where there were a lot of other kids. They all seemed to be bigger than him. He didn't know any of them & they all scared him. All he could do was cry. When they were all by themselves in the basement they made fun of him-- so he would fight-- kicking, punching, biting, screaming. Then the one--who was called Father-- would come down the stairs. You could hear his footsteps coming closer & closer. They'd all shut up in total innocence when Father appeared. Father'd look directly at James-- who was always to blame-- & pick him up like a rag doll. Hurting him—dragging James back upstairs. Throwing James into a tiny room all by himself. Boy was James ever scared.

James'd lie there, on a small cot. Curl his knees up to his chin, whimper, sniffle. Hiding his head in his hands. Trying to make himself invisible.

-- Alone --

+++++

James turned on to his side on the deck. He started to curl into a baby ball. Pulling his legs up to his chin. Feeling the loneliness. He wanted to cry for his mother & brother. But only dry determined tears emerged. He squeezed himself harder knowing he was way beyond rage.

+++++

James hated that foster home. They all had to eat together at a big table & he was always doing something wrong. Do this don't do that.

'Close your mouth when you eat, what are you a savage,' the fat foster mother would say.

'Hold your fork like a civilized person. Don't talk with your mouth full you look like a gorilla. Stop your crying,'

James would lash out hitting his foster sister for no reason. James would look around everyone would be watching sneering at him. He didn't know what to do.

' You evil boy,' the fat foster mother would explode.

'Now see what you've done, you've made your sister cry. Go on, get up to your room if you can't behave,' the fat foster mother would snarl.

The one they called Father would get off his chair & come for James terrifying the young boy. He'd grab James by the ear & drag him to his room.

Everyone always yelling at James for something,

'What are you stupid,'

'What are you lazy,'

'Why can't you do the simplest of things.'

James could never do anything right.

He'd started school now. They would all walk to school together. Everyone making fun of James. How he walked, how he talked, mushing snow in his face. Throwing mud at his head, calling him Cochise. Not letting him play in their games because he was too small, too stupid, too everything.

He was always alone, always afraid, never felt safe. He wanted his mommy, his brother. Why had they left him in this horrible place?

Why did everyone hate him?

+++++

James relaxed his grip on himself. He picked himself up off the patio deck. The wind, the sky, eternity awaited him. He was moving on. He was going to be alright. His plan was still intact. A feint smile of knowing & courage crossed his lips.

James slid back the patio doors. He went into the kitchen & down the hall to his room. He retrieved the hemp rope from where he'd hidden it behind his clothes in the closet. He checked to make sure the note he'd already written, was on his bed--- laying up against the pillow--- where they'd find it.

He looked around one last time.

I was supposed to be happy here James thought. Safe, comfortable, cared for. They tried they really did.

The foster parents were good people. it wasn't their fault, it's me. I'm the problem. I've just been through too much. I need to be in control. I just can't trust what's gonna happen next.

Here he had all the fixings needed to settle in, settle down, become part of a family. Go to school come home to a nice comfortable middle-class existence with all the amenities. Fridge full of food, clean clothes, T.V., computer in his own room. People open to caring about him. Open to listening, trying to coax his feelings out of him--- actually prepared to give a damn.

But it wasn't enough, wasn't even close to tell you the truth, James said in his head. I've had enough of this life. My decision was made long before I walked through their door. As far as I'm concerned, my destiny has only one means of playing out. The only way I can have control-- to finally be free-- is to hang myself from a tree.

James closed the door to his room. Made his way back through the kitchen. He opened the sliding patio doors without hesitation. Stepping through them making sure they were shut tight behind him. Outside, back on the deck, James snugged the rope over his shoulder. He started his journey to the tree to end his life.

+++++

His mother did finally come & get him after two years in that wretched foster home. It was totally unexpected & probably had as much to do, with his inability to fit in & settle down, as with her sincerely wanting him back.

James was nine.

This time she had a man with her. James was supposed to call him 'Dad'. That never rolled off his tongue too well, but he tried.

James was a very nervous nine-year-old. Mother & 'Dad' lived in town. In a needing repair falling down ghetto house in the north east end of the city. Evidently the pair weren't particularly welcome on the reserve.

His mother tried to say all the right things, but there was a distance now. James felt like an intruder--- rather than a son. He wasn't her little boy anymore. That was obvious. He'd totally missed out on that.

One good thing was his big brother was there. But even that had changed. His brother was an old man of fourteen & he really didn't have a lot of time for James. His brother was an 'angry young man'. He was into that lifestyle where his friends took up all his time. When his brother was at home it was always a fight. His brother yelling at his mother. 'Dad' stepping in,

'You can't talk to your mother like that,'

'Who the fuck are you to tell me what I can & cannot do,' his brother would scream back like a hyena.

Then it would get physical. 'Dad' & his brother swinging at each other. His brother always got the worst of it. His 'Dad' was fucking tough. It always ending with his brother storming out threatening never to return. 'Dad' storming after him,

'Good riddance,' 'Dad' yelling. His brother banging shut the rickety-- half falling off-- screened front door, always almost breaking it, storming off.

'Fuck you,' his brother yelling back over his shoulder.

Mother yelling, screaming, crying, making no sense. Just being a blubbering mess.

James could never figure out where his mother's allegiance lay. To 'Dad' or his brother. Unfortunately, by this time his mother was so beaten down by life that she was just treading water. Like a lazy leaf in a hurricane.

During the fights James would watch for awhile. Then just disappear to his room. Close the door & curl up on his bed with the pillows over his head. Covering his ears.

There was some semblance of sanity. 'Dad' had a steady job. James didn't know what he did. He always came home tired from work complaining about everything,

'Jesus christ I work too hard to take that much shit from the boss,' he'd say sitting down at the waiting dinner table.

Mother would make sure there was a cooked supper waiting when 'Dad' got home. A bottle of beer for him cold from the fridge.

Mother always arranged James & his brother had their supper before 'Dad' sat down. His brother didn't want anything to do with 'Dad'. He would eat & go hang out with his disturbed friends. He'd stay out until 'Dad' either passed out or went to bed.

During 'Dad's' dinner friends & relatives would start dropping in.

Every night was a party. Lots of booze, loud music. James was always an intrusion. He was always sent to his room. He was never allowed to join in anything. James was an albatross around their stumbling necks.

It got more & more that Mother & 'Dad' just didn't want James around. She would feed him & get him off to school. Occasionally wash his clothes. Otherwise James was better off to be out of sight out of mind.

When James did ask for something, like a glass of milk or money to go to the store, 'Dad' always said,

'No,' it seemed to make 'Dad' mad whenever James asked him for anything.

'Do you know how hard it is to feed & clothe a family without you standing there with your goddamn hand out, get to your room,' Dad'd say & slap James on the back of the head.

As James got older the slaps got harder.

Eventually the slap on the head became a physical attack. Mother started joining in. James became the punching bag for all their frustration, for all their fear, for all their pain, for all their drunkenness, for all their shame.

Everything James did merited a smack, a hit, a push, a bang his head against the wall, a punch in the stomach, a whack over the back with whatever was handy & when they got drunk it got worse.

James was alone. His brother was never around & when he was he'd get into his own war with 'Dad' & 'Mom' (as they liked to be called now). James had no concept as to what it was like to live this life with any hope.

Finally, after one particularly violent attack. 'Dad' & 'Mom' had taken turns smacking James around during a drunken orgy on a Saturday night.

That Monday--- at school--- one of his teachers noticed the tell all--- puffy purple--- beneath his eyes.

She asked what had happened & James just said,

'Nothing'.

She asked, 'Did someone do this to you,'

And James just said, 'I don't know.'

James was scared. He didn't know what to do. So the Social Worker was called. She appeared dressed in a tight blue skirt & a light brown cashmere sweater tight to her form, highlighting her breasts. She took James aside to a private room. She asked James what happened & he just started to cry. He couldn't stop. He couldn't help himself. He was a boy becoming a man, much too soon.

James was twelve.

+++++

It was seventy-three steps—James had counted it out-- from the patio to the hanging tree. James taking each step gently feeling his bare feet in the soft green grass. He was timing his hanging with the distant setting sun. The sun was doing its part. Sinking lower in the distance. Setting ablaze the golden prairie fields. James had never felt so alive. He'd never felt so sure of himself. He'd never felt so free-- so in control.

+++++

The Social Worker sat & watched James cry. She knew there was some-thing terribly wrong going on. She told him he wasn't going home he was going with her. James knew he was looking at another foster home. Now he was thinking like a man. He' d been beaten up enough for an army of kids. For his own survival James knew anything would be better than to go home to,

'Dad' & 'Mom'. So, he went along with the Social Worker without a fuss. Never to see Mother, ' Dad '& brother again.

James was entering his teens. Aging at an accelerated pace.

James bounced from foster home to foster home. Like a salmon swim-ming upstream. He was maturing—prematurely. His level of tolerance for those around him, was growing less & less. The more everyone around tried to comfort, help & understand him, the more he withdrew.

What could they know? How could they even in a million years grasp any understanding of what was going on in his head. James knew he was lost. He felt like an old reprobate. Awash on the street of some decrepit city. Making his way-- day to day—through this life.

Everyone wanted to help, kiss his life better. But no one seemed to know their right from their left. James just wanted to be left alone.

'Leave me alone' James would say. As he ran away from another foster home.

Never to nowhere in particular. The store at the corner. Walking along-side the side of the road. He'd always be found & placed somewhere else.

James was embracing the loneliness he felt inside himself.

As James grew older his anger started to emerge. A rose blooms-- then withers. Then blooms again & again over the years finally falling off the branch. Blown away by a soft summer breeze.

James had episodes of pure hate. Anything or anyone that got in his path was the recipient of his wrath. He inflicted much pain on whatever came within his domain. He could kill he felt it inside of himself. There were times he came damn close to completing the deed. Fortunately, others had been there to pull him off.

+++++

James came within view of the chair he had planted—an old one from the kitchen-- nestled under the special tree. He shuffled glided floated closer. He would often sit on his chair there watching the sunset. . . dreaming his dreams. A melancholy misted through his mind as he thought back. Not because he was getting tired but because he was getting old.

The rope, slung on his shoulder—like a friendly monkey. Soon to be put to use. James in control of his own destiny.

The air was cooling. The sun started to turn red. Suspended against the sky like an ethereal apparition. Silent, drawing James, a moth to a flame. Into the unknown. James was determined. Pulled along by a soft gentle magnetic current. Moving along as if on a calm stream. Not long now.

+++++

The system had tried everything with James. But he was not to be understood. They didn't see James was already leaving this temporal plain. His rage of fear-- emboldened from within-- was not to be tampered with. Policemen, probation officers, lawyers, judges, doctors, hospitals, group homes, foster homes, social workers, youth workers, counselors, teachers, nurses, psychologists, psychiatrists, do-gooders, self righteous holy rollers, healers, you name it they had crossed James' path. All to no avail.

James' years had started young & were ending-- much to quickly-- old. James was gradually coming to realize that his lot in life-- was to move on.

A loner, quiet, James never fit in anywhere. He was found in a fetal position in the washroom at school soaked in his own urine one time.

'Why, why,' they asked. Only he knew.

It was because he was scared James said in his head. Scared of his teachers, of his classmates, of his new foster home, of walking to & from school, of sitting in a class, of the sun coming up, of the sun going down. The list went on & on. James sat silent to their inquiries. Tears rolling down his eyes.

James was fourteen when his rage reached culmination. James severely beat up a friend. They were sharing a chocolate bar. His friend had ended up in the hospital. James ended up with his first ride in a police car.

Why, why did he do it? They all asked James the same question. He did it because he felt like it & he could, James answering silently in his head.

They wouldn't want to hear that James enjoyed seeing the fear in his friend's eyes. His friend was terrorized when he realized James wasn't going to stop hitting him. Even though, James had him down on the ground, layed out half dead totally defenseless.

Now it was serious. Something had to be done. James was out of control & no one knew what to do. So, the powers that be went to court & placed James in secure treatment.

It was supposed to be therapeutic but was really just juvie jail. James didn't hate it there, he didn't like it, he didn't care.

James did some drugs with the kids in the treatment yard. He had a sexual experience with a teenage girl who in her own way was as messed up as him. It was a disaster. James exploded in her hand, she mocked him. One more log to add to the fire.

Finally, they let James out after a year in secure treatment. James was fifteen. They had done all they could do. James was attending school & there hadn't been any issues for six months now. It appeared in their professional opinion that James would be safe back in the community.

It was in secure treatment that James learned of his ancient lineage & spiritual heritage. Elders would come in to the center sharing their knowledge. James finally finding a home for his salvation. The Elders gave James his name 'Tear in the Eye' in a ceremony that made James feel special for the first time in his life.

It helped James make his final decision easier.

&&&&&

A nice old couple who owned a lovely acreage on the edge of a small northern Alberta town agreed to take James in, on a trial basis. It was just the chance James had been waiting for.

It was perfect.

James had been in the foster home about six months before he started planning his suicide in earnest. He was expected to attend school. Which he did, desperately keeping to himself. Never talking to anyone. Not even the teacher if he could avoid it.

He'd take the school bus home. Always arriving before the foster parents, who worked during the day. They'd leave the back door open. James would go in & make himself a sandwich. Sometimes going to his room to watch T.V. Sometimes though he'd walk with his sandwich down to the tree he had singled out to be his hanging tree. He'd sit down in the kitchen chair he'd dragged down there & stare out across the fields. Watching the sunset.

+++++

James was almost there. Each step now brought him closer to the brink. He no longer felt his feet touching the soft green grass. He commenced to a virtual mist an aura solely his own. Anchored only by this persistent mortality. A withering umbilical cord ready to break.

James needed to exit this existence. In choosing this he was confirming his being. Something can't be gone if it has never been. He'd always been alone. As if he was never there. He had been here-- he had been alive. What happened to James must happen no more.

The setting sun shone into the grove of trees. His chair waiting resolutely for his presence. In the distant horizon the shadows of twilight were fluttering shadows of black over the prairie fields. James, moving like an old warrior, reaching out from a never ending quick sanded abyss. Finally, grabbing onto the chair, steadying himself, breathing deep like an old man. Leaning over catching a few final breaths. Straightening up. He was there.

James stepped up one foot at a time being careful he didn't lose his balance. The last thing he wanted to do was fall. Hit his head. If they found him like that, he'd have plenty of explaining to do. He smiled his final smile to himself as he made his last step up.

James solidly balanced himself up on the chair. Standing with his legs well apart. Now he had to throw the rope over the low-- hanging branch. He tossed it over twice just like he had practiced. This time though he threw it over a third time. He knew this would make it ok for his weight— which wasn't much. He needed to be sure the rope would hold him & the branch wouldn't break. Once done James pulled down on the rope making sure it was tight to the limb. He then without hesitation placed the noose around his neck.

The sun was quietly setting as all of this was going on. Oh my gracious the apparition tearfully thought. Here's another one dying way to young.

James was standing stable-- staring into the spirit world. Looking into the sad sun which appeared to be french kissing the horizon. The mourning apparition sent out beckoning rays-- a reddish-purple glaze surfing on a rainbow-- waves of wonder embracing James.

Suddenly, at the last split second, a bright purple blast blazed a path.

James stepped off the chair. He was free. Free at last. A final speckle of twinkle reflecting in his deep dark determined gaze.

+++++

The older foster parents got home at their regular time that night. Just as the sun was setting. They always worried about James. Sometimes he just seemed so sad. Mother got out of the truck walking up the cobblestone path to the front door. Ron stayed behind to lock up the Ford. Mother getting out her keys slowly turning the handle. Calling James' name as she stuck her head inside the door. More of a reflex than anything else.

'James,' she yelled again, taking off her shoes. Always hoping for a response.

Right off Mother knew there was something wrong-- it was so silent. She listened for rustling in the kitchen, nothing. James' TV was usually on when they got home. Its silence worried her. She turned to the open door & called out,

'Ron, Ron come on now, I think something's wrong,'

Ron heard Mothers' voice, It was up a pitch from her normal concerned communication. He picked up the pace. Putting off pausing to enjoy the spectacular sunset & hustled up to the house where Mother was waiting.

Mother gestured him immediately in. Ron hesitantly stepping through the door, standing on the landing inside. They both felt it at once. The stillness. Both worried & a little scared. They went to the kitchen & found it undisturbed. Mother immediately noticed James hadn't made himself a sandwich. He always made himself a sandwich after school. Usually just peanut butter & jam, just enough to get him through to dinner. Today there were no dirty knifes, no wayward lids from jars, no dishes waiting in the sink.

'Ron, what's going on?', Mother inquired her voice on the edge of frantic.

'I'm sure it's nothing,' Ron replied trying to soothe her the way husbands do with women they've been with for over thirty years. A touch of patronizing tinged with a sense of reality that something did feel not quite right.

They both moved nervously down the hall to James' room. They walked cautiously as if something was going to jump out at them at any moment. Mother eased open the door to James' room.

The room was empty. Everything was in its place, which piqued her concern. James was a teen-age boy his room was always messy or at least always looked well used. Even his bed was surprisingly well made. The only thing out of place was a piece of paper resting on the pillow.

It immediately caught Mothers' eye. She went over & picked it up pulling it up to her face.

Ron in the doorway-- standing concerned-- watched as the piece of paper slipped out of Mothers' hand & fell to the floor.

Ron bent over & retrieved the piece of paper off the small throw carpet beside the bed. Meant to keep James' bare feet warm when he got up in the morning. Reading James' note brought a pause to Ron's pragmatic thought pattern.

'Please forgive me. Forgive yourselves. My life my choice. Tear in the Eye.'

Ron read.

'Who the christ is Tear in the Eye,' Ron erupted.

'It's what he calls himself.' Mother sadly replied.

'Has he run away. What the hell does this mean,' Ron was getting mad.

'Ron I'm scared he's done something to himself. He was always so sad,'

'Well let's look around. You phone the social worker & I'll check the backyard.' Ron said taking the take charge tone which was familiar between the two of them.

Ron opened up the patio doors. A flash of sunset was still setting in the western sky. Ron immediately saw James' body—silhouetted-- hanging still. Silent in the trees.

Ron couldn't believe his tear swelled eyes. He knew James was only fifteen but the corpse he cut down from the tree was that of an old man.

The End

Jack the Ripper

Part One

Eric Chalmerston was 'Jack the Ripper'. Eric had been an orderly at the Royal London Hospital. Located in Whitechapel, a decrepit district in the east end of London.

Eric's parents were Irish. They moved to London fleeing the Irish potato famine of the 1840's. A genocidal situation totally avoidable. If not for English greed & indifference.

Dad was 20, Mom 18. Eric 2, at the time of their re-location.

The family settled by the docks in Whitechapel. The area of London known for its stench of poverty, deprivation, drunkenness & death. Breeding a lifestyle & manner of surviving which bred rage & revolution.

Eric's Dad got on at one of the tanneries. Eric's Mom died in child birth two years after they arrived. Eric's baby sister was born dead. Leaving just young Eric n Dad.

+++++

Dad did his best but he had to work hard so he was never around. Eric became a street waif. There was no school, for the likes of him. Hanging about in the misery & the pain all alone. He never had any friends. His imagination, in its formative stage, left alone to explore the horror of Whitechapel.

He was alone—also-- because he was Irish. The other kids' parents didn't approve of the scum sucking Irish moving over from the island & taking their jobs. Maybe this had something to do with fermenting rage, during his formative years.

Who knows?

Dad was mean when he was around. He didn't spare the lash & Eric was the sort who had trouble following Dad's regulations. Dad insisted Eric make his meals at night & tea in the morning. Eric resented this. The older he got the more Eric found it demeaning. Many a night Eric spent in total agony, attempting to sleep bruised & battered for talking back. Dad was a stern warrior with a bad temper & a taste for the drink.

Dad was a fierce Irish Nationalist & strongly anti English. This got him in many a fight. Dad's main activity, when he wasn't at home or at work or reading about revolution, was pounding the black at the Cock & Bull just down the street.

It never occurred to Dad that his ranting & raving in the heart of English enemy territory would be met with such rage. Dad thought all men equal & he had as much right to say what he thought as any man.

That got his ass kicked on many a night.

Eric would watch from the 2nd floor window of the flat he & Dad shared. Dad's mates from the pub dragging a battered screaming drunken

Dad home. Dad's head bouncing off the cobblestone like a boxer getting hit in the nose.

One night Dad brought home a copy of 'The Communist Manifesto'. It was a gift from a friend at the pub. The workers of the world unite message struck a chord in Dad's thinking. This kept Dad home for awhile as he would try reading it. Which was with great difficulty as he had no formal schooling. Eric & Dad learning to read together quarreling incessantly.

Dad would read it out loud to Eric who would sit on a stool beside his chair. Eric repeating every word. Dad going on & on about how things in this life just weren't fair. What was really needed was a revolution. So the men who worked for a living could get what was theirs-- fair & square.

It stirred up a fire in Eric's blood. Listening to Dad get madder & madder about how unfair it all was. Dad espoused--the drunker he got-- the best action was to kill all the English. Eric soaked it up like a sponge.

Dad used to have rousing get togethers in the front room. The enraged working class engaging in heated debate about starting a revolution. Blokes yelling, screaming at each other, falling down drunk, pissing their pants, passing out naked. Eric watching it all through a hole in the floor.

In the morning the revolutionary reprobates waking up sprawled about the flat as Eric was coming down the stairs for breakfast. Shaking their heads not knowing where the 'fuck' they were. Burping up last nights gin. Farting out big waves of foul-smelling air. Pants down around their knees. People were pigs, Eric grew to believe. Their revolution just drunken puke.

Finally the drink, head butts at the bar & fumes from the tannery caught up to Dad. He died. Keeled over at home eating a dinner of eel & cauliflower at the kitchen table. Right in front of Eric. Dad slumped down face first into the eel, which squeezed off the plate onto the floor as if it were still alive. Eric picked it up-- intending to eat it-- but he got distracted by the look in Dad's eyes.

*****

Eric was on his own, he was 16.

He was a smart ass, able to survive on wit & bluntness. He was clever, but he didn't let anyone know it.

After Dad died Eric was left without a home. He took to the streets to stay alive. Eric was smart & the smartest thing he knew was if you stayed away from the drink you could make a go of it.

Eric gained a sober, objective perspective, on the depraved hideous surroundings he was living amongst.

Ofttimes Eric thought he was the only sober person in Whitechapel.

Over the next few years Eric took jobs at the tanneries, slaughterhouse, longshoring, waiting tables, selling licorice sticks. Eventually Eric got a break--- literally.

One night, Eric was on his way home. He had spent the last few hours, trying to coax ten schillings, out of a stingy dock employer for work Eric had done two days previous. Eric was walking along High Street distracted. Worrying about the money he didn't get & what he was going to do about his rent. He didn't sense a two-horse carriage barreling down out of control right behind him.

The carriage driver-- in a hurry to get the passenger inside to his destination-- had flicked the balls of old temperamental Bess intentionally with his whip. That drove the older horse mad & she reared up pulling the other carriage horse-- who was just six months from the plow-- along with her. They took off along the cobblestones as if they had been hit by lightning. Thundering hooves out of control-- the frantic driver screaming sexually implicit obscenities fearing for his & his passengers' life.

Unfortunately for Eric he had his back to all of this. He was more intent on the money which he didn't get. He needed those schillings to pay his Jewish landlord & get some bread & butter. Maybe even an eel.

At the last moment—too late-- Eric heard the clickety-clack-- more like a gatling gun now-- closing in behind him. He turned to look just as the enraged horses plowed right through him entangling him under the horse's hooves. Tossing Eric aside like a rag doll. The driver & terrified passenger inside the carriage not even aware-- at the time-- that they had hit Eric. The carriage continued its chaotic course, careening off down the street. Appearing to pay the destruction-- it had just wrought-- no heed.

Eric was a mess. He looked dead. Tangled up something terrible. Legs splayed like a drunken whore. Semi-conscious, screaming in excruciating pain. Eric lay there alone on the cobblestones watching the drooping light on the lamppost slowly flicker & then go out.

Eric didn't find out till later how he ended up in the hospital. Screaming in agony was an oft heard melody on these Whitechapel streets of pain. Usually after such occurrences—as Eric had endured--- one is left lying in agony until graced with death. Left to die on your own. Brutal, harsh, as if one's life was no better than the rats crawling through the open sewage.

Unfortunately, though, Eric was blessed. The anxious passenger of the cab who did truly believe in liberty & equality-- as long as it meant he didn't have to be in the company of any common working man—was late for his dinner date. He had the groom whip the horses to haste. Causing the whole uproar. He had heard the sounds of Eric's screams -- a direct result of his impatience—in the distance. Looking back out the curtained carriage window he saw a distorted Eric laying askew on the cobble-stone road.

In his best libertarian manner he had the driver stop the carriage at The Royal London Hospital. It was on his way to his fancy dress up dinner-- anyways. He directed his driver to go to the front desk. Report the carnage & suggest they might send down someone to assist, the crumpled body laying by the side of the road. Tell them he will pay any costs incurred of course.

The enlightened gentleman then proceeded to the dinner party at an even faster pace then before because now he really was late. That night he was the talk of the festivities. He shared his story over dinner. Taking great pains to acclaim himself as having saved some poor fella's life he'd run over with his cab. At the risk of being late to this delightful soiree he added. All the ladies gasped at his courage for getting involved & all the men responded,

'Well done chap'.

Eric of course was sprawled out mostly dead-- from loss of blood & pain-- by the time the ambulance cart got to where he was lying. He looked like a broken-up corpse. He did come momentarily back to life when they picked him up-- he was always to remember that orgasmic feeling of explosive pain—but he immediately passed out again. By the time he got to the hospital he might as well have bin. dead. But a young surgeon saw him coming through the door & took it upon himself to save this poor fella's life.

Unfortunately –for future ladies of Whitechapel & London-- the young surgeon-- who was named Dr. Mark—was successful.

Dr. Mark prided himself on being on the cutting edge for implementing & developing new medical procedures. He gave Eric a blood transfusion—a new procedure which was still being tested. Then he tried a new body cast procedure -- which was working quite well for people with scoliosis-- to try & put back together Eric's many broken bones. Particularly his legs which were just a crooked mess.

Of course, all medical efforts were punctuated with immense quantities of laudanum for a grateful Eric. Gossip was Dr Mark was also known to partake in the opioid on the sly.

Eric eventually woke up in a full body cast. He was comfortably spread out in a relatively clean bed, with a mattress. Alive. All comfortable, safe & sound in a crowded hospital room. High on laudanum he was ok -- he had nowhere to go anyways. Eric settled in comfortably listening to the agonizing screaming of poor souls dying. Smelling the stink of bodies decaying. Urine & puke designing tiles on the hospital floor.

He was there forever. Eric became a medical anomaly. Doctors always coming around. Dr. Mark explaining what he was going to do next.

Eric became intimately interested in blood. It mesmerized him for hours as it dripped into his arm. As it dropped from scalpels onto the cutting floor in the surgeon's room. The dried-up blood giving texture to a bland white hospital decor in the community ward— bloody painted pictures covered in filth. It all fascinated Eric.

The life & death, the tears & cheers, the smells, the sounds, the tools, the decisions. The slaughter of laughter heard all around him. It all intrigued Eric.

Eric especially enjoyed the regular meals. Other patients told him the meals were tasteless mush. Eric was of different opinion. Hospital mush. Mmm delicious.

He didn't really have anywhere to go anyway. So when Eric started getting better he just stayed around. The hospital gave Eric a closet to live in & he paid his way by helping out. He was a natural at cleaning up. Eric showed to be a hard worker, showing a keen interest in what everyone did.

Eric got to clean up as much blood & guts as the floors could handle. Blood, puke, shit, piss, he couldn't mop it up quick enough.

Eric's efforts caught the eye of Dr. Mark who still took an interest in Eric's well being. Dr Mark pointed Eric out to one of his colleagues who was willing to take Eric under his wing. He started giving Eric books to read. Since his time with Dad -- reading The Communist Manifesto-- Eric had prided himself in his ability to read.

It was one of the things which made him feel smarter. That was important to him.

The books, which the doctors gave him, were about anatomy. Eric soaked up the knowledge like a hospital sponge.

So, when he wasn't, washing, cleaning, asking questions, making a general nuisance of himself, Eric was in his room reading--- about human anatomy.

Eventually his studies got him enrolled in medical classes at the hospital. Eric fancied that he was on his way to becoming a surgeon.

Alas, his skills with the knife proved too aggressive & his unfortunate actions were causing the deaths of more than he was saving. His teachers were critical. His evolving passion for death, his ability to induce it by the knife, produced in Eric, orgasmic feelings which were obvious to the supervising surgeons. The surgeons knew the feeling. They all, had at one time felt the same sensations. Their training had reined those sensations in.

For Eric his behavior started to become more & more obtuse. The senior surgeons started to become alarmed. Watching his eyes light up--- like a wild wolf--- when he was ever given the opportunity to use the scalpel.

Fortunately for future patients Eric failed the final exams. Derailing his enthusiasm to become a surgeon. The powers that be just couldn't pass him. But his fascination for blood wouldn't dissipate.

He was offered a job as an orderly at the Royal London. Which he quickly accepted. Not a surgeon but still close enough to saturate his need.

The position was for all hours. One might find him cleaning up first thing in the morning or stocking supplies in the middle of the night.

The wage allowed him a two-room flat on Middlesex in Whitechapel. A short bike ride from the hospital. Eric's work schedule at the hospital accommodated his being on the streets at all hours of the night without suspicion. Eric settled in as a proper English gentleman. It was a masquerade. Hiding with a stoic face amongst the enemy. The Irish inside him burned like a slow pile of coal. Eric hated the English for all they had done & for not letting him be a surgeon.

Eric was a young man with a twisted mind full of rage.

Though Eric still didn't indulge in the evil ale he did have occasion to frequent the local establishments for camaraderie & discussion. Eric fervently espoused his Irish blood & raged at the English in heated discussions. As he wasn't drinking, he was able to make his exit prior to any hostilities arising his way.

Eric was a coward if truth be told.

Eric's time at the hospital grew into years. Eric's outlets for his twisted needs unfulfilled. Working at the hospital in its perpetual gore wasn't satisfying anymore. The pubs were becoming a bore. Eric started to wander the damp cobblestone streets of Whitechapel. Where so much temptation existed.

Eric felt like the only sane person in Whitechapel at times.

Streets teaming with pity & remorse. Dorsett, Thrawl, Berner's, Wentworth, street names on lampposts. Alleyways strewn with abject, mind-numbing poverty. Waifs, mongrels, horses, mules, wailing teary eyed retches of humanity--- scratching to survive. Eric watched it all as he pedaled back & forth to work.

Eric lost all sense of self as he cruised through these open pits of emotional excrement. He found himself slipping dramatically into a raging insanity. Life a pittance scratched out for the price of another day.

Streets owned by prostitutes, drunks & evil. All within the incessant mist of the immensely rich & powerful. Looking out & scorning from their heights of birth & passing carriages.

Eric grew to realize he was very normal for his time. His rage, his special needs fit as a glove to the horror he was living amongst. Eric was most definitely a product of his environment.

Eric became addicted to the company of the prostitutes in the Whitechapel area. He took out his sexual energies with the many ladies of the night. It was down & dirty & bing bang thank you mam. Never a moment to speak or share any hidden desires & urges.

He found himself walking a fine- edged blade. Sanity evaporated into the thick concealing grey. He grew more & more for a need for more. Eric needed Jack.

+++++

Women in Eric's life were his tormentors. Clawing at his back, screaming their hideous wretched faked passion. The female persuasion had no use for Eric nor Eric for them. The prostitutes belittled him. The nurses patronized him, scorning any advances. His mother long gone never a thing.

Eric's insanity compounded as interest on a loan. Rage & pain, one feeding the other. Inducing pain became a regular obsession. Back at his rooms he would for hours strike out with leathered strips snapping his back. The fleshy pinkish skin falling off in strips.

His mind screaming inside. Howling like a raging storm. Tormenting his brain. Nothing made sense & he couldn't figure it out on his own. He must take it to the next dimension to satisfy himself.

Over the years Eric had accumulated quite the collection of surgical tools. They entertained his macabre ambitions to derive pain in any way. Whether on himself or the unfortunate rats & cats who would find themselves waylaid within his rooms.

Eric was desperate, to feel, to be, to just exist, as if something—anything-- mattered. Whipping the skin off his back-- in self flagellation-- his own blood dripping into his shorts. Dissecting rodents, skinning mice alive, short bursts of agony just weren't enough.

Eric's time at work met his mortal needs. His desires outdistanced his sanity. He flamed to feel what no mortal was capable of being.

Eric one night took a scalpel & sliced a vein. Not to die but to live. He punctured a foot so he could feel the terror of the lame. He cut an eyelid so sweet redness could flow freely through his gaze, trickling gently down a dry white cheek. He slit his cock--- with a sharp scalpel--- in hopes that the pain would enhance his orgasmic jubilation.

He sliced & diced all rodents that fell into his precisely placed traps. Nothing achieved his true need.

Eric knew he must step out of this realm --- into a morbid forbidden reality--- jump in & swim in the sea of insanity. Eric needed to experience & inflict pain, by means, which was not known amongst the sane. To enter the dimension beyond human decency.

Eric was approaching forty.

His life became solitary, invisible to all who crossed his path. He never spoke. He avoided approach. He had a fire flaming inside. Yet he remained, tortured, alive.

He made himself a ghost to the bile he trudged through, at work & in his daily routine.

He was silently screaming at the ravishing, greed & immorality which he was forced to endure day after day.

Eric was going crazy. The paupers, poverty, prostitutes & human filth which made up his life was overwhelming & fueling his Irish disposition to despair. This mortal plain was driving him insane. He was exploding from the inside out.

Eric needed to step outside of himself. He needed to feed his warped desperation for a release.

Eric was being torn like two freight trains going in opposite directions each heading for the same destination.

Smashing together in the inevitable explosion. Eric in a flash finally found Jack.

+++++

One silent night-- soon after this revelation--down some perverted alley. As the sounds of drunken cries & wails of despair echoed off narrow walls tearing through his brain. Eric was trying to achieve satisfaction at the end of his engorged--- slightly scarred--- cock plowing into some sickly wet whore's vacuous orifice. She obligingly was bent over the back of a cart—besmirched & bored.

Eric was--much too quickly-- approaching the inevitable pained orgasmic eruption. This time however Eric slipped the scalpel-- out of his jacket pocket --he had placed there for just such an occasion & became Jack.

There it was there, there was the answer. In Eric's deluded twisted mind Jack stroked the blade expertly across the throat of the unsuspecting whore.

The resulting ecstasy was unprintable.

The sensation of death overcame all earthly sentiments. Sending Eric into the never plain which he had been seeking. Absolute release from these mortal bonds exploded within him.

Death not the end but the start. Eric became obsessed with the need for more. It became an addiction.

He was quick to follow up. Over the following weeks Eric started to hunt. He had a bounty of prey & was managing one or two victims a week. At slicing their throats Jack was becoming quite proficient.

Jack's activities came to the attention of the local constabulary. They thought they were seeking a mist, a spirit, a monster not of their world. A black entity living outside the boundaries of human decency beyond human perception.

Little did they know it was walking daily amongst them.

Eric's needs grew stronger more complex. It was not enough to just slash Jack needed to go further. Fortunately, Eric had the tools & training to take that next step.

Eric started spending unique time with his slaughtered victims. Jack obtaining an emotional attachment disengaging a lady from her internal organs. Much like a cuddle & a smoke after copulation.

Now he was where he wanted to be. Eric embraced Jack. Prowling the wretched streets of Whitechapel tools in hand. Eric stalked & Jack ripped from his wretched victims their earthly existence in a timely & professional manner.

Leaving no clues, no indication of himself or his being. Jack's invisibility (which Eric had nurtured) his normalcy (which Eric maintained) being his prime cloaking trait.

Eric carried on as the submissive orderly, solitary gentlemen. While Jack reigned terror around Whitechapel. They lived & dined right in the eye of the storm they had created.

Papers raged, citizens were terrified, names were given, suspects rounded up, but none was near catching--- who was now named by the press--- Jack the Ripper.

Eric felt the pseudonym appropriately reflected Jack. At night, Jack prowled. The coppers assumed they were looking for an inhuman unworldly perversion. Really they were just looking for Eric the orderly.

As Jack's deeds grew more gruesome so did Eric's exalted outrageous need.

Eric's need for unworldly relief was insidious. Jack's insanity accommodated this. Exploding as an active volcano into orgasmic oblivion Eric truly exited this mortal plain thanks to Jack.

Not content with just solitary attacks. Eric aspired transcending this modest ambition. Jack in response to Eric's delight cut up two victims in the space of one hour feeding Eric's hunger for more. One mangled body within sight of the other.

Eric couldn't indulge in enough. An orgasmic rage exploded as Jack stripped & cut the very organs, which had just previously generated life. Jack had indeed facilitated the transcendence of Eric's mortal need.

Jack was not satisfied with just leaving the bloody entrails sprawled about. Strewn about the filthy curbs & cobblestone of the alleys. Jack started to cut more precise. Fondling & placing orderly to the side the more relevant organs. Heart, liver, kidney, intestines, stomach, gall bladder. Sometimes when he really wanted to show how clever he was--time allowing of course-- Jack would cut out the victims' sexual intimacies.

From one of his perky pretty victims Jack picked a prize. After grue-somely slicing & dicing the sad sullen victim of her life. Jack expertly removed a prized organ. Wrapped it in cloth & lovingly walked slowly & calmly back to their Whitechapel flat. The still beating heart dripping blood through Eric's fingers.

Jack treasured & coddled the heart for days. Relishing in its texture to the touch. Jack sucking with his lips on its shrinking wrinkled form.

Ultimately the dead heart started to smell. Upon returning home from work one evening Eric noticed his rooms stunk like a closet of dead rats. He was forced to dispose of Jack's prize.

Eric was seriously tempted to drop off the heart in the night mail slot of the Leman St. Police Station. But fear of being caught prevailed. It would have been a solid clue.

A much more concrete clue then the odd letter & wall inscription— 'Jack's been here'-- Eric had been writing to the constabulary for his own amusement. Flaunting Jack's arrogance. Taunting & misdirecting the pur-suing Inspector's attentions.

Inspector Reid of the local Whitechapel constabulary had been assigned to track down 'Jack the Ripper '. Eric was very well aware of this. Inspector Reid was a tenacious pursuer & given time he might have figured it out. But politics ended up playing a part in the pursuit. Inspector Reid's despair will be addressed as the story progress'

Eric walked past the police station with his dead dry heart. He didn't go far before he just nonchalantly tossed the stinking shriveled atrocity--- once a living beautiful entity--- into the sewer, which was called the Thames.

Eric's late- night walks were becoming more frequent. Jack's killings becoming more brutal. It was all happening too fast. No matter how hard he tried, no matter how vicious he killed, no matter how many, no matter how gruesome, somehow, it was never enough.

Eventually the number of killings grew quite prodigious. Eric had nothing against any of his victims. A wrong place at the wrong time had destined these poor souls. Whose only fate was to be victim to Jack's scalpel.

The papers were all over Jack the Ripper activities. The Globe, Daily Telegraph, London Daily News, Lloyd's Weekly.

Headlines screaming, 'Maniacal Blood Lust ', 'Copper's Moving In', 'Suspect Slips Through Peeler's', 'Murder's Escalate'. 'Body Parts Missing', this one aroused demonic suspicion.

'Whitechapel Terrorized', they were absolutely right Eric thought. 'Foreign Conspiracy', 'Leather Apron Arrested', after reading the news it seemed so far, Eric was in the clear. They had even arrested & released some poor Polish shoemaker,

'Prime Suspect Released'. The public was hysterical in fear.

'New Inspector Brought in from Scotland Yard to lead the Hunt.' 'Inspector Reid

Demoted'. 'Arrest Immanent', Scotland Yard proclaims.

But it wasn't. They were all looking up the wrong dress. Jack was there right in front of them & nobody could see him. Blinded by prejudice, warped by structure, it just couldn't be real. That one, Irish orderly, posing as an Englishman, was playing the game better then the constabulary. No one could get their mind around the reality that one of their own could ever sink to the level of depravity Jack was displaying.

Suspicion, as always, fell to the Jew. Specifically, the Polish Jew, who was basically blamed for all ills of this putrid society. No one dared to look within. No one dared to see that Jack's actions were the result of centuries of cruel & unjust subjugation of one class by another. Exploding forth through the actions of one demented wolf eyed perverted demon.

There came to be a copper on every corner. One couldn't turn sideways without being asked,

'What you up to now?',

'Way home from work,'

'Aye & where might that be?'

'I'm on Middlesex, work at the Royal London,'

'Doing what,'

'Work as an orderly, officer,'

'Aye, well best you be getting along then, streets aren't safe, Ripper's about.'

'Right Sir, ta.' For Eric It was just too easy. For Jack it was a game.

The papers were all over it. Keeping Eric well abreast of the progress of the investigation.

Inspector Reid had been on the right track. Eric followed Reid's investigation in the Daily News. Reid seemed the most likely to hunt him down. Reid was starting to question the right people. But then a bureaucratic panic set in. Much in Eric's favor.

The newly formed Scotland Yard stepped in & Special Inspector Abberline was appointed to head up the investigation. Ignoring Reid. Abberline put together a team of Inspector Detectives to hunt 'Jack the Ripper'. Inspector Reid became just part of a team. It was going nowhere. Everyone had an opinion.

Inspector Reid's enthusiasm was compromised. Everything he said was challenged or outright dismissed. He knew Jack was somewhere in Whitechapel. But the new guys wouldn't listen. So fuck em Reid thought. It sucked the air out of his efforts-- deflating his enthusiasm like a pin prick in a balloon.

The new Scotland Yard was looking into 30 inquiries a week. The papers said the Yard received 1,400 letters which all needed to be checked out. Eric pictured them in a chicken pen all scurrying about minus their heads.

Eric was a realist & a coward. He knew eventually--as in the random chaos of universal laws--he would get caught if he kept up this pace. He was no fool. Some cuckold eventually would stumble blindly into something he ought not. Which would be passed on to the anxious Inspectors. Which could lead to him getting caught.

During one of Jack's atrocities, it might have been murder number four. Jack had looked up from the blood & gore-- spread out in front of him like limbs on the surgeons' floor-- to see a young lad curiously staring at him. He must have just got there, as the look of undefined horror had not yet left the young lad's face. Jack glanced directly into the lad's eyes sharing an ecstatic moment with the living.

The terrified lad ran away as if chased by a pack of wolves. Destined to replace-- innocent childhood dreams-- with nightmares of terror.

Jack's most famous foray had him rip up an Irish lass. This brought him great release. A grand Irish soul freed to join the dainty spirits of the little people. Unencumbered by the burdens of her mortal needs. Jack wallowed in her essence of life. A gloriously bloody scene.

This particular lass happened to be—surprisingly-- not of the working class but had ties to resources which picked up the ears of the moneyed sources. It appeared to stir up an outraged urgency & intensity in the investigation-- not seen before.

Eric could feel the iron clutches of a terrified town closing in.

Eric got scared. Cowardice dominated his whole being. He certainly did not want to go to jail or worse have his neck stretched by the noose. That would not in any way be of any use he thought.

So, Eric toned down Jack. It had been a grand six months. Jack had run loose. Immersing himself in the intimacy of insanity. Running amok upon an unsuspecting crowd of innocent & unsuspecting ladies. Slicing & dissecting them to horrible deaths. Helping their mortal forms find peace from this horrid place. Eric to find release.

Eric was not so naïve as to expect he could absolutely cease & desist Jack's activities altogether. A Chinaman was no lest addicted to his pipe, then Eric to his need for Jack.

But prudence would need to prevail. If Jack was to continue at this hectic pace of cutting, killing & disemboweling, it was inevitable someone or something of authority would come across his hideous activities at the most inopportune time.

Then it happened just as he feared. Eric had sworn to himself-- just one more time-- after this one he'll be done, take a break. Perhaps on this one he had let his guard down.

'What's happening down there?', was said.

A gentleman passing by had turned to look down a dimly lit alley. He had sensed something obscene was about.

'Hear, Hear what's going on,'

The death moans of Jack's latest victim hung in the damp misty air. Jack was deep in the process of removing his latest victims liver, anxious to get to the heart.

The concerned citizen moved in curiously from the street down the dark alleyway. Through the black he could make out-- in the distance-- a flickering yellow light throwing a gruesome shadow on a wall. Twas Eric's lantern. Jack liked just a hint of light when involved in his gruesome work. So he could better see what he was getting into. The curious gentleman's face exploded in unmasked terror once he realized what he was seeing.

Jack turned to face him dripping of blood & guts. Jack's wolf - like glare daring in a furious yellow stare. The citizen-- thinking he had stumbled into a Dantean lair-- took off running like fireworks at a fair.

Jack was able to make a quick exit before this frazzled frightened member of the moneyed class could drag his senses back to reality. Bringing what he had seen to the attention of the constabulary.

It was time for Jack to take a step back.

+++++

Part Two

Right around the time Eric was taking a step back from Jack-- spring 1891-- a most unique patient appeared at the Royal London Hospital. He was complaining of severe stomach cramps. This required a stay in the hospital to diagnose & address what was actually causing his distress.

He had been persistent to the physicians that ever since he had arrived from India to commence his law studies-- at the Inner Temple-- he had been living with much stomach pain. The doctors in their wisdom surmised it was just probably a change in diet, but required him to remain in hospital a couple of days just to be sure.

Eric was assigned to clean his private room.

"What is your name?" this odd looking little brown man inquired. As Eric mopped up around his bed. A dish with an unfinished meal-- Eric was being careful not to disturb-- sitting on a small bedside table.

Normally Eric's cloak of invisibility protected him from patients or staff who would be so presumptuous as to ask him anything. He would usually just nod & walk away.

Yet this time-- for some reason-- Eric stopped his mopping & looked up. Immediately becoming rivetted to a challenging gaze with a twinkle, from this weird looking little man's eyes. Eric detected a curiosity never felt before. A spiritual reunion in some sense.

"Eric," he replied.

"Ah Eric, I want to thank you for your labor & the wonderful job you are doing regarding maintaining this room in a sanitary manner."

Eric was taken aback from the power that this little man was putting off. No one in his years as an orderly had ever made an impression on him like this little man. For that matter he thought no one has ever thanked him for mopping about.

"My name is Mahatma Gandhi," the little man said sitting up in his bed leaning back on the iron pipe headboard, stating his name like a musical story.

" Here sit for a minute if you dare & share this wretched mush, they insist I eat."

Eric glanced over at the unfinished meal on the table & pulled up a stool beside

Gandhi's bed.

The little Indian man talked a lot with his hands & was very animated in everything he said. Telling Eric he knew very few in town, being recently here from India. He enjoyed the opportunity to discuss-- with a local laborer-- what the circumstances of day to day life entailed.

"You are from London, I presume?" Gandhi asked, now moving to rest his chin on the palm of his hand lieing on his side on the bed, looking directly at Eric. Making it easier to pay better attention to what his new friend said.

"Raised right here in Whitechapel," Eric replied.

"Whitechapel, this is a part of London? I am so ignorant of my sur- roundings. I maintain lodgings at my school, Inner Temple, where I'm learning English law. My knowledge of anything else regarding this mag- nificent city is quite restricted."

Gandhi gestured with his free hand, at Eric, 'eat, eat', his bowl of spe- cially prepared food-- meant to heal Mahatma's painful stomach cramps-- sitting there getting rather damp. Eric trying to be polite looked around for a spoon & not finding one stuffed a handful of the mush into his mouth & promptly spit it out all over the floor. Over the years he had forgotten the sour taste of hospital mush. He'll mop it up later he thought.

Mahatma laughed, "See what I mean." Eric looked at him seeing a humorous sincerity in his face.

"You're a lawyer?" Eric asked once he'd shaken off the foul taste in his mouth.

"One day I suppose," Gandhi sighed.

"Well let me tell you this London is a cesspool of a city," Eric started to explain,

"Whitechapel is where you are now. Known for its prostitution, poverty & perversion. The main part of the city is on the other side of the river & its just as bad," Eric replied with obvious scorn.

Eric surprised himself with his response. Maybe too much he thought.

"You sound quite the malcontent, Eric my friend." Eric's response had piqued

Gandhi's interests.

Eric's suspicion screen started rising. Had he left himself open, had a little of Jack come out. He tried to reign it in,

"Don't mean nothing by it. Hard day is all." Eric replied.

"Well my friend," Gandhi said pulling himself up so his back was resting again on the iron pipe headboard. He was getting stomach cramps lieing on his side. Still looking Eric right in the eye.

"I too have reason to be less than pleased about my situation. I come from a land where the English prevail & all my fellow citizens are forced to kow- tow to our English masters. It is the reason I have come to study their English laws. To learn their English ways. In time, my people will learn to resist these English apes & take back our country, my India." Gandhi's eyes took on an otherworldly presence as he lamented his discontent. It was as if his body transcended his speech & he was above himself looking into another world.

Eric shared that stare. Eric could understand the need for more than this mortal plain was providing.

Eric was impressed. He felt a certain camaraderie with this little man with too big a mind for his body. A foreigner, who shared a common English enemy with, 'Jack the Ripper', serial killer of Whitechapel.

+++++

Mr. Gandhi, as Eric referred to him, stayed at the Royal London for the next three days. The original diagnosis—diet disorder-- was confirmed.

Mr. Gandhi would be released with the provision he should try & find a restaurant in London which would meet his vegetarian diet needs.

Over those three days Eric made a point of making sure Mr. Gandhi's room was on his schedule to clean. He would take a break from his labors & chat with this extremely intelligent, focused, lawyer to be.

Mr. Gandhi talked of the inhuman living conditions existing in India. Placing the blame firmly in English hands. Eric could relate to this. Jack's explosive outbursts of hideous mutilations, were very much in line with Gandhi's ambitions to shove a hot iron into the groin of English rule over his country.

Listening to Mr. Gandhi talk Eric envisioned for the first time the possibility of the destruction of the English Empire. Jack saw it as a potential victim.

Blood splattered English genitals. Dripping down English thighs. The English oppressor sliced up by the enraged oppressed -- sliding the blade further & further up it's puckered English anus. Jack could get into that.

Mr. Gandhi at times expressed surprise at how Eric visualized hostilities toward the English. Ofttimes Mr. Gandhi would say,

"I never thought of it like that."

Eric started to see the possibility of Jack's behavior having possible political potential. Perhaps Eric too could strike a blow into a domineering class system. Eric could kill two birds with one stone. Eric could revenge the slaughter the English perpetrated on The Irish. Jack could use his insanity to make it a bloody mess. Ripping the heart out of the English beast.

Gandhi espoused non-violence, that to shed another's blood was to capitulate to the barbarianism of the oppressors.

Eric figured that-- to control the enraged hostility of Mr. Gandhi toward the English using the doctrine of non violence-- would require extreme personal fortitude, discipline & courage.

Eric was a coward, suppressed hostility for Eric turned into Jack's insanity. Hostility needed a release not contained. Eric needed Jack to release the demented demons dwelling within him.

Mr. Gandhi's non-violent way, presented for Eric as a difficult angle for Jack to handle. Eric had trouble getting his head around it. He knew Jack could never.

Eric could see that Mr. Gandhi's dreams had the means to facilitate Jack's insanity in a more mature manner. Mr. Gandhi's beliefs & intent made Eric think that Jack was wasting time just killing innocent girls. Jack could re- direct his insanity towards loftier intentions.

+++++

Mr. Gandhi was waiting for a carriage in front of the hospital. It was time for him to go back to his rooms at Inner Temple. He was feeling much better.

Eric happened to be peddling by, on time for his afternoon shift. He pulled up to say goodbye.

Mr. Gandhi, was pleased to see him. He explained his dilemma to Eric. The doctors had told him he must find a good vegetarian restaurant to meet his dietary needs & he needed it to be within his budgetary realities. He had no idea where one might find such a restaurant.

Eric told him maybe he could help. Mr. Gandhi agreed that would be most delightful.

They made arrangements to meet up the next day. It was Eric's day off. Jack the Ripper & Mahatma Gandhi would walk around drizzly London town together. Seeking out an appropriate place for Mr. Gandhi to eat.

Eric was born & raised in Whitechapel. He had spent the majority of his life in Whitechapel. Whitechapel was not known for its vegetarian cuisine. Sausages with gravy was the favorite fare there. Eric & Mr. Gandhi would have to explore areas of London which Eric wasn't familiar with. Which Eric was more than willing to do.

Thinking like Jack he thought It would give him the opportunity of checking out hidden alleyways & subversive spots where he could indulge his insanity. Away from Whitechapel. Where his activities were starting to close in around him. Time to give the coppers a bit of a twist.

For Eric knew Jack had no intention to cease--- completely--- his murderous ways. A beast needs to feed. Even while it tends to other more mundane matters.

Mr. Gandhi & Eric met up the next day & the friendship—in earnest-- started.

It didn't take the two of them long to come across an establishment which met Mr. Gandhi's gastronomical requirements within his financial restrictions. The Central restaurant on Farringdon Street was just what Mr. Gandhi was looking for.

Over the next while, when days off & breaks in study allowed, Mr. Gandhi & Eric would meet up at prearranged spots. Big Ben, Buckingham Palace, St. Paul's Cathedral, Trafalgar Square & take a walk around London. Inevitably ending up at The Central. Mr. Gandhi would order the special & Eric tea & toast. Mr. Gandhi always offered to pay the bill. Eric wasn't really used to spending time with others. He knew his social skills were lacking which embarrassed him sometime. He had to learn how to react when someone was just being kind.

Eric grew to realize that this insightful little brown man from a faraway place was tormented by much more than that which could be tangibly touched.

Mr. Gandhi's opinions on non-violence were unshakeable. He was not going to fall into the, perverted inhuman qualities, of the English way,

"The English think the use of force is the only way to maintain power. They think right is might. But you must have the might to make everyone think what you say is right."

Eric would actively listen to Mr. Gandhi & would guardingly offer opinion & discussion. Eric saw in Mr. Gandhi a kindred spirit with Jack. Both seeking relief. Both capable of anything. Though their means of constituting a conclusion to an end did differ-- dramatically.

After a few months the sights & sounds of London Town took a back seat to the friendship Eric & Mahatma Gandhi were pursuing.

Eric recognized that Mr. Gandhi-- being a young man-- might have sexual needs. Which could only be met with immediate release. Lord knows Eric still did & he was almost twice Mr. Gandhi's age.

Eric & Mr. Gandhi were on one of their walks. During a lull in the conversation, as they were walking confidently on the cobblestones, Eric discretely asked Mr. Gandhi if perhaps he'd like to dally forth with one of London's ladies of the oldest profession. Mr. Gandhi's response surprised him,

"Actually I am quite married. I have a wife & two children back in India." Mr. Gandhi had never mentioned this before, taking Eric a wee bit aback.

"Must've bin young when you got hitched," Eric said.

"Yes, in my country we marry quite young," Gandhi responded with an edge of sarcasm.

Mr. Gandhi-- it turned out-- was not that particularly enamored with the graces of the opposite sex.

"In all honesty I prefer the company of my own kind." Mr. Gandhi said a wry smile crossing his lips.

Eric of course agreed. " We all of course prefer the company of gents when in it comes to chatter, discussion & rowdiness. But when it gets down to following through on our inalienable sexual urges-- we must of course turn our attention to the ladies," Eric said.

Mr. Gandhi quietly turned to Eric & replied,

"For some I suppose."

Eric looked over intrigued, "Really." "My friend we all have our secrets."

It excited Eric that his friend possessed a secret. A secret which-- if exposed-- could lead to his friend's doom. Both were in the same boat Eric figured. It made him feel closer to his friend.

Eric let on the sly to Mr. Gandhi to be careful.

"Here in London, one could still be clapped in irons for partaking in sexual pleasures with one of your own gender." Eric said through the side of his mouth.

Mr. Gandhi thanked Eric for his concern.

Eric felt good knowing that it was not only he who was walking a razors edge, hiding secrets. Either one of them could end up spending time for what they've done-- or what they're thinking. Taking up space with the rats & thieves in the hell of a London jail. Eric of course would be waiting to be hung.

Rather ironic Eric thought to himself, Jack didn't respond. Insanity refuses to accept it's done something wrong, Jack never ever thought about being caught.

They walked in thought until they turned the corner & The Central came into view.

"Finally." Mr. Gandhi gasped "I'm starved," Eric looked over & confirmed, "I could sure use a tea."

"And you set to be a lawyer & law maker." Eric grinned as Mr. Gandhi replied with a twinkle in his eye which was more like him trying to wink. They were laughing over Eric's tea & Mr. Gandhi's pale ale at The Central. They'd been sitting at an outside table for awhile now after their walk. Mr. Gandhi hard on the second helping of his special salad bean concoction which they made special for him. He & Eric over their time together had many a discussion about their respective dietary pleasures. Eric was sitting across from him leaning back in his chair sipping his tea.

"I bet I know which law you'll be wanting to change first," Eric said & they both almost fell off their chairs laughing insane. Mr. Gandhi even coughed up some leaf he was laughing so hard at his impertinent friend.

' Very humorous my friend, you know me well,' Mr. Gandhi coughed out. A snort of ale coming from his nose.

That evening as they parted their ways, both yelling 'Hail Britannia'— sarcastically-- as a good bye saying. Eric heading across London Bridge, Mr. Gandhi sticking to his side of the Thames going back to his rooms. In the middle of London bridge a local hawker was slinging the news. A headline jumped out at Eric.

'Tenth Anniversary of Assassination of Russian Czar Alexander II.' It said in bold print. Eric bought a copy of the paper & hastened to his apartment to see what this was all about. He knew little about Russia other than he confused it with Prussia.

Eric opened the paper sitting back on his chair in his sparse spartan abode. Apparently on July 4th 1881-- ten years ago today-- in Russia not Prussia Eric clarified in his mind-- Czar Alexander, Czar of all the Russia's-- a peacock on a throne it said--had been assassinated by two disgruntled revolutionaries.

Striking back at the King Eric thought.

Two bombs were thrown-- the first a dud-- the second one blowing the legs off the Czar of all the Russia's. Causing him to bleed out volumes over the road & all his entourage. The scene was absolute chaos the story read, legs & limbs everywhere. Blood splattering the parade ground. All efforts to revive the reviled leader were fruitless. He died bleeding out in excruciating pain at his royal residence-- in his splendid royal bed. His wife, aides & family looking on in shocked disbelief caressing his royal head.

Now this was something which appealed to Eric & caught Jack's eye. The gore excited Jack. The idea of throwing a bomb in a crowd was very creative Jack considered.

Eric must remember to discuss this incident with Mr. Gandhi. Mr. Gandhi was always well versed in the goings on in the world.

That evening, after Eric had finished his meal of eel, he tidied up his dishes & got a familiar feeling in his mind. It was time for insanity.

Jack dictated that tonight he 'd be back on the prowl.

Eric crossed back over the mighty London bridge dressed in his traditional black. The paper vendor was gone-- only a few solitary soles on the Bridge tonight.

A young shop girl—who had served pastries to Eric & Mr. Gandhi that day-- had caught Jack's eye. Eric made his way through the streets of London back to the innocuous pastry shop.

Eric waited patiently hidden in a doorway down a London alley. Jack knew the feeling of making sure he wasn't seen. Jack had the pastry shop-- where she worked—in his glare.

She was just finishing up. Jack watched as she locked the door. Luckily she made her way right past where Eric waited. She was alone on the street. Shuffling along in no hurry. The excitement was intense. The smell of fresh bun & sweet roll wafted the air as she came closer-- to Jack's hidden spot. Passing Jack unseen. The poor pretty young thing saw no shadow as Jack came up behind her. Slitting her throat to the bone with his well sharpened scalpel. It all happened so fast she had no time to be shocked.

Jack pulled her back into the dark & gutted her like a mackerel.

After Jack finished up Eric hightailed it back to Whitechapel. His feet were wings as he virtually flew over London Bridge. He was insane with relief. He slept like the dead that night.

Eric's time with Mr. Gandhi had set Jack on a back burner. But now he was back & Eric knew he needed Jack like a junkie needs his needle.

Eric figured he just wouldn't be so frantic to his need. He was getting older after all. He would act smarter, start stalking his prey outside of Whitechapel. Keep those damn inspectors guessing.

Eric knew he could no more stop Jack then a virile man in his prime can hold back his masturbatory urges. Eric's orgasmic relief was a homicidal, twisted act--- not like them wankers wanking themselves off in the outhouse or beside the river pretending they're trying to piss.

The next week Eric met with Mr. Gandhi beside the tree lined House of Parliament. They walked along talking. Mr. Gandhi bringing up the story of the recently murdered shop girl.

"Did we not buy pastries from that very shop? "Mr. Gandhi asked,

"I believe we might've," Eric replied,

"Well it just makes one think when something of this horrific nature happens," "Happens all the time don't give it a second thought," Eric said trying to comfort his friend.

Eric wanted to talk about the assassination of the Czar he had read about in the paper. He presented to Mr. Gandhi as to how intrigued he was by the use of bombs to achieve political ends. Eric declared to his friend that he found this an appropriate method of ridding one's surroundings of seditious vermin.

Mr. Gandhi of course had some opinions on that subject. Mr. Gandhi was clear, violence was not to be tolerated at any price. Eric retorted that isolated incidents of violence have their place when the situation warrants it.

Mr. Gandhi was firm, "there can be no situation which would require a violent retaliation."

"How about if you seen a bunch of hard-working drunken blokes shoving their engorged dongs up your father's arse," Eric slipped.

Mr. Gandhi looked over at Eric, a bit shocked at this example,

"You make a good point my friend. I would have to think about that,"

Eric looked Mr. Gandhi right in the eye,

" Sometimes thought doesn't solve a thing, violent re-action is the only solution."

They walked on considering each other's position. Finally, they turned the corner onto Farringdon Street, The Central was within view.

Mr. Gandhi looked over to his friend & in a very meditative mode conceded that,

"Violence if isolated to rare reactive situations, might indeed play a very limited part in one's need to achieve what is right."

"Well that's all I mean," Eric said as he held the door open for his friend.

Their time together was winding down. Mr. Gandhi was in the throes of final exams. He was an active member of some organization which promoted the vegetarian lifestyle as the answer to humanities ills. He was also very involved with an organization promoting universal brotherhood & the study of religious books. Mr. Gandhi's diverse interests took time away from Eric & to be truthful some of Mr. Gandhi's ideas especially about food & politics Eric found to be extremely eccentric.

Eric thought sometimes Mr. Gandhi didn't understand the real world. Eric thought if Mr. Gandhi saw the way things really were, he wouldn't have such high falluting ideas about how the human race was worth saving.

"Come spend a week in my part of London," Eric was saying one afternoon. The weather was changing & fall was becoming winter. A wet drizzly chilly time. Mr. Gandhi was leaving in the spring if all went as

expected. They were having their regular. Eric his tea & Mr. Gandhi his —
made for Mr. Gandhi-- salad special at The Central,

"Whitechapel will show you the truth. These pansy ideas, of peace &
harmony, they're only thought up by a bored ruling class. Them having
more time on their hands than they know what to do with," Eric was saying.

Eric pressed on, taking a sip of his tea. Mr. Gandhi chowing down on
his salad was listening.

"I'd venture to say not a one of them-- deep thinkers-- has slipped on
a pile of shit first thing in the morning on their way to work. Smelled the
urinary stench bouncing off the cobblestone just as the sun's coming up.
Fallen flat ass into a puddle of piss, cursing this & every day for having
been born.

"Heading down to their manure stench place of employment. Shoveling
shit from cows till your arms & legs are completely done. Body burning,
piece of bread for lunch. Pushing through the pain & fatigue. When your
work days over you crawl back to your wretched hovel. A room where
you're greeted by the drooping eyes of the wife & your four starving dis-
eased children.

"You have to tell them once again, 'not quite enough for tonight, but
tomorrow's another day, I'm sure we'll be having plenty milk & sugar
tomorrow'. Knowing

'Wee Willie' will be dead in three days if he doesn't get the nourish-
ment he needs to survive. The girls all in rags, barely alive & the wife's an
old drunk whore.

"Never having enough.

"You collapse in a ruin of tattered sheets & bodies only to get up once
again before dawn the next day & do it all over again."

Gandhi put down his fork. Making sure to chew what's left in his
mouth before he replied.

"I am from India, my friend, we invented poverty, disease, filth
& stench."

"Yea, you may know about it, but have you or any one of your fancy
friends ever lived it?"

"Well stated Eric my friend." Gandhi replied sincerely.

That night when saying goodbye, they hugged.

Eric knew Mr. Gandhi eventually was on his way back to his well-off home in India. Family expectations to fulfill the dreams of his parents. Become a successful barrister, husband, father, civil servant, merchant. He wasn't so sure Mr. Gandhi would fit into the slot allotted him, Eric thought about this as he crossed London bridge on his way home that night.

Eric had his doubts that Mr. Gandhi was destined for what his position in life expected of him.

Eric figured that Mr. Gandhi was like Jack in some ways. His burning rage towards the English & social injustice was destined to explode. Eric could see that-- just like Eric-- Mr. Gandhi was a passionate man & had grave needs which were destined to push him to his limits.

If indeed Mr. Gandhi followed the restrictions of his social class Eric believed Mr. Gandhi -- like Jack -- would find other ways to address his hostilities. Which would lead Mr. Gandhi down the path of a social pariah. Eric could foresee Mr. Gandhi finding a release for his hostility which would remove Mr. Gandhi from the realm of human decency into Jack's world of insanity.

Eric had this tremendous capacity to see Jack in every faction of this mortal journey. In every living thing. Eric never mentioned Jack to Mr. Gandhi. When it came to Jack, Eric & Jack kept to themself.

It came spring, time for Mr. Gandhi to go back to India. He had completed his studies. The two friends time together was drawing to a close. Surprisingly enough It'd been going on for over two years now.

Eric met Mr. Gandhi at the dock on the day Mr. Gandhi was off home. They exchanged the usual pleasantries, discreetly, neither one of them wanting to be seen. They hugged & wished each other good luck with their life. Vowing weekly they'd write. Then Mr. Gandhi was up the gangplank & waving back weakly from the rail to his friend. Eric waved back-- from the dock-- one hand raised for Eric one hand for Jack.

Mahatma Gandhi, who was destined to liberate India from English rule-- using a doctrine of non-violence-- was gone from their life.

+++++

Eric was approaching a difficult time in life. He was getting old. With Mr. Gandhi he had felt invigorated. Now with Gandhi gone he was feeling empty. His legs ached from old injuries. He was taking laudanum regularly for the pain but it wasn't helping. Everything was becoming such a bore Jack needed more.

Eric's age & physical realities were starting to restrict his capacity to continue in

Jack's insanity. Eric had been indulging in Jack's bloodlust a few times a year at this point, but this was becoming exhausting. It was time to change the pattern as not to tax his physical needs further. Every new murder & dismemberment, was causing him more & more pain in his extremities. The old war wounds of the crash were starting to creak & moan.

Eric was finding it exhausting. Meeting Jack's needs & holding down his job at the hospital it was all so tedious, mindless, mundane.

Eric decided to think back on what Mr. Gandhi had taught him. Don't just be a one trick pony, expand your mind. Focus your own need on the bigger picture. Don't be afraid to take on your dream.

"Eric my friend, you're a smart man. You're a man who can make a difference."

Mr. Gandhi had told Eric-- not realizing he was also talking to Jack the Ripper.

Eric kept going back to that Russian Czar's assassination. How a well-placed bomb could cause such devastation. Eric believed that Jack would be extraordinately pleased to expand his insanity to a larger forum. Where a knife could be used to meet a private need, a bomb could shower the sidewalk with body parts. Eric decided he would build a bomb that would create the bloodiest carnage since The Battle of Waterloo. For Eric it would satisfy his need for revenge against the English. For Jack it would be the ultimate release.

Part Three

Eric needed a target. He decided it would be the 1897 Queen's Diamond Jubilee. The year was 1893, he had four years to prepare for the ultimate deed. Strike a blow, all that bullshit. For Jack it was the anticipated gore. Jack could slice & dice one girl a night for the next five years. This still wouldn't approach the anarchy, what one well-placed bomb on the Queen's route, would achieve.

Eric envisioned thousands of bodies, flying, kitelike-astrew. Blood so much blood --as a thunderstorm in June-- pelting your face with all the dead consciouses of the newly deceased royalty race. Jack, looking up & feeling fleshy sensations covering lips & tongue, oh the gory oh the guts— oh the glory.

Jack's primeval urge let loose onto an unsuspecting universe. To this end Eric dedicated the rest of his life.

Eric was getting old he must start now. He needed a challenge. He needed to take the next step. His perverted--- evil--- activities had caused quite a stir up till now.

If his solitary efforts can be so highlighted, imagine the sensation caused by his impending plans. To be responsible for the greatest mass murder perpetrated since time itself. That sounded like something which songs would be written about. Headlines screaming larger than life, 'Ripper Rips the Heart out of the Empire.'

So, Eric resigned his position at the hospital. The pension was a pittance but with the money he had saved up Eric bought himself a lorry taxi cab & two horses.

He was able to secure new lodging which came with a shed, still in Whitechapel. A few blocks over from where he had always lived. The shed in the rear he could use at his own discretion. It came with a lock & Eric alone the key.

Eric was unable to douse the flame of Jacks behavior completely. Like a junky to the spoon, Jack's need was just too soon to go cold turkey on cutting the throats of women. So over the next few years-- as his bomb building project became real-

- Eric was prone to roam round London town. Satisfying Jack's insanity with appropriately timed glorious gory gratification.

With the lorry taxi it was easier on the legs not near as much walking around. Easy to lure potential prey, no more hiding & slinking about. Taking a taxi to a killing was like a proper night out. Jack on a date. Same as the rich folk going to a play.

"I got a right to have fun," Eric grumbles as he works pulling his lorry up in front of a big beautiful house. Lit up like a Christmas tree. Two young men excitedly jump out from the back. Leaving Eric with no tip & lamenting his lot. But he's always got Jack, Eric thought moving his horses on their way. It was his way of balancing the scales knowing that for all his customers wealth & prestige he always had Jack who could turn & slice them in a second. It gave Eric a feeling of power.

Jack was starting to linger over his victims-- catching his breath. If anyone was to come upon him doing his business he'd be sure to get captured. Lingering longer on the spot was just a recipe for getting caught. Eric was always grateful for the lorry waiting in a hidden place. It made it a lot easier getting home. Especially since now he was working specifically the streets of London proper.

One rule though, no matter how strong the desire, no matter how fortunate the circumstances. Jack was never to murder a cop. That would have been a straight ticket to the gallows. Coppers would be all over Eric.

Of course, the vast majority of Eric's time--- now---was taken up with planning the

Queen's carnage at her Diamond Jubilee.

Eric got down to learning how to build a bomb. If Jack was to wreak deadly carnage on the Queen's parade, Eric had to learn how to build a bomb.

Fortunately, the discovery of dynamite-- by Lord Nobel in 1867— made Eric's efforts very possible. Lord Nobel's discovery enabled one to safely manage nitroglycerine. It made making your own bomb quite a bit safer & gave you the opportunity to choose your spot. As evidenced by the Russian assassins who tossed two well-made bombs at the emperor blowing him to bits. At least one of the bombs did the other was a dud.

Eric started to notice in the papers that dynamite was becoming status quo. Groups of fanatics & others built dynamite bombs for political & personal purposes, 'Hail Anarchy', 'Free Ireland', 'Revenge', was the cry which fit right into Eric's objective.

There was a story-- which Eric read in The Globe-- where a discontented shop employee-- in possession of a handmade explosive-- walked into his place of work at midday blowing himself & two shop girls to bits. He had just been fired for stealing, the story said. It must have been glorious Jack thought. It inspired Eric to work harder.

Eric worked in his shed raging at the Queen for what she had done to his ancestral Irish home. He would strike a blow at the testicles of the bastard British Empire. Payback Eric thought, for the chaos England had retched upon the globe.

It was a straight no brainer to someone twisted like Jack. Win-Win. Opening the door to the immortal plain through gore & retribution.

Eric knew it was not enough to just build a bomb. He had to be able to control it. Make sure it exploded when you wanted it to & not in your face. The Russians had one fail to go off. If they hadn't had that second bomb the emperor would be sipping tea today. Dynamite was dandy, but sensitive to the touch, it was to be a challenge. Which Eric was, in every way up for.

Eric fell into a sensible routine. Up in the morning at first light, a light breakfast of bread & milk then onto the lorry to work the day picking up fares. At night after a meal of eel at the local fish shop he'd head to his shed where the real work was done. On the odd night if something had caught his eye during the day Eric would put off work on the bomb

& make a foray into town to kill an innocent young thing. Jack always appreciated that.

Eric didn't have trouble with the actual building of the bomb. That turned out to be a pretty straight forward process. He found out he had an aptitude for the work. The precision needed reminded him of his surgeon training so that pleased Jack.

The real problem Eric encountered was getting the necessary materials.

It was most contentious (& illegal) to be in the possession of any explosive element. Other than for approved military & scientific purposes. So, the procurement of these goods was required to be done, at times, in a most, inappropriate, discrete, dreadful, sinister, murderous manner.

Many a merchant—who unfortunately was unable to sell the required components to Eric—met a tragic end. Gasping for air with their throat slit while closing up their shop. Keys left sticking out the door.

It was surprising how easy killing came to Eric. He was against all instincts of guilt. Eric had twisted this whole life around to face the other way. Sometimes he didn't even need Jack to slip the scalpel.

Eric read of the discovery of electromagnetic waves by some German. Hertzian waves the scientists called them. Radio waves the paper called them.

Eric attended Eduard Branly's lecture at the Physical Society in London in 1895. Branly exhibited these radio waves moving about in glass tubes. Eric considered that this might be of some use to him in his ambitions.

Eric followed this up soon after with attending the lecture of Mister Oliver Lodge. Lodge was involved in putting something together that would transmit & receive these moving radio waves.

Lodge called the receiver he built a coherer. The coherer was a glass tube filled with cut metal filings, part silver, part nickel. When the coherer detected these Hertzian (radio) waves from a remote sender, it turned itself on, pulling an arm down, ringing a bell. Eric thought if it could ring a bell it could light a fuse or turn a switch or click a clock.

Eric needed to devise a plan to set off a bomb by sending a radio wave to a box. Inside the box a lever would strike a match. Firing up the fuse sticks attached to the nitroglycerine.

Kaboom!!

Jack had every faith in Eric. Jack knew Eric would figure it out.

Finally, after suffering the loss of many an eyebrow--- & sleepless nights figuring it out--- Eric had something resembling his needs. To try it out, without drawing attention, was to be a challenge.

Once again he fell back on his lorry travels to check out possible test sights. He finally decided on a rugged relatively isolated spot down by the water, south of London.

Eric needed a diversion to redirect attention from where he'll be testing his freshly built bomb boxes. No matter how isolated-- if things go as planned-- it will cause quite a big bang. It would come to the attention of the coppers.

Jack suggested they set a colossal fire in one of the warehouses down by the docks on that particular night. It was agreed to do it.

The ruse worked drawing all the local coppers & firefighters to the fire. Ringing their bells, sounding their sirens. Eric read in the paper the following day it was quite the chaotic situation. Three unfortunate long-shoremen being burnt to a crisp. Which for Jack was a bonus as he looked at the pictures of their grizzled corpses in the paper.

Eric's field test that night went happily off unnoticed. A few wrinkles to be ironed out back at the shed. But he definitely could send a signal by flicking a switch. Have it received in the bomb box & ignite the nitroglyc-erine. Eric had heard & seen the explosion, it had worked. Jack had smiled a fatherly grin.

Eric had, now, less than a year, to refine & properly prepare for the jubilee. Eric decided he would need to build four bomb boxes. He would place each one strategically along the parade route, which had been mapped out in the papers for months now. Thank you very much he thought. The publics need to know everything-- was making things so much easier for him.

Eric would build a miniature model of the parade route, in his shed, on his shop table inside, to scale. His attention to detail will ensure each bomb will be placed strategically at the exact spot escalating maximum chaos, carnage & confusion beneath an English sky raining red when they exploded.

It was to be quite the show the papers said of the coming Jubilee. Little did they know Eric mused.

The Queen was to have a seventeen-carriage convoy carrying her from Buckingham Palace to St Paul's Cathedral right past London Bridge. The Queen's own carriage would be marked with eight cream-colored horses pulling it.

They were almost making this too easy Eric thought.

The papers were all abuzz at the size of crowd expected. The anticipated numbers were astronomical. English citizens from all the colonies would be attending. India-- South Africa -- Canada -- New Zealand – Australia & the rest. They'd all be there. Cheering their Queen.

This couldn't be working out any better Eric figured. His actions will reverberate worldwide. Jack's insanity destined to be acknowledged as a new path to immortality. A new reality.

The thought motivated Eric to worker smarter & Jack to relax.

Eric was standing in his shed reviewing the finally completed-- specific to size-- world he was destined to destroy, sitting atop his table. It all looked so still he thought.

Eric's model of the route was very specific. Miniature landmarks, trees & parks. He even built small little people all along the parade route. Some figures & figurines he carved himself, others he made with old pieces of scrap metal.

He would place his four bomb boxes, he thought, at three points – two in Trafalgar Square—one at London Bridge one just outside St Paul's Cathedral.

Eric proceeded to place each scale modelled bomb box into the miniature world in their secret places along the route. Jack had spent relentless hours with the scalpel carving out little unique intricately designed minny bomb boxes. To Eric it was a game, imagining a world of real life. For Jack it was all about control.

After the final piece was in its place. Eric lifted the lantern to a rung on the ceiling & stepped back casting his shadow over the scene. Coming to attention he then raised his free arm in what would later-- in history-- be called a Nazi salute. Eric relaxed sat back on his stool & took a sip of his tea- which he always had within reach when he was working. Eric walked through the day of carnage in his head. Relishing the dread on display at every step.

Eric figured Trafalgar Square was the obvious choice for the first bomb explosion. Greatest potential of bloody deaths. Thousands of English would be crowded into the massive square like tiny birds eager for their mother. Excited to see the Golden Carriage. The Queen Mother inside-- waving imperially --- her gracious rump spread over the well cushioned back seat. Giving the royal salute to her subjects. Oh the carnage we shall reap Eric thought.

The rabble from Whitechapel will be waiting by London Bridge. He'll set the next bomb there. All of Whitechapel will be there celebrating the procession. Taking advantage of the situation. Pick pockets & prostitutes favoring an exuberant distracted horny crowd to exploit. A mob would be crowding the sidewalks. Hawkers yelling in the streets, British flags draped around em from their head to their knees all red, blue & white. Selling anything with 'Diamond Jubilee 1897' written on it. I'll blow it all up-- the lot of them-- Eric said to himself. He sipped from his tea & silently toasted Jack.

'To your health,' Eric said,

'And to yours,' Jack replied back.

'Everyone from Whitechapel screaming their stupid faces off waiting for the Queen,' Eric lamented,' his heart couldn't be beating faster.

'Unaware that she's never coming,' they both bellowed at the same time. Eric & Jack had a good laugh over that.

A well-placed bomb will quiet their eternal Whitechapel drivel. Eric & Jack smiled knowingly.

Silenced for oblivion. Eric & Jack drank their tea in silent contemplation.

The final bomb box would be placed just outside St Paul's. You know there'll be a good crowd at the church Eric thought. Jack could taste the breath death of delimbed hypocritical Englishmen. Who were waiting unaware their Queen has just been blown to smithereens.

Eric thought, that if all the switches complete the circuits & light the match & all the bombs explode. Jack will have succeeded in changing the world. A wolfish glare filled the air as Eric's eyes became Jack.

Eric would place an extra bomb box at the Trafalgar location. The first point of passage of the procession. He must assure the assassination of the Queen. He'll use the second box for back up only if necessary.

The Queen only with divine intervention, will pass by Trafalgar Square, Eric swore to himself. It will be glorious Jack thought.

Then Eric planned the logistics. Envisioning the route, memorizing like a general over a map. Jack slipped away for a moment, he hated & was quickly bored with anything to do with the mind.

After the Queen & her honor guard are blown to bits in Trafalgar, Eric thought. Jack will be reverberating in all his glory. I'll will move the Lorry against the ongoing hysteria towards London Bridge. No one will notice me. I'll pull up at London bridge.

I'll immediately detonate the next explosive. Jack will be bathed-- for a few moments of orgasmic sensation—in burning fiery blood of the unexpecting Whitechapel population.

After that it'll be a controlled trot against the surging movement of the bloodied masses who'll be in an absolute frenzy. On to the mighty St. Paul's Cathedral. Where we together will detonate the final blow. Jack you'll be standing--- screaming in absolute ecstasy--- awash amidst a thunderstorm of blood, limbs & blessed brain. Jack came back for an instant & grinned like a hooligan.

Then it will be time to head for home, Eric lamented.

Amidst all the commotion, Eric figured he will pick his way back slowly-- almost nonchalantly- through the crowd. Pushing his horses pulling the lorry to move ahead-- feigning he was there on business. He'll go the long way around back to his lodgings. He knew he certainly wasn't going to be able to use London Bridge. Eric didn't want to get caught. This was no suicide mission.

The planning was over. Eric was exhausted. He cautiously closed the door to the shed & retired to his flat & put on the kettle. Cup of tea before he goes to bed.

Later that night as he lay awake on the plats of the cold wooden bed with no pillow, Eric decided he would place the bombs the night before the festivities. He would have to be sure no fool stumbled upon him as there would be quite a crowd. If indeed it did come to that, Jack better have the scalpel at the ready. His consciousness slowly slipping into sleep. A drowsy smirk aroused a stirring Jack.

*****

The date of the Jubilee was two weeks away.

The flurry of activity along the parade route was intense. People from all over. Setting up chip stalls, souvenir vendors staking out space. Out of towners crashed out on the sidewalk anxious for the show to start. Eric taking it all in. No one will notice a wayward lorry driver browsing about in their midst in the middle of the night before the show, a worried Eric reassured himself as the crucial day grew closer & the crowd grew thicker. Patience my friend we're nearing the end Jack softly counselled.

Just one final silent test run to be done. Over the remaining days Eric set up the bomb boxes in the shed. He disconnected all the bombs in their respective bomb boxes. Then he tested the switch, making sure he heard the click in each box before reconnecting the bombs. It was a very sensitive operation & Eric was careful to handle all the volatile explosives with the touch of a surgeon opening up a heart.

It was done. All four tested, all four signals transmitted & received. All four bombs re-attached in their boxes. Only forty-eight hours till;

Showtime!

!!!!!

Eric's heart could not have been beating louder the next night when it finally came time to distribute-- to their respective locations-- his explosives. He parked the lorry, beside the shed. Got down & set about his task. His demeanor was soft. His anticipation surreal. Pure pleasure flowed up & down his mortal being.

Eric was becoming Jack & vice versa.

Eric reverently-- as a child in the choir-- carried each bomb box to the lorry. Placed each down on the soft pillowed resting places he'd prepared. Risking he knew that at any moment any one could blow up in his face.

Finally, it was done. The bombs were in the carriage.

Jack stepped up quietly to his seat. Jiggled the reins ever so gently.

There was a chill in the night. It was damp foggy thick midnight air. Eric was sweating. Perspiration was dripping off his shirt inside his dark black jacket. Jack's black hat was slippery on his head.

They were on their way to place the bombs.

*****

Jack eased away from the curb into the cobblestone street.

Eric was set for the task. Snapping bits of mist stung Jack's wild wolfish eyes. Streetlights shining the grey. A dark yellow light glaring off the cobblestone. Stench of excess dung hung like sleet. Jack made his way like a diamond cutter ever so cautiously.

The streets, were raucous & celebratory. There was a party coming about & the good folks of Whitechapel-- though poor & miserable-- were always up for a good time.

This was the one part of the plan Eric had always been nervous about. He knew it would be dangerous. Uneven cobblestones, traffic, curbs, pedestrians coming at you at any instant. Four bombs of nitroglycerine were in the lorry. Any jarring, pushing, bumping intrusions could jostle the cab, just enough, you just don't know. Alfred Nobel might have discovered how to control dynamite, but it was still volatile as hell.

Jack crept on into the night. Taking immense care to avoid any serious affair with that, which caused Eric to worry. Staggering drunks, potholes, curbs, passing carriages & pipe-sucking prostitutes flew by in a flurry. Jack continued to slice through the distractions like a snake.

It wasn't easy. The scene seemed to be closing in all around them. It took all Eric's lorry driving skill to avoid being jostled. Slowly, determined They set Their sights on the goal. To just get across London Bridge & place Their bombs.

Slowly through the night They crawled. Willing the time to be over the bridge. Away from the creatures of Whitechapel.

Not to long now. They could see the bridge in the distance. Just a few more minutes They thought & They'd be over London Bridge. Into London proper. Where They'd place the bombs in the pre-planned strategic places. Patience the price of success.

The streets of Whitechapel were getting louder. People, drunken people, bawdy whores stumbling off the sidewalks inebriated. Waving their arms wildly. Drunken blokes saluting the Queen. Proclaiming their love for dear ole England. It was a party & the poor folks of Whitechapel were starting to cut loose.

Jack's nerves were burning steel. Everyone was coming at him from every direction. Trying to hail him down.

'Hey cabby give me a ride,' they'd yell & stumble toward them.

'Not in service,' Eric would yell back. He just wanted to kill them all. Just be patient they'll all be dead tomorrow, They smirked.

All of Whitechapel was drunk & wasted. They were the sanest savage in town. It seemed the closer They got to the bridge the bigger the crowds. A whirlwind of frantic floundering on all sides all over the street.

'Get away, get away,' Jack hissed. Eric committed to the task.

--then there it was--

Jack caught sight—out of the corner of his left eye-- a women running from a seemingly hidden alleyway. They watched her as if in a trance. As she drew closer—to Their disbelief--she distorted into an apparition. An apparition careening. Bursting out of a dark alley. Breaking free of the crowd. Coming directly at Them like an arrow.

The apparition had blood pouring out of Its screaming eyes---looking right through at Jack. Its flowing demeanor containing the distorted faces of all the women Jack had slain. Contorted images of female anatomy--- Jack had annihilated—floated in the air. Ethereal waves of mind-numbing terror flowed through Them. A snarling bloody apparition attacked screaming—revenge!

Jack let out a maniacal wail. Was it real Eric thought . . .

The apparition invaded Their mind like a flame. Diverting Them off their concentration. For only a split second. Twas enough to loose the reins. The horses lurched rearing up. The lines went taught when the hoofs regained the road.

The lorry jostled forward.

Ka...BOOM

+++++

The ensuing investigation into the explosion in Whitechapel--- which was delayed by the Queen's Diamond Jubilee which by the way went off without a hitch---discovered a lorry cab license plate. It was embedded in some poor fellow's forehead. Over two miles away from the scene of the explosion. Eric would've been pleased at the distance. Jack would've been impressed with the precision of the kill.

Scotland Yard followed up on the plate. It was discovered this particular cab license was registered to an 'Eric Chalmerston'. It was a name unknown to the police.

The End

The Story of Irene & Her Corolla

Irene was becoming a Meth Head. This actually wasn't a surprise. Irene always had a problem with the drink. When she started getting into meth she just did it on top of her drinking. It was energizing her drunken high.

The problem with meth is that you can't just go into a store & pick some up. The buying of meth still requires a degree of intrigue. This was something Irene wasn't used to. The problems this brought into her life were inconceivable to her party time brain.

)))))

Irene at one time had a successful jewelry business. Problem was she married Ben. They both had a taste for the drink. Irene had been a pretty little thing. Five foot two eyes a blue. Prone to flirt, especially after the drink. Ben was a hard ass -

- making his living falling cedars--he felt woman should be kept in their place. Irene of course was having none of that. So once the sex was over the fighting began. Ben would hit & pound the shit out of Irene.

Irene would swoon in his face. Egg him on,

'Come on you big fuck, hit me,' she'd scream,

'Hit me like a man you son of a bitch,' Irene getting up off the couch & yelling like a demented witch right into his face. He'd slap his open hand knocking her hard right back down. Flapping her angry jowls almost spilling her drink.

'You fuck, Roy fucked me harder than that, you fucking wuss.' Irene yelling in drunken hate. Trying to get up off the couch—stumbling-- spitting blood from her broken lip. Drink steady in her hand. Trying to yell loud enough to get some blood on Ben's face. Knowing Ben hated Roy. Knowing Ben had seen her pressing her tits into Roy's arm at the party last night.

Ben swinging blindly catching Irene square on the face knocking her back across the crying couch. Irene's drink flying all over the wall. Irene sprawled all over the floor unconscious. Irene waking up later in the dark. Ben long gone off in search of more drink & Roy to beat up if he got lucky.

This was Irene's life for twenty years. Finally Irene & Ben lost it all—money & mind. The law intervened. Ben went to far & was out of her life. Prison sentences are over much faster than the emotional disaster they have left behind. So Ben's been out for a couple of years now & Irene's still afraid, broke & broken. Drinking more than ever. She's embraced the homeless life like a child hugging its mother. But she'd always been the drunk at the party not the druggie. Now living in transition housing on the coast, drugs are the order of the day. Irene finally broke down & decided to partake.

Irene's in her room partying down with Herbert & his dealer friend Sean. In their meth fueled haze, they decide they have to go to Vancouver to score some more drugs. Well Irene is the only one with a car, a ten-year-old white corolla. Irene of course is too drunk to drive & too stoned to make any sense. So Herbert & Sean took her keys & drove the corolla to Vancouver.

Irene wakes up the next morning & can't remember a thing. There's a message beeping on her phone. She reaches out with her swollen finger sheepishly retrieving her message, always fearing the worst after a black-out night. Lying on her back she listens. A firm female voice tells her to phone the police in Vancouver about a white corolla found in the city.

This doesn't make any sense to Irene. The corolla is just outside in the parking lot. Irene like she is in a conspiracy gets up off her large dark red recliner which pretty well fills up her single room. That & the single unslept in unkempt bed, a rickety kitchen table, a beckoning shower, kitchen sink & a fridge full of magnets complete the décor. The whole place looks trashy eclectic. Beer cans, syringes, flowers & pictures adorn the motif. Poster of Burl Ives on the wall.

Irene pulls back the towel serving as a curtain on her only window, shading her eyes from the blinding sunlight. Slowly she squints & stares down at the empty parking space where the corolla is supposed to be.

'Fuck,' she screams in her head. 'What the fuck happened to my corolla.'

Irene immediately throws on a pair of studded blue jeans which were strewn about the floor. She lifts up the plain white t shirt she's been wearing for pajama's for weeks & sprays on some deodorant-- which for some reason is in her hand-- & bolts through her door. She's heading down the hall to her girlfriend Patty's place, on the prowl for beer.

She's pounding on Patty's door. Irene's head feeling like a red-hot branding iron is sizzling inside her brain.

'What the fuck,' Irene hears from inside the room. Patty's door slowly opens.

'Fuck Irene what the hell are you doing it's seven o clock in the morning,' Patty spits out the words like her mouth is full of fur. Patty stands looking through the crack in the door, the latch still intact. Patty's once pretty eyes looking like she's wearing a disguise of bags & wrinkles. Covering up the women she was.

'I need a beer. Let me in. Come on, come on.' Irene is obviously desperate but all this has happened before & Patty is getting sick of it.

'Fuck off Irene,' Patty says & goes to close the door but Irene is persistent & sticks her bare foot in the crack. Patty tries to slam the door hard but she's got no leverage so all she does is stub Irene's bare toes.

'Jesus Christ Patty that hurt,' Irene says putting on her little girl face. Which is actually quite grotesque. Patty knows she's in the same hound dog boat so she pointedly states,

'Fuck Irene come on, I've got someone in here with me.'

All of a sudden Irene backs off. She knows this is serious. Patty is definitely not going to let her in if someone is in her bed. Everything in the transition house is a secret. Whoever is screwing who has to be kept under close raps. Shit the powers that be even frown on having friends in your place. If someone is found sleeping over, the word is keep your mouth shut.

Irene also knows this makes her chances of scoring a beer that much slimmer.

'Come on Patty someone stole the corolla. I don't know what the fuck to do.'

Irene pleads, 'I need a beer.'

'Wait here,' Patty hesitantly says. Irene pulls back her foot which was still stuck in the crack. Patty shuts the door & pulls the chain off the latch. Turning tip toeing to the kitchen. Returning with a single cold beer can in hand.

Patty hesitates & opens the door slowly as if an apparition's going to come flying out. She steps out into the hall. Holding out a cold High Test can of beer. Which Irene eagerly takes & opens with her thumb.

Patty leans back on the door while Irene greedily gulps a life renewing swig.

'So, who ya got in there,' Irene asks as she wipes her mouth with her short shirt sleeve.

'None of your business,' Patty shoots back.

'Fuck it ain't Zach is it, you cradle robber,' Irene takes another swig of the sweet nectarine soothing her throat.

'Zach's fucking thirty-one you witch. Fuck you, cradle robber, you wish.' Patty shoots back with just a touch of a grin.

'You've got your beer now get outta here, I gotta get back to my man.' Patty breaks into a sly smile.

Patty & Irene share a big laugh. It is quite funny. Patty's over fifty, way past her prime, & she's still getting it. Who ever would have thought. Irene & Patty both share the humor of the situation. Both know they ain't got much time left, so party on when you can.

'Well excuse me,' Irene says exaggerating the words, 'If I'd have known I wouldn't have bothered you,'.

'Yea right you skank. I hope you're jealous,'

'Fuck that,' Irene smiles as she passes Patty the beer. Patty politely takes a little sip. She doesn't want to be smelling too bad of beer when she returns inside.

Irene smelling Patty's breath says, 'Don't worry honey you smell like a brewery anyway,' Irene just saying what Patty was thinking.

Patty takes a bigger longer drink,

'Who the fuck cares anyway,' Patty replies shaking the tuffs of hair off her face. Patty was what was known as a tough broad with a soft side. Irene was known for being butt fuck crazy. They made a good pair when they were getting along.

When they weren't watch out.

Patty had only one thought on her mind & that was young Zach waiting for her inside. Fucking this guy brought back memories of the way she was when she loved to dream. Now she's got to try & arouse this guy into a mid morning ride with her sagging tits & flabby ass. With lips that resembled flaking paint, long ago having lost their appeal. She knew it would be a challenge to raise Zach's drug addled prick.

'Look Honey I gotta go back inside,' Patty says starting to turn back to the door. Then she remembers she's holding the beer & passes it back to Irene. Who's in the process of looking for a butt. Patting herself down checking her studded blue jean pockets.

'Got a light,' Irene asks as she pulls one out & puts a stale butt she's found into her mouth.

Patty makes a quick decision that the sleeping prince charming inside can wait.

'Got a smoke for me,' Patty asks.

'I think let me check. Why don't you go back in & get another beer while I look,'

Irene says out the side of her mouth.

Irene feigns to start checking her studded pockets for smokes. Knowing she'll be lucky if she finds another butt. Patty gives up on waiting & passes Irene a worn bic lighter.

'I'll go get a beer, be right back,' Patty says, Irene gives her a girly sheepish grin. Patty tiptoes again back to her fridge & grabs a cold one. She checks in on Zach on her way back to the door. He's still sleeping. She gives him a glance, looking at the top of his head nestled on the crusty pillow.

She didn't see Zach's thin angular sunken cheeks pocked from meth. A nose that was exploding in scabbing red blotches. His hair shorn down to bumpy black stubs. All she saw was the Rock Hudson of her youth. Broad blue eyes, smooth weathered skin, hardy high cheekbones & a bed of hair blowing in the wind.

Patty could hear Irene starting to get anxious scratching at the door like a cat. She opens the door just as Irene was preparing to start knocking. The last thing Patty needed was Irene pounding on the door disturbing her Rock Hudson.

Patty shuts the door silently behind her. Just her & Irene in the hall. A long barren corridor studded with doors decorated with catchy phrases, 'Keep Out', 'Mud Slide Region', 'Don't Knock before Noon',' Nirvana is a State of Mind', 'Piss off'.

Patty opens the beer handing it to Irene in one motion. The last one, long polished off. I wonder where she put the can, Patty thinks looking around. Patty reaches out for Irene's butt-- exchanging beer for butt. Irene takes the fresh High Test & greedily drinks.

'Fuck, what the fuck happened to my car,' Irene slurs into Patty's face. Patty blows rings of smoke back haloing Irene's red, spider web eyes.

'What are you talking about,' Patty asks reaching out for the beer. Irene takes a quick swig & hands it over to her. Ironically Patty now finds herself smoking a butt & drinking a beer while Irene stands there with nothing.

'The corolla's gone,' Irene says.

'How do you know?'

'I looked out the window this morning & it wasn't there.' Irene answered impatiently, taking back her butt.

'What the fuck were you doing after I left last night,' Patty asks, she's starting to get a little fuzzy. If you've been drunk as a skunk the night before, it doesn't take much to bring back the buzz.

'I don't know, when did you leave? Was Herbert still there?' Irene asks as she now reaches for the beer. Now she has both, everything is as it should be.

'Herbert was there waiting for you to pass out so he could get into your pants. I split when that little shit Sean showed up. He's an asshole & a sleazy dealer,' Patty says.

'Fuck I don't remember anything. I must have been pretty wrecked,' Irene takes a swig.

'No question there, they were on a pretty serious quest for some more meth when

I left,' Patty said.

'What the fuck does that have to do with the corolla,' Irene passes the beer to

Patty. Who takes a pretty big swig herself.

'Sean probably had something to do with it,' Patty sneers, she really hated that prick. Patty gives the beer back to Irene & takes the butt.

'How the fuck did he take it,' Irene replies you can actually see the wheels start to turn in her head.

'Herbert & Sean were scheming about something. I overheard them talking about doing a meth run to the city.' Patty said blowing a billowing plume of smoke in Irene's face & palming the butt.

'Fuck I sure don't remember that.' Irene says, speaking as if through a fog.

'They probably stole your keys, took the corolla & went to get some dope.' Patty said resolutely. The beer was gone Irene wanted more but Patty balked. She really did want to get back in.

'When did you hook up with Zach then. Was he at my place?'

'I met him in the hall on my way back to my place,' Patty said.

'You dog,' Irene giggled. Stifling a smile while trying to hold herself up from falling down backwards.

Patty reached out & grabbed her.

'Watch yourself sweetheart,' Patty helped Irene steady herself.

'I did get a call this morning,' Irene said suddenly.

'What do you mean?' Patty was getting anxious. Fuck Irene she thinks-- always getting in the way. It always has to be about her & that's not fair.

'Someone calling me about the corolla. They left a number,'

'Well Jesus Christ Irene phone it back.' Patty said turning to go into her room.

'Ya gotta anymore beer?' Irene asked, Patty just ignored her & closed the door.

Irene proceeded down the hall. Knocking on doors looking for beer, something to drink. If she got lucky maybe a bit of meth.

It took a few days before Irene finally sobered up enough to give a shit. Take a critical look around to see where she was at. You're fucked up ya gotta get your life together she was thinking. That thought passed through her like a spark.

But during that moment of clarity she phoned Sam the social worker. It took awhile but Sam eventually found out the story.

'The car is at the police pound costing you thirty bucks a day,' Sam said to Irene settling down onto a well-used chair at her kitchen table.

'I'll drive you to town to get it tomorrow.' Sam had come around to Irene's place to talk with her face to face.

The story was—Sam had found out & was trying to explain to Irene over a cup of coffee. Sam & Irene were in Irene's place sitting round the sticky kitchen table, her bed a mess the window wide open. Slight ocean breeze winding through the room. At least the coffee mugs were clean Sam noticed. Red recliner covered in clothes.

'You gave the keys to Herbert to drive Sean into town to pick up some meth.' Sam started. 'Only Sean knew where to go. Well once in town the two of em of course got all turned around. Before you knew it Herbert was driving the wrong way on a one-way street. The cops-- who happened to be on the street going the right way-- saw the corolla coming the wrong way directly at them. Two headlights bearing down. The cops pulled the two buffoons over. When they asked for a license neither had one. After much questioning they got extremely evasive answers from the boys. The cops figured out that Herbert did have a license. But it was currently suspended which cost a bigger fine then just not having one. That was probably why Herbert wouldn't give a straight answer. Herbert's not as stupid as he wants you to think, Sam was thinking to himself.

'It was obvious the car didn't belong to either one of the boys. There were no papers they could find in the car. So when the cops called in the licence plate to see if it was stolen the answer came back from the dispatcher,'

' No no record of it being stolen,' the dispatcher told them.

'It is registered to an Irene Smith who lives on the coast. She owes a lot of money in parking tickets.' The dispatcher added.

'The cops asked the dispatcher to call you. Maybe make some sense out of what's going on.

'That's you' Sam said to Irene trying to keep her attention as he explained all this to her. Irene was doing everything she knew to keep from nodding off.

'While the police were waiting to find out about the corolla, Herbert & Sean were detained. They were put in the back of the police car. Giggling like a couple of monkeys I'm sure,' Sam smiled a chubby smirk. Irene laughed at that, Sam carried on,

'Sean was detained for just being too stoned. There had to be a law somewhere the cops had thought. Sean evidently told them he didn't really mind. He was so stoned anything that happened was an adventure. Herbert was detained for lying & being a jerk. Herbert didn't care, as usual, he was just in it for the party.

'Well the dispatcher had phoned you to see if you owned the car. But you were of course literally dead drunk at this point in the night. You were off in black out land. That's where the message came from.

'So the dispatcher dispatched to the police who were patiently waiting in their car. Listening to these two clowns in the back just making no sense.'

'There's no answer,' the dispatcher told them, 'I left a message, what you do is up to you.'

'Roger that,' the cops had replied.

'They decided to put Herbert & Sean in jail for the night. The boys had nowhere to go anyway. They put the corolla in the pound & the boys got to spend a night in the downtown jail. Which was not bad at all. They would've slept anywhere, anyway. It gave them some time to catch up with old friends, I'm sure.' Sam took a breath.

'So the corolla's in the police lock up in Vancouver. Who knows what happened to Herbert & Sean.'

All of this Sam said. Trying to keep some form of semblance of Irene's attention.

Sam was a social worker on the coast & was trying to work with Irene. He had got the cops to tear up the tickets so they would release the corolla. After he explained to them Irene's situation over the phone the day after this mess. It was agreed she'd never be able to pay them anyway. For his end Sam made a commitment to get the corolla out of the pound ASAP.

Sam had a social work meeting in town tomorrow anyways. At least his gas & ferry fair were covered. He was clear with Irene to be ready in the morning.

' We're on the eight twenty, first thing make sure you're up & dressed, don't be late. Only one rule no drinking,' Sam told a bobble headed Irene.

'You gotta be sober when I pick you up.' Sam said in a voice that said don't fuck up as he got his bulk up & left. Making sure he closed the door tight leaving Irene's room.

The ride over on the ferry was totally uneventful. Irene slept the whole way. Sam left her in his car & went up top with his coffee. Enjoy the view, have a smoke.

Howe sound is truly beautiful in the morning Sam thought. Letting the pain & the anger slip out his ears. Sam stood by the rail looking out over an icy smooth silent sound. Cradled by an ominous stone mountain crypt.

On the other side Sam dropped Irene off at the police pound. Irene saying for sure she'll use the money--Sam got her-- to get the corolla out.

'I'm gonna drive right back. I promise.' Irene lied. 'Maybe we'll see each other on the ferry back.' Irene said as she waved goodbye to Sam. Who drove away not overly optimistic of her sincerity.

You were actually happy. It was a good day. Well it all went to shit after you got the corolla out of hock. You drove straight to the cold beer store to get a twelve pack for the ride back. By the time you got to the ferry you'd stopped at a couple of regular spots for shots. There weren't to many bars left that you weren't barred from so you had to pick your spots.

You eventually got to the ferry & got the corolla in the lineup. Yo' decided you had time to go to the bar in the pretty little ferry town. V actually the Chinese food restaurant was the only place in this prett' ferry town who'd serve you a beer. You had a few beer & a lot mein. On your way back to the corolla you stopped in at the l' got a six pack for the ferry ride. The bartender had no trouble selling the beer to you, as long as he knew you weren't drinking it within his view.

Back in line the cars started to move. You inched the corolla forward carefully onto the boat. Finally you were parked on board. You looked around, everyone was headed upstairs for a meal & the view. You cracked open a beer, had a couple of sips & went to sleep.

The banging on the corolla window woke you up. It was the ferry worker waking you. They were pulling up to the dock, time to get off.

You shook yourself awake. Ran your fingers through your hair looking at your face in the rear-view mirror. You really didn't care what you saw. Your mind was so messed up all it saw was distorted.

You followed the car ahead of you off the boat & up the ramp. As you drove the corolla off the ferry lot you pulled up to the highway & noticed the signs. You screamed,

'Fuck, I got on the wrong boat!'

The sign said ten miles to Nanaimo. You weren't on the coast-- you were on the island.

You pulled the corolla over to the side of the road. Cracked a beer & started to cry.

Might as well head into town you said in your head. Fuck I gotta get beer. Maybe you should just get back on the ferry. You were in a dilemma. Each side of your brain screaming at the other.

'You idiot, you're stupid, you're ugly, you're a loser,' said the depressing side.

'Fuck you, everything for a reason, don't freak out, you'll come out ok just like you always do--you'll survive,' said the side which was virtually pleading for some sanity.

You meticulously checked your pockets for money. You had enough for some more beer. You looked at the gas & realized it was almost on empty, but you had enough to get to town. There was no boat going back no matter what you decided anyway.

In town it wasn't hard to find a cold beer store. You spent the rest of your money on an eight pack. You took a road down to a beach & found a pretty parking place. You sat in the corolla & watched a westcoast sunset looking east.

You came up with a plan to phone the transition house where you lived. The staff there will know what to do you figured. Unfortunately, your cell phone was dead.

The corolla wouldn't start, no gas. You stuffed some cans of beer in your stylishly fringed cowboy jacket which had seen better days & set off to find a phone. Leaving the corolla alone on the beach. You made your way back to town & panhandled for change because you'd spent your last dime on beer. When you got enough coin (you'd done this before) you tucked yourself into a phone booth & made the call. Careful to get the coins right in the slot. You didn't want to be losing any hard-earned change.

The staff at the transition house on the coast were having a quiet day. With Irene away everything was always quieter. When the phone rang, they noticed the number came from Nanaimo across the strait. The staff were automatically suspicious it might be Irene.

'Sure enough, it's Irene,' the worker said to her colleague hearing Irene's voice on the line.

'Irene calm down you're not making any sense,' the worker said firmly,

'what's she saying,' her colleague asked in her ear.

'I don't know, I can't understand her, here you try,' the worker said as she handed the phone to her partner.

'Hi Irene. It's Jane, where are you?'

'Iiiiiiiiiiiiiii'm here,' Irene slurred back.

'Where's here?' Jane replied.

'I   thin--------thin-------think   it...........
....s Naan................aiiiimo.'

'Fuck Irene you're really fucked up,' Jane said. She could barely under-stand her.

'Puuuleeeese whatshouldIdo.' Irene got it out like an explosion.

Jane looked over at her colleague & asked her to get the address of the Nanaimo Homeless Shelter.

'Here Irene slow down, do you have any money,' Jane asked knowing the answer.

'No but I got beer,' Irene replied clear as a bell. She had a flash of clarity.

'That's great Irene. Here, there's a shelter in Nanaimo just get a cab & it'll take you there. I'll phone ahead & tell them you're coming.'

'I've goooot the corrrrrrrrrrolla' Irene slurred back.

'Where is it.' Jane inquired.

' Noooooooooooooo gas,' Irene said.

'That's probably for the best' Jane said, 'You don't sound sober enough to drive.

Now find a cab. I'll get the shelter over there to pay.'

Irene slammed down the phone mad. She didn't know why she was so angry. Maybe at herself for being such a fuck up. Maybe at the staff at the transition house for not being able to teletransport her home immediately. Irene sat down on the curb cracked open a beer & waited for a cab to come by.

Cabs are like buses. If you stay in one place long enough eventually one will appear.

Sure enough a cab pulled up. Irene threw away her beer & pulled herself up using the cabs back door handle. The driver looked around & frowned. He knew what was coming. Irene opened the door & slouched her way in like a folding sheet.

'Where to,' the driver asked.

Irene took a while to settle herself & figure out where she really is.

'Goinnnng shellllllter,' Irene slurred.

'Got any money,' the driver smirked. He knew the answer but it was slow tonight. His brain needed some levity.

'Iiiiiiiiii dnt now,' said Irene.

The driver just put it in gear & headed for the homeless shelter. It was only a couple blocks away.

'I wannnna stop a a cold beer store,' Irene was yelling in the back, she forgot she had no money. The driver watched her in the rear-view mirror. She's crazy he thought. Little did he know he was right.

The cab pulled up to the curb in front of the shelter. The driver went around to the door & lifted Irene out-- careful not to touch anything morally forbidden. She started stumbling on the sidewalk. The driver helped her sit down on the front steps. He went inside the Nanaimo Shelter to tell the staff about someone sitting stone drunk on the steps he'd just dropped off.

They thanked him for coming in. The workers at Irene's transition house on the coast had phoned to give them a heads up. The driver's description of his fare sure sounded like their girl. They did ask if he'd been paid, when he said no they offered to give him some money for his troubles. Which he gladly accepted.

By the time they all walked to the front door Irene was gone. They all looked up & down the street. Irene was nowhere in sight.

You had hooked up with some guys while you were sitting on the steps. It wasn't hard. You'd cracked a beer & the sound seemed to resonate like a man calling his dog. These two guys appeared like magicians. They said they had some meth. You said you were running out of beer.

'Don't worry we've got lots,' said the one with an incredibly straggly beard, which distracted from his incredibly ugly face. The two missing front teeth didn't help.

The other one was slathering in the mouth. He couldn't believe the luck. You were like a drunken deer caught in their headlights.

You all went down to the beach & had a fuck party.

You woke up alone just before dawn. Lips crusty. Mouth muscles tight, a result of forced exertion. Your right hand stiff & sticky. Your groin ached & your butt was dry with blood.

!!!!!

You made your way back up the hill from the beach. Body aching. Your tasseled cowboy jacket covered in sand on the back. You remembered something about a homeless shelter. You wandered around the pretty coastal town looking like a bum until you finally found the shelter.

The shelter took you in. No questions asked. Cleaned you up. You became frantic at one point because you had lost your wallet.

(((((

It was arranged for Irene to return to her room at the transition house on the coast. Shelter staff in Nanaimo got her on the boat with just enough money for food & coffee. One staff, an old girl who'd been there & back again, slipped a pack of smokes into Irene's pocket. On the other side was arranged for Irene to be met by Sam who'd drive her back home.

On the boat Irene went up top & was a blubbering mess. But she made it, all the way to the other side sober.

Sam was at the dock to meet you. He was standing there watching the sunset over the water. There was a thick smoky silence on the drive back to the transition house. Broken by the odd laugh, but no tears. Sam dropping you off at the transition house front door. You reaching over across the front seat to hug him. Sam feigning politely, speaking softly, ' I know I know,' squeezing your hand , saying,

' get some sleep sweet girl.'

That first night, back in your room you started drinking. You had somehow scored yourself a bottle of vodka. You were furious at yourself for what had happened. You started kicking in other people's doors on the floor. You were causing a dramatic disturbance in the corridor. The workers on shift were wringing their hands in despair. Then you did the darndest thing. You went back to your room to everyone's relief. Where you proceeded to phone the police on yourself.

The cops came right away. Those staff sitting at the front desk welcomed the police in. They had tried but they just couldn't do a thing for you. They watched as first two then four then six policemen made their way up to your room. You put up a momentous fight evidently. Mohamad Ali had nothing on you. It took them all six to hog tie you. They took you down the stairs & out the door like a spider on a spit. Tossing you into the waiting paddy wagon. All the cops leaning on their cars. Looking like they'd just run a three-minute mile.

The next morning—after spending the night in cells-- the police dropped you off at the front door of the transition house. You waving a cheery goodbye as the police car took off outta there like a shot. You were smiling as you walked through the transition house lobby. You went up the stairs to your room. Once in you walked amongst the unobliterated disaster you had caused the previous night. Proceeding cautiously each step taking a chance at stepping onto something gross. You made your way to your window & opened the same curtain where you had started this whole mess just a short time ago. It was a bright sunny morning. You shielded your eyes. Sunbeams streaming in through the window. Glass stained in speckles from thrown screwdrivers. You looked back around your abode & started to clean up.

*****

Footnote; Irene did get back her wallet. An older couple-- retired to the beauty & serenity of Nanaimo-- were walking along the beach early the next morning. Something they did every day watching the sunrise. They found the wallet half buried in the sand. It wasn't unusual for them to find odd pieces of paraphernalia on the beach. They routinely turned found items in to the police.

The corolla-- patiently waiting on the beach-- during a seismic high tide storm was washed out to sea.

Shelter Early Morning Smoke Circle

Very Informal. Ray, Shirley, Eric, Julien & sometimes Indian Mike. The sleeping sun waking slowly. Starting its ascent. Taking its time. Controlling the ambience.

Dawn starting its exotic dance in the homeless shelter courtyard.

Shirley would come out first. Ray would already be there. Julien was on his second cigarette. Eric had been there all night on his computer. Indian Mike nowhere to be seen.

Shirley had a story worse than gory. Rays tale was a tragedy. Julien was fighting the drink. Eric was putting a plan together for the rest of his life.

It always started with a cough. Usually from Ray, but Shirley could give him a go. When she let go it was like her whole body was coming up. She was an elegant old lady. A beautiful example of how bad life can get. Her story was always told with a stiff upper lip. Her spirit shone like a bright princess wand.

After the coughing slowed down, we'd all light up another cigarette. This would set off another chorus of coughing which would last as long as a song. Then everything would settle down again. A split second of silence like a fine sip of wine.

Talking would all start at once as if someone had dropped a checkered flag. Everyone had something to say about something. Rules at the shelter, Donald Trump, what the weather would be like today.

Dawn perked up its ears & slowed down to listen.

Julien would go on & on about how unfair it was here at the shelter. He always had something to say about one thing or another. Usually concerning his ongoing struggle to get along with shelter staff & follow the rules.,

'I don't see why I can't make my own coffee in the middle of the night. Whenever

I want.'

Julien would mumble to no one in particular. His bald white head-- a pock marked pale dome—semi covered with wisps of grey white hair. Worn out bloodshot robin eyes bulging out of his head.

Julien'd stand there, in his lanky five eleven frame. Coffee in one hand. Smoke in the other. One foot up on the bench like a hockey coach. Standing half out half under the droll flimsy covering—which served as a roof for the smoke pit. He'd be looking out into the light cracking the eastern sky. Julien's thin cracked lips moving under the shadow of a vast pointed nose. Talking to no one in particular, watching his smoke curl into oblivion.

Julien still thinks he's a ladies' man. He's gotta be at least sixty but you never get a straight answer about his age. He thinks his status at the shelter is quite high because he's good with tools & fancies himself a carpenter. To his credit he does pick up work now & then.

'You just want to stay up with the cute looking staff,'

Shirley says, stopping from coughing just long enough to give Julien a jab. She wants nothing to do with him. She'd seen a million Julien's downtown in the east side. Loud mouth boasting drinking guy who thinks he's just the cat's ass. They are a dime a dozen down on Hastings.

'No it's nothing like that. I think she's got a thing for me,' Julien replies contradicting himself.

You would, Shirley thinks. That girl better look out for herself Shirley mutters under her breath.

Julien's got a side of him which just ain't safe & they all know it.

'Hey, if she wants it I won't refuse,'

Julien snickers, he honestly thinks in his booze addled brain that he's got a shot.

He lights up another cigarette, as if it's his last one.

'Jeez I gotta get more smokes,' he lies. He hates people bumming from him. He's really cheap with his smokes.

Julien starts to go on about how much money he's got. He shows the group his new seven-hundred-dollar watch he just bought. A dash of dawn twinkles the glass.

'Are you crazy,' Shirley says, not impressed. How can someone be so stupid she thinks.

'Fuck man don't go showing that around,' Ray says. He looks away with an overly interested eye. How crazy is this guy for bringing something like that in here Ray says to himself.

Eric looks up as Julien shows it around taking a look of disbelief at how someone can be so like a child at Julien's age,

'Cool Man,' Eric says.

Julien's from a family in the Maritimes. He's been across Canada once. He got here many years & tears ago. He talked of his father leaving him a watch. The family promising they'd send it out, after dad died. Dad died twenty years ago. It's never coming, he's known that for awhile, but Julien refuses to believe it.

Julien's as stubborn as a mule. If someone disagrees with him he'll never shut up.

'No problem, I'll lock it up in the locker,' Julien says.

Everyone looked up & instantly in silence agreed don't get into it. Everyone with a brain knows you didn't bring an expensive watch into a den of thieves.

Ray more then anyone. He'd noticed that watch with dollar signs flashing through his brain. If this guy's so stupid to bring an expensive watch into the shelter, he deserves to lose it Ray thought.

Ray was not called The Beast for nothing. He was a very big man. Easily over three hundred & thirty pounds. Shoulders broad as a semi. Ray always wore sweats & sat on an aluminum frame patio chair with two wooden slats stretched across, to stop the chair from collapsing. He was just too big for the bench. The reinforcement really wasn't working well & Ray was going through a few chairs a week. The soft aluminum legs would slowly start to stretch out. Ray sitting like a captain in a boat slowly sinking. It was always cause for a laugh to watch him going down. Ray loved the attention.

Staff at the shelter were looking for something, that could hold his heavy size. That wouldn't be constantly embarrassing him they thought. Everyone deserves a sense of dignity. No matter their condition all staff agreed.

Ray'd sit there in his chair. His sagging belly bulging out over the straining elastic of his sweats. Great rolls of flesh flowing out from under the t-shirt & hoodie he always wore for pajamas. Ray would cough-- a bellowing bull in heat. His stomach & chest rippling like a giant jellyfish. It should be mentioned The Beast always wore bare feet. Even when it was cold.

When this was pointed out Ray'd reply,

'Who can afford socks,' Ray'd say & smile.

The Beast wore his poverty like a halo. He was past worrying about money. His ship had sailed & he knew it. His life was all about story telling & complaining.

Ray was an oilman from Alberta. He'd worked in the oil patch most of his life. He used to have a lot of money & a nice house on an Albertan acreage. But it all went to shit after he crashed his truck-- on a drunken snowy night-- head first into a semi. That basically destroyed his life & got him hooked on pain medication.

A twenty-year downhill slide. Now fifty-eight here he is living on the island in the homeless shelter. He's been on the island for ten years & loves it. It's fucking beautiful. But his addiction to crack & meth is like Atlas with the world on his shoulders.

Ray would always bring up how fucked up everyone else was. He had a penchant for gossip. He had to know what was happening, especially if it wasn't any of his business.

'How's your health Ray,' I asked. His coughing was atrocious. Every morning was getting worse. It had become almost background music.

'I'm OK,' Ray replied, reaching down for his puffer which was always clasped in the palm of his hand. The one that wasn't holding the cigarette. He lifted his elbow & puffed a squeeze into his mouth-- like a mother bird feeding a worm to a chirping baby.

'Got a new puffer from the Doc couple of days ago, seems to be working,' Ray said. I started laughing. He stifled & then exploded into a laughing cough.

Shirley grinned, her eyes lifting to catch Ray's laughter. Eric looked up from his computer & chuckled.

Ray had a deep rumbling laugh like a moose caught in a lava flow. Ray's hollow dark eyes were slitted behind layers of flesh. It was difficult to see into Ray's eyes. Especially when he wore sunglasses. He always had a week-old beard he used to hide a once handsome face. Thick black wavy hair never combed. Always pushing straggling strands off his forehead like a nervous tick. Long strong thick—tobacco stained-- fingers dwarfing his cigarette.

'Want some fish.' Ray asked me. 'Got some over in the freezer.'

'Where'd you get them,' I murmured.

'Out at Trout Lake, caught em right from the shore.'

'How'd you get there,' I asked, perking interest.

'Went up in the van, me, Lil & Luke.'

'Van's still running?'

'Oh yea, yea it's running good.'

'You get that thing with the keys all worked out,' I asked.

'Fuck yea, ended up costing me seven hundred & ten dollars,'

Lil was Ray's women. One night about a month ago in a meth filled rage Lil threw the van keys at Ray one crazy night at the shelter. Lil screaming at Ray like a kamikaze. Ray just trying to get out of her sight. She threw the keys at his head & missed. The keys were never found (some thought they might have slipped down a vent).

Ray had to buy a whole new ignition system. He worried someone might find the old keys & steal the van.

'Fuck that's a lot,'

'No kidding,' said Ray, taking a long deep drag.

Ray would cough. That was about the length of the conversation before he had to cough again.

Shirley would say, 'You better watch those cigarettes,' with a flirty look & then went on her own coughing spree.

'Look who's talking,' replied Ray, with a sparkle in his eye. I've still got it he thought.

Shirley was just the opposite of Ray. Ray'd overflow the chair he was sitting on like a walrus. Shirley's frail rail thin frame would be perched daintily on the edge of the bench, like a pretty bird on a branch. Her spindly legs crossed elegantly. Shirley holding her cigarette & coffee as if she was at a Hollywood party.

Always in an old robe. Pink slippers & a different sweater every day covering her ethiopian shoulders. Shirley was sixty eight & looked like she had died & re-risen. Her partner in life for the past twenty years—Jeff-- died recently of a heart attack. Jeff had been back in Toronto visiting his sister. It was totally unexpected.

After Jeff died the landlord kicked Shirley out of the apartment she & Jeff had been living in for ten years. She left the island & went to stay with her son in Surrey. She had a heart attack along the way & ended up in Vancouver General. When it was time to go, her son forgot to pick her up. Shirley ended up walking ten miles in the rain back to her son's place. Who was on the couch smoking weed when she walked in thru the door. He had got his days mixed up.

That got her sick again, pneumonia. This time the hospital decided to send her back to the hospital on the island where her doctors were. When she got discharged from the island hospital she had nowhere to go, except the island's homeless shelter.

'You smoking meth up there?' Shirley asked Ray. She knew he was, she just wanted to watch him lie. She had a hard heart.

'No no money for meth. I don't like that shit anymore.' Ray lied.

'Lil's smoking meth,' I slipped that in cautiously.

'Yea she gets it from Luke,' Ray said, under his breath.

The story of Luke is one of the most bizarre you'll ever hear. You see Lil is crazy. She & Ray complete each other. They've been together for fifteen years. Both previously married, both lost it all to drugs & bad decisions. They met at a homeless camp on the Coquitlam River. An infamous piece of forested land which suited the homeless situation quite nicely. Ray would regale you with wild drug stories, of the time, everyone just hammering down. During the day they'd tube down the Coquitlam River. Ray said they had a hell of a time before it all fell apart—as it always does when you're homeless. He & Lil came over to the island to visit her sister ten years ago & never left.

Well Lil met Luke last year. Luke is a sad soul who's lived on the island all his life. He lives with a diagnosed mental illness & an addiction to all kinds of drugs. Luke loves them all. He's twenty years Lisa's junior. Now Ray isn't sure what the hell's going on. He knows Lil, whose still in her forties, can be an attractive woman with her long black hair & immense bosoms. Even after a lifetime of drugs Lil can still turn a head. Luke is a young innocent man with a functioning penis. Ray's no fool or is he.

Lil is determined that Luke is not her lover. He is a long-lost son from one of her ex boyfriends she says. You see Luke was adopted & it's not clear who his biological parents really are. Ray is just reeling it all in, it just doesn't make any sense. How the hell did this guy come into their life & who the hell—really-- is he?

Lil would either be staying at the shelter or in the van with—'her son'-- Luke. Even though the van was Ray's, Lil claimed it was half hers. That's why that time with the keys was inevitable. Lil screaming at Ray-- like a banshee-- rattling the windows in the shelter,

'Give me the keys you bastard,' Lil's face turning different shades of crimson. Ray said ok & dropped them on the floor. He turned his back on her & headed to his room. Lil picked up the keys & threw them back at his head. Like a Nolan Ryan fast ball. That was the last anyone saw of those ignition starters.

Ray was having a hard time trying to deal with what is right & what is just wrong. Ray would always become quiet as the sun started creeping up. He liked to sit back in his reinforced patio chair when the conversation wasn't about him or some things he just didn't like talking about. He'd sit watching the emerging sky. Thinking about purple prairie skies. Oil rigs silhouetting the distant horizon like in an oil painting. Back in the day. Another life.

He didn't like talking about drugs. I think in his way it embarrassed him. Yet Ray would brag about how many beers he had the other night.

Shirley would start to talk. Dawn made her dour. Shirley was a hippy street kid who turned old. The love of her life—Jeff-- rescued her from her life on the street. Shirley was a child of the sixties & was still fighting the man. She swore she's been addicted to opiates for thirty years & she never knew it. She was going to sue the system that did this to her.

'Oh yea you just wait, I'm gonna get em. Get em good.' She'd say in a firm committed voice. No one understood who exactly she was going to get. Shirley was living off her hate. It gave her strength. Her partner Jeff had always said that they'd get em together. But now he was gone. It just wasn't sitting real to her.

'Jeffy wants me to get those bastards.' She'd say into her cigarette. Specks of dawn dancing around her shoulder.

Shirley held a vigil at the Sally Ann on the island for Jeff after he died & no one came. On the way back home she forgot his ashes-- which were in a box-- at a bus stop. She wasn't frantic she knew Jeff would find her. You see Jeff was a mystic. Sure enough that night someone phoned the shelter. They had the box with the ashes & were anxious to return them to Shirley.

Shirley was a very fragile beautiful old lady. Compared in size to the Beast she wasn't even there. She'd started her street life when she was twelve. Her mother dropped her on the corner of Hastings & Main. You're on your own-- you little whore-- she told Shirley. Closed the car door & drove away. There Shirley stood alone on the curb. That night she slept in her clothes under a bridge, curled up in a ball.

Mother had found out her new boyfriend was regularly raping Shirley. Her albatross of a daughter. This made little Shirley's psycho narcist Mother jealous. Blaming it all on Shirley. Giving her reason to throw Shirley out-- onto the street.

? ? ?

Dawn was spinning a dirty yellow thread. Filtering through the ancient cedar trees surrounding the shelter. The sun was starting to wake up, as in a yawn. The black retreating. We all sort of slunk back into a shell of solitude.

Silence broken only by persistent coughing. Julien was finishing up his coffee. Ray was thinking about breakfast. Watching the sun slicing upwards through the huge cedar canopy-- he was in no hurry. Shirley said she had to go back in for a pill but wasn't quite ready yet. Shirley was always very evasive about what pills she was actually taking. However she loved her marijuana about that she was quite clear.

Eric looked up from his computer & asked me for a light. I handed him my Bic. Eric disdained his position. There was no one so shocked at what life had brought down on him. Eric was forty-nine a proud immigrant from Germany. He had come to Canada to make a better life for him & his wife. It had all gone to shit. After establishing himself with a successful company, the wife started to look for an even better situation. She left Eric & somehow took the house. Eric -- during this time-- turned to cocaine & started the slide into crack & meth which brought him to the homeless shelter.

Eric-- who was around my age-- had a militant disposition. A well built man of enormous outrage & compassion. He desperately wanted to make the world a better place. He motioned me over to the bench he was using as a desk for his lap top.

'Look at this,' he said pointing at the screen.

'What the hell is it,' I said, bending down squeezing my eyes to see what I was looking at. It looked like just a bunch of wiggly lines & graphs.

'It's a wiring diagram for solar energy panels. I used to install them,' Eric said.

'You make good money doing that?' I asked.

'I did alright,' Eric sighed. He didn't want to get into it too far. He just wanted to show me what he used to do. Thinking somehow by doing that he could get himself a moment of relief from this drudgery he found himself immersed in.

Eric was trying to figure out how to make his situation mean something. You see Eric was surprised he had sunk so low. He had been earmarked for success. But he also enjoyed the meth style of living. He liked the intrigue of the deal. The exchanges in the alley. The drama of scoring. The bang of getting high. The insanity.

Eric perceived himself as a functional meth head. As if such a thing really exists.

He was addressing his situation with engineerial precision. Every component has a place. The reality of his situation had to be broken down into rational reason. That was the problem, some aspects of his situation weren't rational. There were some things which weren't sane. They couldn't be explained.

'You know I took Jane down to some trailer the other day to store her stuff,' Eric said.

'That was nice of you,' I replied knowing a story was going to happen. Everyone knew Jane-- a sometimes early morning shelter friend-- was a witch.

'Well, I try to help if I can,' Eric said with a guttural German slang. Digging in his pocket for a cigarette & pulled out a healthy butt with at least three or four good pulls in it. He lit it with my cracked Bic lighter. Narrowing his bright Hitler eyes as he put flame to butt. Careful not to singe his lips.

'It was crazy. We got there & the people there didn't even know her. Jane insisted this was the place but it clearly wasn't. The people started to get a little freaked out so we left. Jane didn't think twice about it. Got back in the car & we came back to the shelter. It was nuts man,' Eric said stretching his long nazi legs out in front of him.

'It just didn't make any sense,' he finished.

'Pissed you off,' I really didn't know how to reply.

'Just the opposite,' Eric turned to look at me,

'What do you mean?' His answer intrigued me.

'I love the action. I love the crazy of it all,' Eric replied, taking a pull on his butt. Watching the smoke swirl up over the wood paneled fence which walled the shelter patio. Up into the mystical cedars where a now sparkling dawn, was dancing in absolute abandon.

'How do you survive, man?' I was sincerely concerned.

'I don't know,' he said turning back to look at me returning my lighter.

'First thing I gotta cut out the meth for awhile.' Eric paused, 'Clear my mind.'

'Wouldn't it just be easy enough for everyone to just stop doing drugs,' I asked absentmindedly. Sometimes when I look into the eyes of the home-less all I see in my mind is --why you?

'Drugs aren't the issue. They're just a diversion.,' Eric said. He looked at me sternly. His dark Germanic features taking on a chilling presence. The high strong cheek bones. Dark red hair, close cropped. Fierce blue eyes. Hitler would've loved to have got his hands on this one I thought.

'It's stigma that's the problem.' Eric said.

'What do you mean,' I thought I knew what he was talking about but I needed clarification. I'd heard this before but the term has a tendency to take on a variety of meanings-- depending on who you were talking to.

!!!!!

The sun was streaking through the cedars, hovering just below the wood paneled fence enclosing the shelter. It seemed to be waiting for something. Sometimes out here at this time of day it felt like we were in a prison yard. I know when they set this place up they didn't mean for it to be anything but welcoming. But what they failed to forsee was that when ever you put an eight-foot wood panel fence around an enclosed concrete space it takes on a certain feel. Prison like. This prison however was for keeping people out-- not in.

Waiting for the sun to come up had that brother's in arms appeal. All in this together encased in our own private personal place.

The shelter was starting to wake up inside. You could hear cereal being poured. Milk being looked for. Old conflicts flowing from last night starting to begin again.

'Pass me the sugar,' get it yourself.' 'I'll get it for you my man. No trouble.' 'You trying to suck up.' 'Go fuck yourself.'

The banter of homeless culture never makes any sense. The homeless have a language unique to their situation. You have to be really quick to keep up.

Squabbles & anxiety in the homeless shelter were always prominent in the morning & very late at night.

Dawn started making its presence felt. The voices-- waking up-- in the shelter sounded like baby robins chirping waiting for their breakfast. Worried their mother & father won't be coming back. Left by themselves alone in a nest, high up in a tree. Destined not to survive unless they get some help.

Julien had gone back in. Ray was trying to get up but gravity wasn't helping. He was almost ready to give up & have another puff. Shirley was talking into her phone. Trying to get a hold of her doctor. Still holding her cigarette. Burned down to the butt. Highlighting her tobacco-stained fingers. Nails, bitten down to a dim red cusp.

Eric –still sitting--stared past me looking into the shelter.

'People will work it out themselves. No matter what anyone's going to do.' He said turning to look directly at me.

'It's all about the ceremony man. The catholics have their mass & the druggie has his hit & we're the ones getting treated like shit. Don't make no sense to a thinking man,' he said.

'Yea but mass doesn't kill & isn't seen as a burden on society,' I said back, looking challenging into his eyes.

'Who are you kidding,' Eric said. 'You trying to tell me the catholic church is not as much a drug as a needle in my arm,'

'I guess we all have our crosses to bear,' I answered with a hint of smirk.

'My cross is the swastika,' Eric said. 'It hovers over my german heritage. A sharp sword slicing slowly, a death of a thousand cuts. I know what it's like to be stigmatized.' Eric said.

'History has not been kind to my german generation.' Eric took a drag off his smoke. Paused. I looked at him sitting there. I pictured in my mind different circumstances which would have seen him sitting in a nazi uniform & me sitting in chains. I caught myself & berated my imagination for being so racist.

'That's one of the things which makes me do meth.' Eric said, as if he was trying to talk himself into what he knew was only an excuse.

'I was programmed to succeed but here I sit at forty-nine & it's never been.' Eric continued on,

'I was sold a lie. That to be a man I must suck it up & get on with my life no matter what. No matter how tough. I had to be strong.

'My german conscience hangs around my neck like a stone. Yea I turned to meth to lighten the load. Yea meth cost me my house & my family. But in its own way it saved my sanity.'

'How can you say that,' I said. I was mildly surprised at this statement. Here was a man who had lost everything but was claiming he had somehow become sane.

'I can say that because it's true,' Eric said. 'Living here homeless has made me see that there is no track between them & me. There's a pride in what's happening here. It's cloaked in deceit. Yet everyone here is fighting back in their own way.

'But what's on the tracks blocking the way is the stigma express. Wipeout & disperse. I know all about that it's in my nazi blood. I remember my Grandfather's stories about how the nazis dealt with the fringes of society. Stigmatize, isolate & annihilate.'

'So what's the answer, don't leave me hanging,' I'd heard a lot of this shit before from a lot of guys who had no idea what's the answer, making excuses. I tended to be cynical.

Eric caught my tone & stubbed his cigarette out in the communal coffee can which served as an ashtray. He spoke as if he'd said this many times before & was getting frustrated because it seemed to fall on deaf ears,

'Someone just has to listen.' Eric said, giving me a nazi stare.

'Gotja,' I replied a little embarrassed. I'd heard this before as a plea for years. But never as a command. I almost saluted.

&

Ray let out a deep groan-- the sun just farted I thought-- he was almost off the chair. He just couldn't wait any longer for his cereal. Gravity was to be defeated.

But just as The Beast stood up-- throwing a shadow over the patio-- in walks Indian Mike. Coming in through the wood paneled patio gate, letting a slice of sunlight in behind him. Mike plops himself down on the bench.

'Anyone got a smoke,' Mike asks.

Ray sits back down—after all of that-- he's really coughing now. But happy to see Mike. Now let's have some fun Ray was thinking. Ray never lost that little boy's mischievous grin—the tips of his mouth curled up on the ends pointing to excited evil eyes-- like Batman's nemesis the Joker. Ray was always up for a story & he knew Indian Mike's stories were always bizarre.

Eric, notices Mike sit down. They're friends, they hang out, share each other's dope. Eric knows Mike has a way of finding trouble. Eric bends over the excuse for a table we're all sitting around-- a rotting wicker model-- & hands Indian Mike a butt from his pocket.

'Heil Hitler! What the fuck happened to you,' Eric says looking at Mike's face. Shirley calmly glances over at Mike & takes a long drag on her cigarette.

Mike looks up, with Eric's butt hanging from the side of his mouth, looking for a light. Ray leans over the arm of his bending patio chair & flicks his bic for Mike's butt.

'Holy fuck man, what happened to you,' Ray says sort of impressed with what he sees. The Beast had been a brawler in his day.

Mike wasn't real anxious to speak. Indian Mike is an astrologer. Mike is ageless. Mike knows the skies at night. He'd seen a flying saucer when he was young & has been looking for another one ever since.

'Got hit by a two by four,' Mike smirked & took a long drag on his butt.

Mike always sat hunched down. Elbows on his knees. Head bent toward the floor. Black wisp of hair staring at you.

I was focusing in on the black leather jacket he always wore. I noticed right away the cuffs were stained in blood. I was thinking that something must have happened but I certainly wasn't going to react.

Abruptly Mike raised his head & stared right past me. I saw it all. His face-- which always carried a permanent scar on his cheek-- looked like mush, all purple & blue framed in dry blood.

'Fuck man you been to the hospital,' Ray asked.

'No, my Auntie saw what happened & patched me up.' Mike said to no one in particular.

Shirley sneered. She'd seen it all so many times before it didn't mean nothing to her but a fucked-up story devoid of glory.

'Wasn't my fault man. I was just over at my girlfriends & Crazy Joe showed up drunk, screaming obscenities. My girlfriend told him to leave. Kick'd him out we thought. He's fucked up man.' Mike said shaking his head back & forth, only slowing down to take a drag from his smoke.

'Crazy Joe, that guy who killed his brother with a knife ten years ago,' I said. I was a horrible name dropper.

'That's him, we been at each other for twenty years, the guys an asshole,' Mike said.

'How come he's not in jail,' the social worker in me always ready to question justice fucked up.

'Nothing happened, they said he was crazy & he got off, a couple of years not even.'

'That's fucked up,' I said.

'Fuck ya,' Mike jerked his head up & started his story.

'I was saying goodbye to my girlfriend as I was heading out, walking down the hall to the door. Crazy fucking Joe steps in my way. He had been standing in the shadows waiting. We thought he was gone. He stepped into my space. Blocking my way. I said to him what's your fucking problem, asshole. He smiled & fucking clobbered me with a two by four he was holding. Two fucking fister. Right across my face.'

'Fuck man you gotta get that looked at,' Ray said again.

Mike had a long black gash across his forehead. His one eye looked like it was almost falling out. Seemingly held in by the purple swelling of his noble native cheekbones. Mike had been foolishly handsome in his day. Now his scarred, ageless, proud, features bore the reality of living on the street.

'I gotta a few licks in,' Mike looked up at me, he wanted me to know he wasn't a wuss.

You see Mike was an ex-weightlifter. He had the chest of a barrel & thick weightlifter thighs at one time. He used to arm wrestle & evidently had been quite a champion. But he quit after his last match when he broke his opponent's arm.

'Cracked like a piece of micah tile,' he said when telling me the story. Even just the telling of it sent chills down my spine.

That was it he'd had enough with arm wrestling. It freaked him out. We'd talked about lifting weights, getting back into it. Mike was bound & determined for a bit but I think it was more me pushing then him actually wanting to get back into it. The drugs were holding him back. They were easing whatever pain he was feeling about what's happened in his life.

That & the recent death of his daughter of a drug overdose in Toronto didn't help.

'I went at him low.' Mike continued his story, 'We crashed outside through the door. He got me down & gave me some shots. But I got in a couple when we were flying off the stairs.'

As Mike was talking the wound over his eye started to drip blood. He started dabbing at it with a Kleenex, obviously instructions from Auntie.

Everyone had seen it all before in many places at many times. It triggered memories balanced with complacency.

Ray lit another cigarette & was starting to cough,

'You got a concussion man,' Ray said making a decisive diagnosis, 'I've had a few. Ya gotta be careful when you get whacked in the head. Have to protect your self. A two by four will crack your skull. You gotta headache man?'

'No, I'm ok,' Mike said. It was all I could do to hold back my laugh. Mike was anything but ok.

'Better get that eye looked at,' Ray was directing the attention back to him as the acting authority. Mike didn't mind. He never was one to seek out attention. Mike just really wanted to go lie down, get rid of his fucking headache.

'I had a guy stomp on my eye.' Ray continued. 'The doctor told me my eye ball was just hanging on by the flesh.' Ray said compulsively bringing the conversation around to him. It was like a narcissist disease for Ray.

Eric bent down & took a look at Mike, then looked at me to see if I was going to do something about this. When it became quite evident I wasn't getting involved Eric took charge.

'Come on man I'll take you up to emerg. You got money for gas?'

'I got some money,' says Mike.

'Right on, let's go.' Eric directed like a sergeant.

Indian Mike reluctantly rose up. His black leather jacket—spotted with blood—fell loosely down his back, almost touching his knees. The old leather jacket looked two sizes too big for him. A remnant of past times in his life I thought. The shoulders in particular stretched out wide. Mike went along with Eric like he had nothing better to do. Anyways, he was in too much pain to argue.

Its a funny thing in the culture of the homeless that no matter how bad it really gets everything always gets worked out. Most of the time. Sometimes it just doesn't.

Ray stubbed his smoke out on the palm of his hand saving the butt for later. Shirley was enjoying the sun on her face. But she'd had enough. Time for both to go in. Ray helped her up, ever the gentleman. Like a sasquatch lifting a bird with a broken wing.

Dawn's dance done. Time to start the day.

Ray was all smiles. He had a story to embellish at the kitchen table. Everyone would be anxious to hear what had happened to Indian Mike. Find out where Mike & Eric had gone.

No matter where or how we live we all have a bit of curious in us. Everyone always needs to know what everyone else is doing. The homeless are no different from you or me—it's all about the drama.

It was empty on the patio. The sun now visibly overhead. Well past the wall. I finally finished my last smoke. Time to get back to work I figured.

I headed back in.

I knew I'd be the one to get stuck with doing the breakfast dishes. It always happened that way.

The End

Nowhere to Hide

Part One

*'One fine day in the middle of the night
two dead boys got up to fight.'
(anonymous)*

It was the spring of 1967.Sudsie & Zit had just robbed the CIBC at Bathurst & Finch in Willowdale Ontario Canada.

Unfortunately, during the robbery, an off-duty policeman—waiting in line for a teller—saw what was happening out of the corner of his eye. He unhooked his weapon from under his coat, trying to be discrete. It caught Zit's-- easily distracted-- eye. Zit panicked & shot the shocked officer—errantly—in the head. No one more surprised than Zit-- who had never shot anything but his foot before.

The two desperados were speeding off in a 1965 Ford Comet. Rain pelting the road. Plan was to head north up Bathurst & west along Hwy 7 to 400 HWY & then straight north for the rest of their luckless lives.

They planned to lose any would be pursuers in the lakes & forests of Canada's northern wilderness. The perfect place to lay low. Fleeing through a fantasy-- living the dream.

'Do you think he's dead?' Zit asked, he couldn't stop shaking.

'Don't know,' Sudsie said, concentrating on keeping the Comet on the road. Bathurst at this point outside the city was only two lanes & Sudsie was already starting to slide on the shiny black asphalt surface.

'I thought he was going for his gun.'

'You panicked & fucked up. Watch for cops.'

The rain was dying down. Bathurst was starting to get a little misty. Moisture bouncing off the patient blacktop.

'Just like Eddy, eh,' Zit started to calm down.

'No, you fucking moron, it wasn't just like Eddy. Eddy never left anyone dead.'

Sudsie said

They both idealized Eddy Boyd. An infamous bank robber who operated in & around Toronto in the late forties, early fifties.

The western sky opened up as they sped north. The late afternoon sun-- sparkling the mist-- starting to keep an eye on our guys.

Sudsie grabbed his shades from the dash. Zit settled in like a scarecrow ,sitting back for the ride. Lighting up a smoke giving it to Sudsie, then lighting one for himself. Tossing the match out the window.

Sudsie taking the smoke, eyes never leaving the road.

'Fuck gotta make the lights,' Sudsie said & sped ahead.

The interchange at Bathurst & 7 was crucial. They were coming on it fast & hard. Fortunately, there were few cars about.

Sudsie made the light turning hard left onto HWY 7 just as the light blinked to red. A fishtail, a screech, anyone watching would comment about the two young hotheads going too fast. A couple of concrete cowboys, invincible, euphoric, dumb, doomed.

'Where we going again?' Zit had a habit of asking questions he should know the answers to, while Susie had the habit of ignoring him.

They were flying, nobody seemed to be noticing. They were heading west now into the curious sun. Bank robbing murdering desperados. Desperate to get on HWY 400 & head up north. They were hitting all the lights, getting it right, they were in fugitive flight.

Flying by shiny new strip malls, an aged Pinecrest Speedway, its dilapi-dated grandstand waiting for demolition-- an old hockey rink. Neither Sudsie or Zit had ever played. Their time had been spent in pool halls & on the street, no time for hockey. A rich boy's sport, they'd sneer.

Unrestrained industrialization, Toronto was oozing north into what was once farmland. Green becoming grey, the horizon pummeled with billboards. The renegades whizzing by.

Sudsie pushed the accelerator harder, eyes glued to the road.

Everything happening just as he planned. Except for Zit shooting that guy. Fuck that was not part of the plan. Zit was sitting beside him picking his nails. Fuck don't nothing bother him Sudsie thought tightening his grip on the wheel. The Comet was starting to shake a bit, he guessed it wasn't used to high speeds.

'We'll head up north like we planned, get up into Muskoka.' Sudsie said.

Zit grunted like a stunted hog & took a long drag from his cigarette. Trying to remember how many smokes he had left

The sun was watching, onlooking rays blinding our boys way. Shining bright like a spotlight in their eyes. Finally, the sign 'Hwy 400 North Turn Right' sprung into their eager stare. Emerging like a ghost through the glare.

*****

Sudsie & Zit were a couple of street clowns who lived on the wrong side of life. Now fleeing for their lives. Too stupid to know their actions would have ramifications that would lead to their ultimate demise.

Three nights ago they had spent the evening in their regular watering hole-- the Algonquin Tavern on Yonge Street in Willowdale-- putting on a hustle, pool, drugs, cards, sleight of hand, anything on the downside. They'd had a good night & as usual were drunk & stoned-- to an obliterated degree. When-- while taking a pee-- Zit noticed that the Ford Comet he was leaning on, had a set of keys in the ignition.

Well it certainly didn't take much. Zit beat it back into the bar & got Sudsie, who was shaking the pin ball machine for more balls. It didn't take a stretch before they were hopping into an empty Ford Comet & were off, driving like big shots.

'You know what we should do? It's time to get off the shithole & do it,' Sudsie said driving north up Yonge Street turning west down Steeles in the stolen Comet. 'Time to rob a bank,' he glowed. Zit in the passenger's seat just fucking wrecked-- babbling-- his mind racing as to the possibilities what they could accomplish now they had wheels. Absolutely agreed.

Sudsie-- comfortably behind the wheel—really wanted to rob a bank. He & Zit had been talking about robbing banks since hearing the legend of Eddy Boyd, when they were in the slammer. Boyd was a bank robbing hero. Still being talked about by a new generation of jailhouse punks.

Sudsie & Zit had been serving two years less a day at Millhaven-- a jail just outside of Toronto-- when they first heard about the infamous Eddy Boyd Gang.

Eddy Boyd had found himself unable to make a legal buck when he came home as an out of work pilot after the 2nd world war. So he turned to robbing banks. Eddy & his gang menaced the southern Ontario corridor for almost ten years. When finally caught & imprisoned at The Don Jail-- Toronto's infamous stone prison— they escaped, not once but twice. Eddy's exploits were legendary & stories of his escapades are part of jailhouse lore right across Canada.

Entertaining a generation of young punks looking for someone—something-- to believe in. Each new inmate getting the latest version. Eddy had become a glorified Superman. Exalted lion in the minds of the criminally inclined. Eddy & his

Gang-- criminally committed to Eddy's cause; Booze, Babes & Running from the law.

In the slammer you get to know where you stand, where you sit in the pecking order. Back in Eddy's day bank robbers with guns were at the top. They were Gods & Eddy Boyd was the king of bank robbers. Eddy Boyd, bank robber supremo, the legend. His story passed down like a right of passage.

*****

Eddy's gang consisted of--Tough Lenny Jackson, Pimple Face Suchan & Willie the Clown Jackson (no relation). They planned each job like clockwork. The Boyd

Gang-- weapons hidden under high collar, floor length trench coats. Wearing their trademark Fedora hats. Exploding into an unsuspecting bank they'd been casing for weeks. Eddy-- coming in the rear-- prancing in like a prince on a pony. Clad in a well tailored suit with impeccable Italian shoes. His captured german luger sticking out over his belt.

Everything planned down to the stolen black Packard. It's eight cylinders rumbling, running outside— puffing on a full tank of gas—ready to ride.

'Everybody down!'

Tough Lenny would command-- drawing his machine gun from underneath his tailored trench coat. Hat pulled low over his eyes. Lenny was tough & mean. He was a big man, tall broad shoulders, big beer belly -- sometimes you couldn't tell whether that was the machine gun or his gut underneath that coat. Lenny controlled the gang & he didn't take any shit. He was the real leader of the gang.

Eddy was the star with his Clark Gable looks & devil's eyes. Eddy would wear grotesque make up looking like a maniacal clown, but just leaving enough to let his devil may care dashing good looks shine through. The tellers swooned when they first caught his eye. Then when it was all going down, they used to sneak a peak-- as they lay face flat on the ground.

The gang-- Jackson, Suchan, Jackson & Boyd-- would take over the bank. Directing extremely well-orchestrated chaos. Each of them in their place, each with a job to do.

Tough Lenny Jackson wandering the floor, machine gun in hand, just itching to let loose. Steve Pimple Face Suchan with a 38 pistol, poised to use it terrified at the thought. In time he'd fire the bullet which would get him & Tough Lenny hung. Willie the Clown Jackson wielding a weapon way to big for his smaller frame. Standing by the door of the bank. Determined to make a good show, always the clown, he always had something to prove.

All barrels pointed on an agitated bunch of unfortunate people just out to cash a cheque or make a day's pay.

Eddy'd vault the counter, Lugar now in hand, flashing it about like a conductor waving his wand. Eddy was wild, reckless, controlled.

Eddy grabbing the cash from behind the tills & in the vault. Like a loosed beast leaping back up on top of the counter. Snarling politely at those on the ground, in a—mean-- well-read manner,

'The Boyd Gang would like to thank you for your time,' Eddie would say bleeding with sarcasm.

And away they'd go, backing slowly out the door. Turning & jumping into the waiting Packard. The Clown driving, Tough Lenny in the front seat, finger still itching to blow off some rounds. Eddy & Pimple Face riding the boards hanging on. Firing their guns randomly in the air like kids at a fair. Tires spraying up gravel & broken pieces of black. Exhaust fumes & burning rubber. Bystanders out for morning shopping shocked at the intrusion.

The Packard flying off into a startled warm blue southern Ontario sky.

*****

Sudsie & Zit worshipped Eddie Boyd. He was their Batman, Spiderman, Davey Crocket & Robin Hood all rolled into one. They worshipped at the Church of Boyd, Eddy was their Allah their Jesus Christ.

Now 1967, 20 years after Eddy had robbed his first bank, Sudsie & Zit had robbed their first bank. They were living high.

Sudsie powered into the turn like he was driving a race car. Hitting the 400 at a staggering speed. Zit held fast to his seat. Eyes ablaze like he was riding a galloping steed ahead of a pursuing posse—little did he know this was their prophecy.

They were heading north into the womb of Canada's wilderness.

The sun growing tired, slipped behind the stringy greying clouds for a rest. Not quite prepared to settle down for the night. Sticking around, waiting to see what the end of this story will be.

*****

The surprise of stealing the car had set the plan in motion. The keys were in the

Comets ignition crying for them to take it. The next decision made was to rob a bank. They planned over the next few days how they were going to do it. They knew Eddy planned & cased the intended place so they followed his ways like a blueprint. Amidst a mountain of beer, tokes & speed, they put it together. Sudsie planning meticulously. Zit listening as hard as he can.

Zit got up from his kitchen chair-- too dry to listen-- went to the fridge & cracked open a Molson beer. Just happy to be here with his friend-- friend to the end. He didn't care what they were going to do as long as they did it together-- he just didn't care.

They sat, drank & smoked at their wobbly kitchen table planning the heist. Living on the second floor above the print shop. Outside wooden stairs up to the cheap drab door. Wiggly handrail at the top. It's a wonder neither one of them hasn't crashed through. A window in the kitchen over the sink that looked out—north-- over an industrial space. A well-placed picture of Eddy in handcuffs on his way to jail, pinned up on the kitchen wall over the fridge. An old cut out from the Toronto Star, headline underneath ' Boyd Gang Captured' Sept 13 1952 the date. Eddy smiling defiantly at the camera. Cops lined up all around like they were just waiting to give Eddy a shot. Anger etched on their faces.

ΛΛΛΛΛ

Sudsie & Zit never grew up. These guys never got it. For whatever reason & there are a million of them (too many to mention here), these guys figured out that they alone would come at this life as if life itself owed them a living. Every generation breeds its losers. This criminal class trying to claw its way to respectability believing they & they alone, were entitled. Without putting in the effort & hard work, like the rest of us working class stiffs.

These criminals cry in wild disbelief when caught-- tried & hung-- looks of amazement & disbelief on their face, as the hood is pulled down. The noose tightened & the trap door sprung. Tough Lenny Jackson & Pimple Face Suchan of Eddy's gang paid the ultimate price in 1954, for killing a cop. Hung like dead ducks in a Chinese food store. Not Eddie though, he was holed up with a perky blonde when they were killing cops. He got caught eventually, escaped the noose, but got locked up & they threw away the key.

Our present fugitives were on their way to this inevitably imposed eventuality-- that all who follow this lazy stupid egotistical strategy of life-- were destined for a tragic dose of reality.

*****

Sudsie & Zit had been out of control in a bad way all their life. They met up in Bayview Junior High, 1959. They came from the poorer side of the school district. Sudsie with a single Mom, Zit a first-generation wop. They had to make up with attitude what they lacked for money & brains.

Both little 12-year-old assholes, couple of greasers right off the bat. It didn't take much for them to find each other. The first day of school both of them sitting in the principal's office for fighting-- each other. Joined at the hip ever since. They became buddies, bullies, greasers. Strips of bryl-cream hair falling off their foreheads, black beatle boots, real greaseballs-- chewing gum like a cow, replaced later with a smoke dangling out of the side of their face-- perpetual snarl.

Pushing kids around, careful that their prey was smaller, weaker, scared. If someone fought back the two of them would crumble like cowards, mumbling curses & threats of revenge, which never amounted to anything. Attention span of a couple of gnats. A couple of young punks.

At thirteen they started stealing candy bars from The Dot Shop for profit – a corner store in the neighborhood—as they grew older cigarettes were the prize. Old man Wilson who owned the store was easy to confuse. Eventually they went for his cash in the till. That was enough to get them caught & hauled off down to the cop shop.

'How old are you' the police officer asked, not a question but a command.

No answer, both snickering. A slanted smirk flashing from one face to the other.

'Come on boys, how old are you!' The officer pulled out the billy club— waiting-- started patting his hand with it, hitting it harder, harder & then whack. He cracked it over Sudsie's head.

'Fourteen,' squealed Zit, scared to fucking death. Sudsie lying flat out face down across the desk. Back of his head clotted in blood.

They got let out. First time offenders, cops trying to give them a break. Parents were called came & got em. Well, Sudsie's Mom's friend got him. His Mom was busy with her own life.

Zit's stern Italian PaPa came walking down to the police station in his sagging, large white, sweat stained undershirt. Baggy workingman's pants, concrete covered work boots-- half laced up. He wasn't happy.

This one always in trouble he thought. Him no good. The dumb one of the litter. Sometimes I wonder why I do it. This one—christ-- what am I going to do with him. I'm ashamed, all police looking at me.

He walked through the door into the station, trying to hide his shame.

'That one there yours?' The policeman asked looking up from behind the screen. PaPa nods his head.

'Alright Zit your dad's here.'

Zit getting up off the bench where he was waiting, contemplating his thumb. The cop eyeing PaPa. Letting Zit out. Cop thinking, I wouldn't want to be him when he gets home. Turns back to his paperwork.

PaPa gives Zit a cuff as he's walking out the door from the station. Zit stumbling, taking it all in as if it's a big joke. Can't hold back his snarky grin. Outside PaPa starts screamimg,

'You think this a big joke!'

Zit takes a couple of steps down onto the sidewalk & PaPa gives him another shot to the back of the head, sending him flying to the curb.

'What the fuck.' Zit gets up & spits out some blood. He looks at PaPa trying to be the tough little bastard he thinks he is.

'You shut your face.' PaPa says getting real riled up. Looking at his boy directly in the eye.

Zit takes off running down the road. PaPa's enraged, turning blue. Steam coming out of the top of balding PaPa's head.

'You're cursed!' PaPa shouts into the wind shaking his fist in fury.

Sudsie got dropped off to a motherless house. His mother down at the bar he figured. He was used to his mom never being home. When she was home, it was fucked up.

He had an eleven-year-old sister—Rhonda—she was in the front room on the couch watching TV, eating stale potato chips when he walked in.

'Better get up to bed Sis,' he said.

'Where have you been,' she asked.

'None of your business, come on go to bed,' his head hurt.

'I just want to finish watching this show,'

Sudsie went over across the room & turned off the TV.

'Get going, now.'

Rhonda bounced off the couch in a pout & ran up the stairs.

'You're not my boss,' she yelled back.

Sudsie always ended up looking after Rhonda. Believe you me Sudsie was the last person you wanted raising your kid. His mother was one of those bad single mothers. Always resentful, tired, listless. Unless her friends were around. Then it was a different story. Drinks in hand, laughing voices, dancing to the new Elvis. Sudsie sitting on the stairs—watching-- trying to figure how to get a ten out of the new Uncle Ben.

When it was just the three of them Mom was always on him. Empty the ashtrays, clean the coffee table, go to the store for smokes. He always trying to steal the change. When she was drinking-- which was all the time-- she never noticed it missing until the next morning. By the time he got home from school she had forgot.

Sudsie had to put Rhonda to bed at night & get her up in the morning. Help her get ready for school. All the time screaming in his head what a fuckin ass hole his mother is-- shouldn't she be doing this.

Mom every morning-- drunk sick. During the day sprawling on the couch in their never clean house. Coffee cup steaming on the coffee table. Her gollum hand hanging down like a weathered limb from a tree reaching for the cup with long wrinkled fingers. Displaying the cracked remnants of yesterday's nail polish. Cigarette smoke swirling the air from an always full ashtray. House stinking sour smell. Watching TV shows, Price is Right, Dragnet, Guiding Light. Phone would ring or a friend would come over & she'd be off to the bar. Sudsie & Rhonda getting home from school to an empty stale house. Peanut butter sandwiches waiting on the counter-- sometimes with jam.

Tonight, she gets home just after her friend dropped Sudsie off. Immediately she's on him for pulling her away from the bar. She's fluttering about making no sense. His eyes follow her around as he tells her what happened but she can't listen-- her minds back at the bar.

'It was nothing,' Sudsie said. 'The cops were all fucked up.'

He tries to show her where the policeman hit him. Parting with his finger's his greasy hair. To no avail she wasn't interested. She was thinking what one of her friends had yelled at her as she left the bar,

'You should get that boy of yours under control.' It had embarrassed her.

'Mind your own fucking business,' she had snarled back.

She pushed past Sudsie to the fridge for a beer. Popped the cap & went over to the hi fi to put on some Bobby Fuller Four. The front screen door soon flew open & four of her friends from the bar burst in-- it was party on. She completely forgot about Sudsie-- her son-- who was now on his way up the stairs to look in on Rhonda. Make sure she at least had brushed her teeth.

'We'll talk about this tomorrow,' Mother yells at him like a drunk actress on a set. Yea right he yells back in his head & starts taking the stairs two at a time. She's showing off to her friends being the responsible mother. He doesn't know why but it makes him mad. She always has to be the one-- the star of the show-- his anger rising as he watches Rhonda spit toothpaste all over the sink.

Zit was hiding in the bushes waiting for his old man to go to sleep. PaPa soon would be drunk in his chair. Watching the CBC to try & learn more English. Once Zit heard the snore he knew he'd be safe. Knowing he had to cut an enraged-- like a bull-- PaPa a wide berth. It didn't usually take long, PaPa never made it past the late-night news.

Zit'd wait for the snoring sound then sneak around going in the back door. MaMa would be there in the kitchen washing the floor. Big cross with Jesus's drooping head hung on a hook above the kitchen sink. His two older sisters on either side of MaMa talking over MaMa's small round Italian head. Helping out by hanging out while MaMa does the chores. Talking up a storm. His younger brother would be upstairs doing home-work, fucking goody two shoes. MaMa softly sobbing, would get up off her knees, brush off her skirt & give her son—he the one I worry most about-- an Italian mother's hug. Then wiping her tears with her apron MaMa make him something to eat. The only time Zit was her number one son was when he got himself into trouble.

Now Sudsie & Zit really were big shots at school. Their run in with the police was pretty impressive to the student body as a whole. The story was of course totally exaggerated in the boys favor. Sudsie wearing his greasy welt as a warrior. Zit walking alongside like a lanky lancelet.

None of the ritzy kids at Bayview Junior High had ever been involved with the police. The only policeman they knew were Sergeant Joe Friday & his partner Bill, in Dragnet, on the TV.

A child well fed, loved & cared for. Safe at home, lying on the carpeted floor, watching Dragnet with their father & mother, just before bed.

Innocent to the other side of life.

Word got around the halls fast. It gave Sudsie & Zit instant cred. Prancing about, lipping everyone off. Real studs, girls with big twisted hair, tight jeans, premature boobs, hanging out with the big shots. Sudsie & Zit auspicious to your average, straight laced orgasmic pubescent kid. Who went to school, played sports, practiced drums, did their homework, wasn't allowed out after supper.

Sudsie & Zit were real cocks on the block.

Sudsy liked to play the tough guy shoving smaller kids around. Until he got tuned on, in the cafeteria when he went too far. He challenged a jock in the cafeteria at lunch. In front of all of us eating. Sudsie jumped up on the table & screamed, 'come on,' The jock jumped up & tuned Sudsie in with a one shot punch to the head. Sudsie ended up face first on the cafeteria floor head bleeding red. Zit looking on-- yelling insults at the jock who had jumped down & was wailing on Sudsie's head. Zit was ready to turn tail & flee if the jock turned on him. Having no courage to step in. Zit was a real sleaze bag.

Sudsie & Zit spent all their time together, doing stupid kid stuff. Looking tough, acting mean, being big fucking bullies, smoking tons of cigarettes out behind the junior high school, hanging out, bored, restless & dumb.

High school was a lot tougher. Everyone had grown smarter & they hadn't. They had to be tough & stupid in a whole new way. They fucked around at school, lipped off teachers, never went to class. Sneaking a puff at their locker, trying to impress the girls when they walked by as they blew swirls of smoke through their nose. Working too hard on playing it cool. Any pretty little thing taking an interest resulted in a boner tenting Sudsie's pants much to Zit's amusement.

Old enough now to hang out at Pop's pool hall. Talking tough, talking dirty, dreaming up schemes, sinking the white ball more than the black.

Not old enough to buy liquor but always figuring out ways to get high. Weed, speed, booze. One night, all fucked up on speed at the pool hall, they'd heard that doing gas was the way to go-- missing the part that you were supposed to sniff it not drink it. They went out back & siphoned some gas from a parked Harley & almost killed themselves. Zit was out on the spot. Flat out sprawled on the pavement. Sudsie went back into the pool hall stumbling around like he had just been shot. He bounced his head off the side of a table cracking his skull & splashing blood all over the pool tables & floor. The other reprobate patrons watching thinking what the fuck. Finally Pops, the owner, calling an ambulance, para medics hauling them both off. Quite the story, again made the rounds in the halls, now at the high school.

This time it wasn't cool, it was stupid. Everyone was older now—all were maturing-- except them.

Both of them kicked out of high school, when they turned 16. The minute the principal could do it legally. Sudsie getting a job at the local gas station. Zit getting on at his father's construction company. Both scheming, dreaming, talking bullshit, walking like they're bigshots. Showing up to work stoned, always late, stealing from the till, Zit whacking off in the porta potty, Sudsie always hitting on the girls who came in for gas. Both getting fired-- neither one of them caring.

Zit getting kicked out of his home for bringing shame on PaPa. Who took to reaming him out yelling & screaming how could he have such a son. Finally, PaPa came at him with fists telling him to get out. Zit turned & spit, then hightailed it out the door. MaMa crying in the kitchen.

Zit moved in with his more tolerant uncle, who at least talked to him when they watched TV. His wife-- Zit's aunt-- had big boobs. Zit'd try jerking off watching her undress through a crack in the door.

Sudsie still at home, Rhonda getting older now didn't need as much looking after. When she got tits, Zit tried to fuck her on the couch-- thinking it was the thing to do-- his pimply complexion repulsing her but she figuring what the hell. He ended up all confused & exploded on her underpants. Sudsie never knew, he'd been passed out on his favorite chair drunk that night. Rhonda turned into quite the slut later in high school.

Sudsie finally telling his mother to just fuck off. Leaving for good in the middle of a-- terrible mother charging at son with a broken liquor bottle-- fight. Sudsie dodged & popped her one (a lot of tears in that punch). He left screaming at her he'd never be back, slamming the front door so hard he broke a hinge, it never got fixed.

Sudsie moved in with Zit, the uncle unaware. Sudsie sneaking in through the screen in the bedroom window every night. Finally, Sudsie getting caught one night when they both came home high on whatever was selling on the street. Being so loud waking the uncle. Unc getting up to see what was going on. Finding them both with their cocks out in Zit's room jacking off to a Playboy picture. Well Sudsie was jacking off & Zit was watching him, Sudsie oblivious.

Sudsie was kicked out, on the spot, even though he really wasn't living there anyways. Sudsie was now officially living on the street.

Living wild in parks, cars, ravines & allies, it was all cool. He & Zit still hanging out. They'd go steal food from Sudsie's mom when she went out. Rhonda usually home—now a teen-- in the front room watching TV, talking on the phone, listening to Motown.

'Hey Sis,' Sudsie would say as he came through the front door-- still wobbling from the broken hinge-- & head for the kitchen. Zit would slide over to the couch, settle in beside Rhonda.

'Whatcha watching? Bonanza.' Zit would ask trying to be social.

Sudsie would be raiding the refrigerator. Stealing cans from the cupboards, filling up a grocery bag he'd brought along. After he'd stocked up, he'd leave the bag by the front door-- in case he had to make a quick exit if Mom showed up--& hop into his favorite chair he used to always watch TV in. Pretending life was like it was when he had a home. Forgetting the part-- that wasn't so long ago-- when he & his Mom were tearing out each other's heart.

'Mom seeing anybody?' he'd ask Rhonda.

'Yea.' Rhonda's eyes never left the screen, but she did put the phone down.

'What's he like?'

'He's a creep.' Rhonda looked over silently at her brother, giving him the eye. Sudsie got the message.

'What's his name?'

'Todd.'

They sat around & watched 'Bonanza'. Zit trying to edge closer to Rhonda. Rhonda trying to make herself invisible to him.

It took them two weeks. But they finally cornered Todd alone on a dark street. Sudsie came up from behind & sucker punched him on the right side of the head, Zit, hiding in the shadows, came straight on & laced a boot deep into his groin. Todd crumpling to the ground. They were actually a good team. Each feeding off each other's mean.

Sudsie gave him a final kick to the head,

'You stay away from my sister you perverted fuck,' Sudsie screamed. Leaving Todd lying half dead, on a cold hard street.

Zit overstayed his welcome at Uncs. Auntie caught him wearing her panties, told her husband he had to go. So, he & Sudsie melted into their surroundings. Both now living off the street.

They were in & out of jail & juvenile detention centres for awhile. Finally turning eighteen. To celebrate they robbed a liquor store-- all fucked up on booze & speed. Police arrested them drinking whiskey & eating hamburgers. Sitting on the curb two blocks from the same liquor store they'd just robbed.

Both got penitentiary time in the Millhaven Jail, two years less a day. Big boy jail.

That's where they heard about Eddy Boyd & The Eddy Boyd Gang

The Pen was school. They learned how to steal, they learned about fencing, they learned about dope-- the golden egg at the end of every punks rainbow. They learned society didn't give a shit about them. If they were going to make it the only person they could trust-- was each other.

They learned how to work the police, work the guards, work the system. How to respect those who will kick your ass quicker than bat an eye.

They learned about Eddy Boyd. Finally they had found a hero, someone to look up to, someone to shape their life around. Made them feel bad ass. They learned-- back in '52'-- The Boyd Gang had been captured just down the way from where they had gone to junior high school.

Shit when they were young they had gone fishing for eels at Shepherd & Leslie. Standing on the bridge over a little creek that got deeper when it rained. Eddy & the Gang had been caught-- after they escaped from the Don Jail for the second time-- holed up in a barn right by there. Sudsie & Zit started to believe they had seen the barn from the bridge. Even though the barn had been long torn down.

After The Boyd Gang was caught the cops had taken Eddy & the gang back to the North York Township Police Station. The same station Sudsie & Zit had been hauled off too many a time.

Renamed the Willowdale Police Station by the time Sudsie & Zit were old enough to be thrown in. Shit they might have even spent time in the same cell Eddy & the Gang had stayed in. At least that's what they talked themselves into.

The captured worn out Boyd Gang had been waiting in chains in the Willowdale jail. Locked in thick barred cells, tired & hungry, cold that permeated their bones. Waiting to be shipped back downtown to the Don Jail from whence they had just escaped-- again—the guards extracting their revenge every chance they got. Sudsie & Zit only saw the glory not the pain.

Sudsie & Zit felt a kinship for the Boyd Gang. They felt like reincarnates. Even though two members of the gang, Eddy & Willie the Clown, were still alive. It gave Sudsie & Zit validation.

Sudsie & Zit got out of Millhaven after eighteen months. High school certification from the school of jailhouse living. Most productive time of their lives.

They still had six months of parole to finish their sentence. As luck would have it they got the same parole officer. Sudsie got on at a gas station apprenticeship program. Zit got placed at a printing shop. Both good trades.

They shared a 2nd floor walk-up when they got out. At Dufferin & Finch over the print shop Zit worked in. North facing big kitchen window. They'd get loaded during their time on parole & talk of living in a cabin up north. Both of em drunk staring out the window as they stacked their dishes in the sink. That was one of the benefits of the robbing the bank.

They'd get to head up north as part of their getaway with lots of money. Then they'd hideout in the bush—maybe find an abandoned cabin-- until the cops stopped looking for them. They really had thought it through they figured. To you & I their plan would have presented as being quite straight forward. But for the boys the bank robbing plan required, that their minds were running at peak. Like the mind of a professor writing for publication.

The walk up gave them a place to hang the picture of Eddy getting caught. They'd get all high on speed & talk of them & Eddy. They really believed Eddy was there as an inspiration when they were putting together their plan to rob the bank.

'So I'll be like Eddy grabbing the money from the tills,' Sudsie said trying to explain things to Zit. 'You stand guarding the door so no gets out like Tough Lenny used to do.'

Sudsie never knew if Zit was listening or not. I guess it really doesn't matter Sudsie thought, what could possibly go wrong anyways.

The deal was while they were on parole they had to give their cheques to the parole officer-- he paying their rent. Six months parole, a lot of bullshit, had to watch yourself in public, a lot of restrictions, if you fucked up you went back to jail. So they'd stay in at night.

Jail was an eyeopener but you had to be damn stupid to want to go back. Why do you think Eddy busted out, twice? The boys learned to pass the time in jail playing cards. So-- while on parole-- instead of going to the bar after work -- where they would get into trouble-- they'd stay in the walk up & play crib. Drinking, smoking, arguing, enjoying each other's company just not knowing it.

' fifteen two, for two' Zit would put his cards down,

'that's not fifteen that's fourteen,' Sudsie watching each card closely,

'nine & five fourteen yea ok,' Zit would finally see it,

' I've got two, four, six, eight & one is nine.' Sudsie always got the numbers right.

'Where I can't see it.' Zit studying the cards like they were a mystery.

'Right here,' Sudsie would say pointing it out patiently.

They'd go on & on. Playing cards toasting Eddy's picture. Take em two hours to finish a game but it could have been two years for all they cared. Talking of how tough & smart Eddie really was. How he lived life fast & hard. Never had to apologize to anyone.

*****

They were celebrating the successful end of their six-month parole at The Algonquin Tavern. They hadn't been at the Big A for awhile—including the time at Millhaven it'd been over two years-- so it was a bit of a home-coming celebration. It was good to be back-- they both thought together as they walked through the Big A's front door. Draft room off to the left. Nothing changed. Wally the Waiter still slinging draft. Same old crowd. Looking like they hadn't moved since the last time the boys were here.

They're sitting back enjoying their draft. Assuming the pose. No one paid them no mind. A couple of guys at the bar gave them a nod of con-fused recognition. They were on their fifth round when this guy comes walking over. They both recognize Red-- from Millhaven-- right off. You never forget the face of a man with a scar stretching from his nose snaking off across his cheek like a birth mark to a flattened ear.

'Hey Red, sit down man, what's happening,' Sudsie pulled out a chair.

'Good to see you guys,' Red slides onto the seat & puts his beer down on the-- full of draft-- tiny table.

'You just get out?' Zit asks through a cloud of cigarette smoke. Leaning back in his wooden chair.

'No, I've been out a couple of weeks doing business.' Red looks around for some more beer.

Wally the waiter, big fat belly pushing his waiter white shirt over his belt, comes by with a tray full of draft. They all drink up what's in front of them in a gulp & Wally drops down four, mesmerized by the scar on Red's face. Red gives him a wink & Wally drops down four more. Wally barely squeezed them on the too tiny table. Better there then on my tray Wally thought.

'I've got this,' Red says & pulls out a thick roll of bills from his pocket. Flashes it about, pays Wally & returns it to his pocket.

'Holy christ man what'd you do rob a bank?', Sudsie & Zit say in chorus as their eyes pop out of their heads at the sight of his roll

Red leans in close.

'Look I'll let you in on something if you guys are cool.'

'For sure man what's up?' Sudsie pulls his chair in close-- like a conspirator in a movie.

Zit straightens up his chair. Sitting in closer leaning in like a gangly stork.

'I'm into pushing weed, acid, speed it's a fucking gold mine.' Red says.

'Looks like you're doing OK.' Zits impressed. Zit's eyes glued to the bulge in Red's pocket.

'I am man, making lots of money. I'm looking at more cash than I've ever believed existed. You guys interested, its wide open.' Red pulled back & took a long haul on his glass of beer.

Sudsie & Zit looked at each other & with a quick nod they entered into the next phase of their twisted existence. Maybe it wasn't robbing banks but it was still living outside the law. They both quit their jobs the next day & became connected drug dealers. Pushing weed to school children, acid to stoners & speed at the bar. They started making money, living large.

But what would Eddy say. They bought a gun off some biker. Zit wore it in his belt like Eddy. He ended up looking like a cartoon character. Zit was not a handsome man. He had a long triangular Italian face, combed flat slick black hair, complexion which was always coming undone, always in some sort of perpetual explosion. A nose which stuck out like a crow, a slit of a mouth & a heavy Italian beard. Tall like a stick. Sudsie was built like a bull rider & looked like James Dean. He fancied himself a women machine. But he presented like a tool, so he ended up with women where presentation wasn't important, they were just interested in getting laid.

The money was coming in but they were still small time & they knew it. They had to step up their game. Small time drug dealers were at the bottom rung of the criminal life ladder. They needed to move up. Robbing a bank was the answer to enhance their cred & be like Eddy. Make a name for themselves. Be legends like Eddy. It wasn't fate which left those keys in the Comet's ignition—it was the answer to a dream.

The sun-not quite set- came out from behind the stringy cloud. It was intent on having a front row seat. Watching the boys riding hard up the 400 heading up north in their Comet trailing a tale of a life ill spent.

End of Part One

Part Two

'I fought the law & the law won.'
(Bobby Fuller)

By the time Sudsie & Zit were turning onto the 400, Sergeant Detective Southern had just arrived at the scene of the bank robbery & murder. He had been sitting in his office at the Willowdale Police Station, thinking of giving the wife a call & seeing if they might want to go out to a movie when he got home. Then over the wire came the call, bank robbery at the CIBC, Bathurst & Finch, possibly officer down. Detective Southern had to go.

It didn't take him long to get there, the station wasn't far from the incident. He arrived to a scene of chaos. The ambulance was parked in front of the bank's front door. A couple of patrol cars were already in the parking lot, lights flashing, lots of commotion. Detective Southern jumped out of his plain police car. He slowly approached the bank senses heightened. The first officer he saw was trying to bring some order to a dreadfully emotional situation in front of the bank. He wasn't letting anyone in or out.

'They're inside Sir, it isn't pretty' the officer said. He was just a rookie & very nervous. This was his first major crime scene. Southern didn't have to flash his badge everyone knew everyone at the Willowdale Precinct. Southern noted the confusion in the rookies manner.

'Is it one of ours,' Southern asked softly.

'Yes sir it's Whitey.' Was the reply. Southern's knees weakened Whitey was one of the good ones.

Southern knew what to expect, this wasn't his first rodeo. Steel himself he has a job to do. He'd been on the force for fifteen years now. His father, Constable Southern Sr, had been a police officer. The son followed in the father's shoes. It really wasn't a difficult decision he grew up wanting to be a cop. So the first opportunity to sign up he took it.

His father had actually been a prominent player in the ultimate capture of the Boyd gang back in the day. He'd heard the story many times. His father never tired of telling it.

The Toronto Police had found the gang holed up in a barn just by Shepherd & Leslie in North York Township. Largest man hunt in Canadian history at that point. Two thousand policemen checking every face every car everywhere. First time a helicopter was ever used in a manhunt, hovering up & down the infinite number of ravines & river valleys which Toronto's built around & within.

This was the Boyd Gang's second escape from the Don Jail. The first time they escaped there wasn't this much heat. Some people even saw them as modern-day robin hoods. But this time they were in for bank robbery & murder. Tough Lenny & Pimple Face had killed a cop when they were on the run. So now people were serious, the public didn't see it as much as a lark as a bunch of cold-blooded killers on the loose. The cops especially.

Finally after more than a week on the run up the Don Valley fighting brambles, mud & trees the gang ended up in an abandoned barn at Shepherd & Leslie. Some curious farmers saw these mysterious guys hanging around the vacant barn. One of the farmers thought to let the police know. Sure enough the police knew it must be the Boyd Gang.

Southern's Dad was one of the patrolmen sent to support the detectives. They moved in on the falling down wooden barn in the middle of the night. A force moving through the black-- all to a one-- ready to be shot. Eddy & the Boys sitting frozen cold & hungry inside. Thinking they're hiding unseen in a big indiscrete barn. The dilapidating structure sticking out like a sore thumb in the middle of a field within sight of Toronto. To everyone's greatest relief the actual arrest went off-- with just one hitch. Eddy & the boys were so exhausted they hadn't even posted a lookout. The detectives had Eddy, Lenny & Willie in cuffs as soon as you can spit. They went down without a sound. But 'Pimple Face' Suchan wasn't around.

The detectives on scene asked Southern's Dad to check all nooks & crannies in the barn for guns, check the rooms, check the stalls.

Sure enough Southern's Dad used to tell the story;

'I found him in the last stall down at the other end of the barn from where the rest of the Boyd gang sat handcuffed. It was pitch black. I had a flashlight in one hand, gun in the other. I was flicking the flashlight back & forth. I was looking meticulously in each stall, going slow cautious. Scared, not knowing what I'd find. Maybe a bullet you never know. Finally the flashlight caught sight of something out of place. I paused & went in. There sitting on the one side of this last stall was a huge cache of weapons. All kinds of weapons, rifles, pistols, machine guns. Well this gave me pause for thought. As I was contemplating the scene. I noticed out of the corner of my right eye some movement of a blanket--like a humped beast-- on the other side of the stall. I raised my gun & aimed, 'Who's there,' I yelled, & sure enough if Steve Suchan, 'Pimple Face' himself didn't jump out like he was on a spring board. Hands above his head. I shone the flashlight right into his eyes. There stood the fourth member of the infamous Boyd gang surrendering right there to me. I caught him single handed.'

Dad was a pretty big thing for awhile.

*****

Detective Southern entered the bank. He went immediately over to the downed man. Moving with conviction as if on glass. The ambulance attendant was just pulling up the sheet covering the body.

'What happened?' Detective Southern asked. The ambulance attendant now stopped, pulling the sheet back so Southern could see for himself.

'Gun shot, one shot got him right through the side of the head.' the attendant solemnly said.

'Milliken, his names, Officer William—Whitey-- Milliken.' Southern replied unnecessarily sharply.

'Yea sorry. Officer Milliken looks like he might have been going for his gun, the clasp's unhooked but the guns still in the holster, poor bastard,' the ambulance attendant lamented. Trying to be respectful.

Detective Southern turned away from his dead colleague, then turned back & whispered softly into the attendant's ear,' make sure they save me the bullet.'

Southern called over to the Officer in the bank who was still in the process of securing the room. Quickly recalling his name from his memory bank. 'How you doing Frank,' Detective Southern said solemnly as Officer Frank made his way over.

'Fine sir, right fucked up, poor Whitey,' Officer Frank said.

'He was off duty,' Southern commented.

'He worked a double yesterday.' Frank the friend started talking. 'He was on days off.'

'Do you know why he was at the bank?' Detective Southern inquired.

'He had to grab some cash, we were thinking of playing some cards. Putting a game together for later tonight maybe. Fuck.' Frank was trying hard to hold down his feelings. He was starting to tear up.

'Well let's catch the bastards who did this.' Southern said, giving Frank a confident slap on the back.

'I want you to go around & interview every customer & employee of the bank who was inside during the robbery. I want descriptions of the suspects & any little thing that they might have been seen as odd or out of step. Nothing too small.'

'Sir, who's gonna tell his wife?' Frank the friend respectively inquired.

'The Captain will tell them. Wouldn't want that job.' Southern sincerely had learned the part of this job he liked least was telling any family their father is dead, murdered.

Southern left the bank & gestured to the young rookie Officer standing a little dazed outside the bank to come over here. The young rookie was eager to take direction.

'Bad scene,' Southern commented. 'How's it out here?'

'Everyone's just milling about, Sir,' the Young Officer replied. 'Whitey, is he gone.'

'Yea he's gone.

Right at that moment the ambulance attendants were wheeling the gurney with Whitey's dead body on it through the door. Detective Southern held the door.

He turned to the Young Officer, ' I want you to tape off the area. The whole parking lot. Then I want you to interview everyone out here who may have seen something, check in on the stores, talk to the clerks, someone has information. We need to catch these guys who did this.'

'Right on it sir.' The Young Officer jumped to it. Nothing better to deal with the feeling of helplessness, then having something to do that might help catch the killer.

Detective Southern walked purposedly back to his car & radioed in to the Captain his immediate superior. Giving him up to date information. The captain informed him he was already on the phone mobilizing the whole Metro Toronto Police Force. Get him some more information & he'll put it over the wire.

'I'm sending two more detectives over to help, just say what you need.'

'You going to inform Whitey's wife.?' Southern needed to ask. He had to make sure every corner of concern was covered.

'Yea , I'll take care of that,' The Captain sadly said.

Detective Southern started to make his way back to the scene & stopped in mid stride. He turned back to the car & reached through the window & called up the Captain again.

'Captain I think we better alert the OPP, I've just got a hunch.'

'I'm on it.'

Southern headed back into the bank. Approaching Officer Frank, with pen & pad at the ready. Southern's senses on high alert, his head on a swivel.

'What do you have for me, Frank?' he said every fibre of his being in focus.

Frank started interpreting his notes.

'Well there were three customers & four employees including the manager here when it happened. Two young males entered faces all gooed up by what looked like makeup.

'One was smaller, stocky, square face, straight chin. He was first in. Yelled it's a robbery. The other one came in right behind him, tall spindly gangly features. He's the one that shot Whitey. He was holding the gun in his hand when he burst through the door, might have stumbled, anyways gun went off & poor Whitey went down. The stocky one grabbed some cash from a couple of tills & ran out. He had to practically grab the other one who was just standing there looking stunned.' Frank looked up from his notes,

'That's the gist of it anyways.' Frank tailed off.

'One interesting thing,' he'd remembered something specific,' all the witness's remarked their faces looked painted. Sorta like a couple of clowns.'

Southern took a breath taking a mental note.

'What were they wearing?'

Frank referred back to his notes. Written in a small little notebook. Flipping pages as he searched for the requested information. Pencil in his top pocket sticking out a little awkwardly looking well used.

'Both wearing jeans. One with the cash wearing a ratty leather jacket. The other just in a white tee shirt. Gun was tucked into his pants when they left.'

'Hats?'

'No one mentioned hats.'

'How about their hair. Color, long, short, curly, long?'

'One lady who's a teller told me they both looked like greasers, said they both had black hair. One curly astrew the other slicked back.'

'Boots, shoes?'

'They were both wearing construction boots the old guy over there noticed. Probably Kodiaks he thought. Damn near pissed himself when he heard the shot. He was just here to cash a cheque.'

'Well get all their names, tell them they can go & thank them very much for their help. Tell them I'll be contacting them if I think of something else they might be able to help me with.'

'Yes Sir.'

'Frank.'

'Yes Sir.'

'You did a good job, Whitey would be proud.'

'Thank you Sir.' Officer Frank said proud his eyes wetting up.

Detective Southern took a long look around the bank, hoping to pick up something which had been missed. Unfortunately all he could see was Constable Milliken's body outlined, taped in blood. Ghost of Whitey lingering.

'You get those fucking guys,' Detective Southern swore he heard in his head

'No problem my friend I'm on it,' Detective Southern replied strong like an oath.

*****

Southern went outside to query the Young Officer questioning potential witness. Milling about in a dismal twilight. Parking lot sparkling wet.

'Well officer what do we have?' The Young Officer who was eager like a young kid. Anxious to impress the Detective. He was trying to look serious making sure he didn't sound like an idiot. It was important to him, that all he worked with thought him smart. Especially the detectives-- he wanted their job eventually.

'It appears Sir they ran straight from the bank to that parking spot right over by the exit,' he said making sure to point out the exact spot. 'There they jumped in a car & away they went'

'Did anyone get a description of the vehicle.'

'Yes Sir, that long haired chap over there, sitting on the curb said he noticed it was a Ford Comet. He's a bit of a poet he said & thought it ironic they sped out of the parking lot like a Comet in a Comet.'

Detective Southern let out a little smirk.

'Anything else?'

'Yes, that lady over there waiting by the grocery store. She swears they went straight through the lights in the intersection. She was just leaving the store through the automatic doors, pushing her grocery cart when she heard honking. It startled her she said. She looked around & saw this car careening right through the red light. Cars on either side of the road screeching & honking. She said she knew someone was up to no good.'

'Did she notice which way they were headed.'

'Straight north up Bathurst, Sir.' The rookie knew the detective was pleased with this last piece of information because Southern looked him in the eye when he said it & the rookie could see the spark.

Detective Southern went over to the relaxed chap hunched over sitting on the curb. He thought if he was a poet maybe he caught a glimpse of something more. That needed the right probing. A detective needed the smallest of details. Poets are said to be very observant of the smallest details no matter how painful.

'Good evening Sir,' Southern said. The sun was surprisingly still visible in the west. Making a presence through the greyish blue clouds. The air was damp from the previous downpour. Dusk was descending on the crime scene. The rain during the robbery long gone.

'I am Detective Southern of the Metro Toronto Police Force, I was wondering if I could ask you a couple more questions. It won't take long.'

'I've already told that other officer everything I saw. I don't know what more I can tell you guys.' The poet said sitting, looking up from the curb, He looks tired Detective Southern thought.

'Well, I'll be the judge of that.' Southern said trying to be firm.

'Did you see the license plate?'

'A bit as it sped off,' the frazzled poet was really wracking his brain. 'Couldn't read the numbers at all, it was raining.'

'OK, but did you notice the color of the plate?'

'Well what I could see I'd say it was a slash of mud on a dirty white pallet.'

'Like a province of Ontario white plate?'

'Yea I guess you could say that.'

'What color was the car?'

'Well it was hard to see everything happening so fast,' the poet paused for a breath, 'but I would say a dull blue or a greasy grey.'

'Anything unique about the car? Loud exhaust, tinted windshield, raised hood, anything hanging from the rear-view mirror?'

'Nothing really stood out, it was a Ford Comet. I remember that. Squat square frame, low riding roof, whitewall tires.'

Southern was thinking it must have been stolen, make sure he checks out with vehicle branch for listing of recently stolen cars.

'Anything else?' Southern knew from experience there was always something simple which could easily be missed.

The poet straightened his back & had a thought.

'Well, there was something sticking up in the back seat that seemed out of place.'

'Describe it?' Southern knew this might be it.

'A long narrow stick of some sort,' the poet reflected. Trying to paint it as a picture in his mind. Southern mulled over the implications of such a thing.

'Could it have been a rifle?'

'No definitely not a gun.' The poet said reflecting. 'I remember it was raining & the windows were wet with raindrops dripping down like on a lake.' Then a light went on in the poets head, it was like he was having an epiphany.

'It was a fishing pole, that's what it was.'

'Well, that's a great help, thank you.' Southern was pleased. 'If you could just go give your name & address to the officer over there, you're free to go. I'll be in touch if need be.'

The poet stood up pleased with himself.

Southern turned back to the rookie officer & directed him to get names & phone numbers from all who had provided information & tell them they'd be contacted if needed. He said this over his shoulder as he headed immediately to his vehicle in a rush & radio'd in.

'Captain it looks like they were two punks driving a stolen blue grey Ford Comet. I suggest putting an all points out for the car.' Southern leaning on his unmarked Ford Fairlane stretching the mike out through the window. For some reason he forgot all about the fishing pole.

'Looks like they were headed north up Bathurst. Did you get the OPP?'

'Still trying to get through, working on it.' The Captain's frustration at trying to engage the provincial police was historic.

'One of em stocky, the other tall & thin. Should be easy to spot.' Southern was trying to think of some relevant facts.

' I'll tell the OPP about them heading up Bathurst. Once I get a hold of them,' the Captain said. 'But I'm thinking maybe that was a ruse & they're headed back our way. If they're a couple of punks they might of u turned it back into the city. Drove north to throw us off.' The Captain was thinking in his head the cost of gas for all his cars if they end up in a chase on northern roads. He was more hoping then believing they turned back into town. Make everything a lot easier.

'I think you're given them to much credit Captain. I think these kids are heading for the bush. I'm just going to head up Bathurst see if anything sticks out, maybe they broke down.' Southern had another hunch.

134

'All right away you go but stay in touch. Stay south of Seven in case something comes up.'

'Roger on that.'

'Roger over.'

By this time another car of detectives was on the scene. Southern updated them with his information. They wanted to do some questioning & checking out on their own. Some one would have to stick around as forensics was supposed to be arriving any minute. They agreed that once they were satisfied that their own investigative initiatives were in play they would make their own decisions as to what trail they would follow. They hinted it might be useful to check out the local bars, see what they could pick up, start with the Algonquin & go from there.

Southern told them he was heading up Bathurst. The rest could go where they please he thought turning away & in a double step hurriedly went to his waiting souped up undercover police car.

There was always so much competition to get the caller within the Force. Everyone pushing for the big bust, everyone going for the glory, everyone needing their picture on the front page. Southern wasn't into that bull shit. He saw what it had done to his father, all the pressure, the attention, promotion beyond his ability, turning to drink to hide his inadequacies, making scenes at home, hitting his Mom, dying young.

Job just too much for him & too proud to ask to go back to what he really wanted to be doing which was just walking a beat, Being the constable on the block, checking locks, having coffee & sandwich at the local deli. Putting in his time, taking his pension retiring to a peaceful setting on a distant lake. Feet up, fishing rod in hand, floating on a bright blue lake under a deep soothing sky.

'That's it' !!

Suddenly a bulb lighting up in Southern's thoughts. The fishing pole. They were heading up north to do some fishing. Had to be. He knew he should tell the Captain but the Captain would only tell him to leave anything outside the city limits to the OPP. Stay in the city, investigate.

Southern didn't want to investigate he wanted to pursue. He had a promise to keep.

Southern jumped in the front seat & quickly cranked on the oversize engine. It rumbled relieved to get going. The discrete 1967 Ford Fairlane was Southern's partner. That's the main reason Southern always worked alone he couldn't stand the thought of someone else driving his beauty. With it's police issued high performance big eight under the hood. Southern stepped on the accelerator & it roared like a beast in heat coming to life. Southern sped off. Straight north up Bathurst. Siren singing.

Part Three

Sudsie & Zit were heading straight north up the 400. They'd made the turn onto the highway & were feeling pretty good about everything. Real desperados on the run.

Dusk was draining, the rain clear & the western sky lit up like a cigarette. A sultry sun finally in an exasperated last gasp took its exit over the wet farm fields of southern Ontario. A treacherous grey descended over the land.

Sudsie looked over from his driver's seat, 'See anyone following us?'

Zit in the passenger seat beside-- legs lieing askew like seaweed on the dash-- did a quick 360 head check, a feat to be made famous in later years by the girl in The Excorsist, ' No one I can see,' he said.

'Let's turn on the radio, maybe it's on the news. We'll be stars just like Eddy was,' Zit said wallowing in illusions of grandeur.

Sudsie shrugged. Why not he thought running from the law listening to rock n roll. I'm into that. He was starting to notice that no matter how hard he slammed down the accelerator the Comet wasn't going to go over seventy-eight.

Zit turned on the radio twisting the chrome dial as if he was disengaging a bomb. He finally found CHUM 1050. Playing the newest hit from Toronto's own Ugly Ducklings, Gaslight. When the song finished a quacky excited DJ spoke up telling everyone that it was looking like the rain was letting up & it was going to be a nice clear night. The days traffic was thinning out & the accident on the Don Valley Parkway had been cleared up & traffic was progressing at its usual snail's pace.

Since the Boyd gang's escape in 1952 the Don Valley had been paved over & was now the commuter connection to Toronto. For the hundreds of thousands commuters working downtown & living in the suburbs.

After Boyd & the gang had slithered through the bars-- they had cut with a hacksaw smuggled in the hollow of Tough Lenny's wooden leg-- they shimmied down the Don Jail stone wall on a bunch of sheets tied together. Jumping the last thirty feet. Now down on the ground they slid out of control down into the Don Valley ravine. Making their way unconventionally to the Don River rushing below. There they started north up this same Don Valley. Following the river hoping the dense vegetation of the valley would hide their efforts not to be seen. Took em seven days to reach the infamous barn. This was the same valley which within 10 years will have been slashed, flattened, straightened & paved. Providing the escape route--north-- from the city to the suburbs. Eddy as with all his schemes was just a little bit ahead of his time.

During Eddy's time, the jail rose up flat from the ravine, ominous, evil, right out of Edgar Allen Poe . The Don Valley was bushland, with the Don River running through it. For a week they were trudging through thickets, wading through creeks, walking over fallen trees. Only to end up in the barn on Shepherd, not more than eight miles up the valley from where they had started. Tough sledding.

They were right about one thing though. The brush hid them from the inquisitive eyes of the greatest manhunt in Canadian history. It gave them the needed cover from the swirling eye in the sky. Canada's first use of a helicopter , in a civilian matter. However this effort to conceal came with a price for Eddy & the gang. By the time they reached the barn they were physically spent. Thus the reason for the lack of resistance during their capture.

The sun was gone, what little bit of it had stuck around was sliding away, it was getting dark. Sudsie relaxed a bit, taking off his shades. Zit dozing off mesmerized with how hot they are.

Sudsie reached into his leather jacket & pulled out a pack of smokes. He laid them on the dash taking one out. He then plugged in the fancy lighter in the Comet & like a tycoon with a cigar fired up his cigarette. Traffic was light no one had paid them any mind & they haven't seen any cops. Sudsie was feeling pretty proud of himself, if fuckup asleep over there hadn't shot that cop it would have gone off real smooth. Fuck, oh well we'll hide out in the bush just like Eddy, he thought.

The reality was that the living & running from the cops in the bush almost killed Eddy & the gang. That thought never crossed Sudsie's mind. He could only see notoriety.

They were well up the 400. King's Highway it was called. Lights of the city fading in the rear-view mirror. Sudsie looked down at the speedometer needle clearly saying you're going seventy-seven miles an hour. Might as well ease off a bit Sudsie thought. The highway was flat not a cop in sight. Just as he was letting his foot off the accelerator his eyes happened to glance past the gas gauge which was clearly showing they were virtually running on empty. Of all the things he had to plan for this job. Now he realized-- with an ominous chill-- he had forgot the last thing on the list. He forgot to fill up the gas tank. Fuck. Next time he'd remember to put that job closer to the top.

He looked over at Zit, sprawled fast asleep as only a tall lanky punk can drape themselves over the front seat of a Ford Comet. Not a care in the world. Like we just spent the day riding the rides at the Ex., Sudsie thought

Sudsie turned up the radio, DJ playing a song by a boy from Willowdale. David Clayton Thomas & The Shays playing, 'Brainwashed'. Sudsie didn't really care. Tell you the truth he didn't really like a music. He just hated when some songs came on & they reminded him of his mother, his sister. On the other hand he did like rock n roll.

'Zit wake up,' Sudsie yelled & gave Zit a closed fist into his shoulder.

'Ow, fuck man that hurt, what's up, coppers onto us yet. Haven't seen hide nor hair of em. They must've thought we headed back downtown. So I think we could be cool, Who's gonna arrest us up here.' Zit woke up from his revelry rambling.

*****

Officer Purdy had been on shift since four. Going the four to twelve. Fuck he loved his job. Working for the Ontario Provincial Police force had to be the greatest job in the world. It had it's moments, pay could be a little higher, but that's not the thing. Driving & hanging out in one of the most beautiful areas in the world balanced off the smaller pay.

He was on patrol tonight. Main focus on the King's Highway No. 400. One of the primary responsibilities of the Ontario Provincial Police was to police all designated King's Highways in the province. So he got to drive the highways in a big, souped up cop car, as fast as he wanted, up & down, north to south, west to east. Pavement, gravel, mud, ice & snow, he loved it.

Tonight he'd done a few miles & was sitting at the King Township Cloverleaf mile 89 on the 400 heading north. South of Barrie. He was parked in the back of the Gulf at the King City Service Center. Lights out, inconspicuous, relatively unseen. Sipping a coffee, listening to his police radio. Watching-- the station, the HWY, the night sky, the light off the lampposts-- everything in his view.

Detective Southern was past Steeles now & out of his jurisdiction. He had another hunch. He was pulling up to the Bathurst Highway 7 interchange. He pulled over-- just north of 7-- got out & looked around. Staring straight north the road turned into gravel. To his right east to Richmond Hill. To his left looking west there was a big sign on Hwy 7 that said, 'West, King's Highway 400 North.'

They're heading for the 400 north. A light bulb clear as a bell went off in his head. Southern jumped back into his anxious automobile screeched his wheels flew the wheel to the left. Flying through the intersection turning her back to the right. Pedal to the mettle west down Hwy 7.

He bent over & picked up the radio,

'Check, Captain I think they're headed up the 400. I'm gonna follow it up for awhile.' Southern says. Meanwhile he's going 120 miles an hour like a dart down Hwy 7. Flatlands passing cars like they were standing still. Not noticing all those landmarks Sudsie & Zit had passed just a short time before.

'Alright Southern, take it to Barrie but if you don't see anything come on back. I'll notify the OPP you're headed up their way,' he knew Southern was stubborn, a tracker on a trail.

'Have they put out the all points yet?' Southern replied trying to hide the thrill of the pursuit in his vocal demeanor. Don't want the Captain to hear your mind is set.

'Don't know,' replied the Captain his mind already focusing on a hundred other things. 'I'll ask.'

' Roger that.' Southern replied relieved his Captain hadn't tried to reign him in. He was free to catch the bastards who'd murdered Whitey. He was flying through lights like they weren't even there. Slowing down slightly as he approached the respective crossroads, but when he sensed it was clear his foot was back to the floor.

Our narrator the setting sun appears to have lost interest finally in our petty lives & has long gone to try another venue further to the west. When Detective Southern finally virtually flew onto the ramp onto the 400 & headed north, dusk was gone dripped into dark.

*****

'Look Zit we have to pull over for gas or we're not going to make it.' Sudsie said in a heightened voice at his dishelved partner trying to get him to take something seriously.

'Fuck man what the hell do you mean, I thought you filled it before the job.'

'Yea well I didn't so fuck you, we gotta get gas soon, we'll have to pull over at the next sign of pumps. Keep an eye.'

It wasn't too long before Sudsie spied the round sign ' King City Service Center, Gas and Food, 2 miles.' In smaller letters, ' last gas till Barrie.'

They were on it before they knew it, The King Township Cloverleaf, Zit spotted the turnoff as they came upon it. Zit was all alert now.

'Up there man,'

'Yea I see it.'

Sudsie slowed down & turned off the highway spying the big Gulf sign of the Service Center. Fuck what a relief he thought. Next time I gas up before the job.

Right at that moment as Sudsie & Zit were turning in for gas, Officer Purdy's radio cackled. It was Purdy's OPP Captain,

'Word just in boys it looks like those two felons who robbed the bank & killed an officer down in Toronto might be heading our way. With a city detective chasing em. Be on the lookout for two males driving a bluish grey Ford Comet. One of em stocky, the other tall & thin. They are presumed to be armed & dangerous. If you spot them do not approach. Radio it in.' The older OPP Captain abruptly finished with a flourish of cigarette generated coughs.

A jumble of officers radioed back, 'Roger that,' all at the same time sounding like a flock of geese Purdy thought.

Officer Purdy was writing down Captains description, when he looked up & there sitting at the pumps was a bluish grey Ford Comet. He couldn't believe his eyes. Out jumped one spindly lanky lad heading into the store & the other one a bit stocky stretching his legs as if he'd just completed a long drive & his legs were stiffening up. Funny, thought Purdy, you would have thought the other one would be cramping up with those long legs.

'Captain I think they're here at the King Township Gulf gassing up,' Purdy said into the mike like a spy.

'Stay put & observe. Do not approach,' Captain coughed into the mike. Cautiously adding, 'if it is them then let's watch what they're up to.'

Purdy stayed put, coy, watching. The wiry one went into the store. The stocky one went to the front of the Comet & leaned back on the hood. He nonchalantly lit a cigarette within two feet of the gas pumps. Not to bright thought Purdy.

!!!!!

An attendant emerged from the store through the same door Zit just went in. The gas jockey just a kid thought Officer Purdy. Stay alert.

'Fill up Sir.' The young attendant asked. He felt good but in all honestly quite nervous. He had only been working here a week & already they've left him alone to run the place. He could pump gas ok but running the till was still a challenge. Plus he had to keep an eye on the store while he was out here at the pumps.

'Yea fill er up.' Sudsie said through a veil of smoke.

'Check the oil?' our young attendant asked. Wondering if he should tell this guy to put out the smoke. You'll blow us all up. But he refrained. This guy looks like wasn't afraid to fight & our young attendant wasn't overly confrontative anyways. Just do your job he thought.

'No just the gas. Oils fine.' Sudsie replied sharply. Sudsie glanced over looking for Zit. He saw him through the window glass in the store. What the fuck is he doing he thought. We're not on a shopping trip.

Our pimply faced teen age gas attendant thought Sudsie responded quite aggressively, rude almost, sure not friendly. What an asshole, he knew the type, thinks the world owes him a living, like those Italian Mobsters in the movies. Talks to me like I ain't as good, fuck him. Our Attendant pulled down his cap & filled the tank. Taking special note to let quite a bit of gas slide down the side of the innocent Comet after it was finally full.

'Hey man watch what you're doing,' Sudsie was watching him spill the gas.

'Yes, sir sorry sir.' Punk, thought our attendant. Glancing through the Comet's back window as he replaced the gas cap, he saw the pistol in the back. Just laying there on the backseat beside what looked like a fishing rod. That's weird he thought. Our attendant went from irritated to nervous to scared in an instant.

Sudsie finished his smoke & went into the store followed closely behind by our innocent scared attendant. What the fuck am I going to do Our attendant fretted. Failing to beat Sudsie to the door. Inside, Zit had a pile of stuff piled on the counter. Chips, pop, candy bars, crackers, sandwiches. Sudsie took a look at all the stuff.

'What the hell Zit you buying out the store?'

'Just stalking up a bit.' Zit smiled showing off his crooked teeth.

'Give me four packs of smokes,' Sudsie said to our attendant. Who was now behind the till. Sudsie thought what the hell not a bad idea might as well stock up.

Our attendant was watching like a scared sparrow. The lights in the store lit up his customers faces. He stared in terror, was that fucking make up they're wearing, he gasped. They looked really weird grotesque. The fluorescent lights were reflecting off the bank robbers peeling painted faces. Our attendant was beyond fear. The pimples on his startled face started to prickle.

He rushed the four packs to the counter. He was not getting a good feeling about these guys. Sudsie threw a few pepperoni sticks on the pile & grabbed a lighter. 'How much for the Bic?' he asked giving it a flick.

Our attendant was ready to just break out in a plea but instead he heard himself say,

'50 cents Sir' he was quite prepared to just give it all to them just so they would leave.

Our attendant couldn't look either one of them in the eye. On their part Sudsie & Zit were being reasonably polite, certainly for them. They were unaware their attempt at being disguised like Eddy was melting down their face. Any thoughts of causing alarm were the furthest thing from their mind. They were only thinking that they better pay up & get going. Head up north--freedom.

Our attendant--on the other hand-- felt for sure they were going to rob, kill & mutilate him. He was alone, boss gone home for dinner, slow night, he prayed for that bell at the front to ring. A new customer to his rescue. But there was no sound, except of course for his heart which was pounding like a revving race car through his chest.

Our attendant rang up the goodies, each one carefully entered into the cash register. At any moment he knew he was going to get his head knocked off. Sudsie waited at the till leaning on the counter. The rack of bics fascinating his attention. He picked another one off the display. Stood there just flicking the bic off & on, getting bored. Finally throwing the lighter down onto the counter, making the decision to buy two. Our attendant slid it over with the rest of pops & chips & cheesies & sandwiches & pepperoni's & whatever else had caught Zit's eye & rang it all in. Zit wasn't even noticing anything. He was casually leafing through a car mag by the counter.

'$17.50 with the gas.' Our attendant said. Face masked in fear & purpose as he addressed Sudsie directly. Beads of sweat starting to form on his upper lip, certain the tall one was going to stab him just for speaking.

Sudsie looked up at him. Looking at him, bored. This was it, Our attendant thought & started to close his eyes in anticipation of what is to come.

' Shit I left my money in the car. Wait here,' Sudsie suddenly said. ' Zit you keep our friend here company while I go get some cash.' Sudsie gave Zit the nod towards our stone statue of an attendant who waits absolutely terrified in fear, frozen in marble.

"I'll be right back.' Sudsie yelled over his shoulder as he left.

Zit looked up & smiled, his stupid crooked grin, his lips too big for his face. 'Throw this magazine in there,' Zit said to Our statuesque attendant.

' Yes sir,' our attendant managed to get out of his attendant mouth.

'Sir no one ever called me sir.' Zit curiously commented turning away in a flurry.

Sudsie moseyed out to the car & reached under the driver's seat for the cloth sack of cash they had robbed from the bank. He reached in & pulled out a couple of twenties. Lots of cash he gasped. Shoving the money into his pants pocket. Should do he thought. This was big dough to him. Placing the sack back under his seat.

Back in the store our young pimply faced attendant had virtually wet his pants. By now in pure genuine fear that the rude one had gone back for the gun & was going to come back to blow off his head & steal all his cash & cigarettes. To this he believed was his teenage fate.

Sudsie came back into the store. Reached into his pants pocket. Our bug eyed attendant tensed, this was it, for sure I'm dead. Our attendant closed his eyes & waited for the worst.

'Hey man what's up.' Sudsie was standing on the other side of the counter. Looking at Our attendant as he placed a twenty on the glass. Our attendant quickly opened his eyes trying to be cool in the face of danger. Waiting for the shot. Seeing Sudsie pushing the twenty across the counter.

Someone who might be watching may be thinking it's the attendant who's a little bit weird & the boys are trying to help this nervous nut out.

'$ 17.50 right.' Sudsie reaffirmed politely. In a voice which broke the ice. Not a gun in sight.

Our attendant snapped back on track. Doing his job. Something about hearing the price & no weapon pointed at him, brought him back from the abyss.

'Well your friend over there,' Our attendant pointed to Zit, 'also purchased a car magazine so it's actually $ 18.00, with tax.' Our attendant couldn't believe he was being so bold. Defying these ruffians & demanding their money. His sense of responsibility was overcoming his dreadful overwhelming fear of having his head blown off. Now he was determined to get his money, for the store, for the right thing to do.

Our attendant rang in the twenty, eyes glued to the till. As he was reaching for change in the till, Susie looked up, with a nonchalant air,

'Hey man keep the change,' Sudsie said acting the big shot. Zit looked densely over-- as if he was just getting out of bed with his droopy bedroom eyes-- & Sudsie gave him the wink. Zit smiled.

Our attendant couldn't believe his good luck. Here in one quick stroke he went from a certain death to being up two bucks. A fortune when you're earning a buck fifty an hour.

'Thank you very much Sir', Our attendant said respectively.

"No problem,' Sudsie sneered like the hot shot greaser he was, 'Come on Zit let's blow this pop stand.' Zit tucked the mag in his baggy blue jeans, tightening his belt & picked up the bags of junk food.

'Give me a hand.' He grunted to Sudsie. Bags of chips were spilling over his arms, bottles of pop clutched between his fingers.

Sudsie looked back & grabbed a couple bag of chips & the pepperoni, a bottle of pop. Then they were gone. Out the store. A door slowly closing marking they were here now they were no more. Phantom figures walking leisurely back to their now gassed up Comet.

Our attendant breathed a sigh of relief reflecting on how wrong he had been about those guys. Probably just going up north, do a little hunting, little fishing, little drinking. Nice guys he thought as he set about restocking the now overly depleted shelves. He just couldn't get that image of the pistol laying on the back seat out of his head. Maybe they're famous he thought.

*****

Officer Purdy had been sitting tight, observing the whole scenario like watching a play. Respecting his orders to stay put. Hard to do when you're chasing someone described as armed & dangerous. You're desperate to confront them. He watched as the two suspects got out of the car. The tall thin one going into the store. The stocky one hanging about smoking casually. They're acting like they don't have a care in the world he thought. Couple of pals off to the cottage. Purdy watched as the stocky one of them rushed out of the store & grab something from the car & stroll back in. It was all he could do to stay still. Then they both left the store carrying a few bags of what looked like groceries. Stocking up-- a bit premature-- he thought, must be hungry, they've had a big day. Dumb fucks.

Purdy saw them get back into the car with a sense of relief.

He radioed Captain, 'It's them Captain. A bluish grey Ford Comet, two of em, fit the description. They're here at the King City Service Center.

They just got gas & what looked like junk food & pop. Now they're heading out.' Click.

'Roger that.' The balding Captain replied.' Follow at a distance & tell me which way they're going.' To the old Captain the news couldn't be better.

Sudsie pulled out of the Gulf Service Center & followed the signs to HWY 400 north, Barrie. Officer Purdy following discretely.

'We're on our way now man. Turn up the tunes.' Sudsie said in a jubilant mood. Zit bouncing in his seat for some reason, bent down real happy & turned up the volume. Elvis Presley's hit tune Suspicious Eyes was playing, 'We're caught in a trap,' the opening line went right over their heads. Premonition perhaps for our two oblivious fugitives.

Officer Purdy was back on the radio, 'They're back on the HWY Captain heading north to Barrie.'

'Roger that. Keep following them silent, don't let them see you. Stay far enough back that if they turn off you can tell. Don't let them know you're following them.'

'Roger that.' Purdy was hot on the trail.

Purdy's fat & jolly Captain pushed back his chair away from his desk & said to no one in particular.

'We've got em.' Fists clenched in anticipation. Time to put the plan into operation.

Detective Southern meanwhile had heard the whole thing on his radio. He was south on the highway about twenty miles from the King City Cloverleaf. He was closing in. He was going so fast that he slowed down. He didn't want to pass them.

Purdy's Captain jumped up from his chair (no mean feat) & raced through the office out to his car. Opening the door he slammed down into his seat. Grabbing the radio mike he pressed the button down as if he was setting off a bomb & radio'd to all,

'Suspects heading north up HWY 400. All cars & I mean all cars head for the Infamous Bradford Overpass. We'll take them there.' He said in his best General Patton Captain voice.

*****

The Bradford Overpass was infamous in police lore because in 1952 The Boyd Gang had pulled off their last bank robbery at the CIBC in the town of Bradford. Just a couple of miles down from the then under construction new Bradford Overpass.

It had been a dull grey morning. The approaching noon day sun was preparing for an entrance. Struggling to light up the small town of Bradford's main street after a morning of rain. An off-duty police officer was out to get his morning paper. As he was walking nonchalantly down Main Street he noticed three guys in trench coats get out of a big black Packard on the other side of the street. He watched them head nonchalantly towards the bank. They appeared in no hurry. One even tipping his hat to a mother out taking her baby for a stroll. But there was something about them which he found suspicious. Possibly the bulge in the trench coats where guns could be concealed. They certainly were strangers in a small town. Possibly up to no good.

He watched them go into the bank as the Packard sat waiting by the curb. Engine running. A fedora hat behind the wheel. It hit him like a sledgehammer. Something was up. He raced back to his room, above the bakery two blocks away to grab his gun.

The Boyd Gang entered the bank in all their bravado & bluster. Tough Lenny had everyone face down on the floor. There were only two customers, a cashier & the bank manager in the bank.

The one customer in there to take out some money, she had her eye on a new dress, just in, at Eatons. She wanted to be the first in town to get it. She was wanting to impress her friends at the harvest dance coming up this weekend. Tough Lenny terrified her.

The other customer, though he would challenge you if you called him this to his face, was an old farmer, mean, ornery & mad at life. When Tough Lenny told him to get down Lenny had to give him a look to freeze the devil himself, before the old farmer went down. This boy giving the orders means business the old farmer thinking.

Eddy hopped over the gate in his usual fashion, by now everybody knew who he was, no need for disguise. He gave the cute cashier a smile to melt honey. Even though she was terrified her body tingled. Eddy getting her to fill up his cloth bags with money from the tills. Tough Lenny went behind the counter & got the bank manager up & headed for the vault. Tough Lenny got him to open it up & threw some more cloth bags in his face telling him to fill em up. Willy the Clown Jackson guarding the front door keeping his shaking gun trained on anything that moved.

By the time the off duty cop had gotten his gun & was racing back to the scene, the gang was exiting the bank & jumping into the waiting Packard. Steve 'Pimple Face' Suchan waiting anxiously behind the wheel. The determined cop let fly a couple of shots towards the fleeing bank robbers. Tough Lenny just getting to the waiting car, always the last to leave, stopped & turned on the sidewalk & aimed his machine gun right at this adrenal pumped hero cop. To this day our off duty hero still can't figure out why he wasn't cut in two. The bullets were flying all around him whizzing by both ears. Like standing in a miracle, they all missed him.

The Gang piled in the roaring Packard. Tough Lenny riding one side-board Eddy the other. Pimple Face flooring it, Packards tail swagging, dust flying. The off duty soon to be legend cop, running down mainstreet in hot pursuit firing his pistol to beat hell. Willy the Clown, leaned out the back side window took aim & shot three times with his pistol. One creasing our hero's ear, drawing blood. This gave our hero time for reflection. He halted his pursuit. Stood watching panting like a dog in heat. The Gang clinging to the Packard racing away. Smell of smoke, gas & gunfire filling the street.

The Gang's plan was to head west out of Bradford. Get to the new King's HWY that was just being built a few miles west. Hooking Toronto up with Barrie. They didn't know the powers that be were still working on the road putting in turnoffs, overpass's & right of ways. They hadn't thought that far ahead to check. That was the one thing on the list Eddie had forgot to do.

When the fleeing fugitives got to where they thought the HWY should be there were construction & detour signs all up. Your Money at Work the big signs said. The Bradford Overpass was just being built. It didn't exist -- much to the amazement of our flying felons. The desperate Gang slammed to a halt. Pimple Face threw the Packard in reverse did the big screeching turn around & headed the few miles back to Bradford. The way from whence they had just come.

Our ambitious off duty hero was slowly standing up. Dusting himself off straightening his tie. Nursing his nicked ear. When lo & behold who comes thundering back through town going the opposite way down mainstreet, but the screaming Packard carrying the Gang.

Our cop immediately went down into a crouch in the middle of the road & started firing off more shots at the approaching Packard. The car-- as an enraged bull sensing danger-- turned to the red cape posing as an off duty police officer & bore horns down on our now frightened hero.

The off duty cop managed to jump out of the way as the Packard screamed by. Narrowly missing his left leg being mangled when he just managed to pull it back at the last second. Just out reach of the Packard's treads. The Boyd Gang hurtled past down the road heading for what was now their fate.

The authorities finally caught up to the gang, a few months later. The Bradfod Bank was their last party. They were detained, incarcerated & two of em hung. The other two spending the next many years as guests of the government.

Eddy had $24,376 dollars of the Bradford banks money in a cloth bag underneath the bed he was sharing with his mistress when Detective Payne of the Toronto Police force pressed his pistol against Eddy's sleeping temple & yelled,

'Get up Eddy Boyd you bum, it's Payne, you're under arrest.' Detective Payne had been practicing that line for years.

Purdy's Captain had chosen the Infamous Bradford Overpass as the obvious spot to set up his fleet to meet the advancing adversaries. The same place where-- sixteen years before Eddy & the Gang's plans ran into disaster-- our desperados were now destined for doom.

*****

The highway was four lanes across with a grassy median down the middle splitting the well used HWY in two. Two lanes north two lanes south. Straight like a race track's straightaway both ways. Either way strung into the black, splitting farm fields at rest. The Bradford Overpass crossed over top the King's HWY 400 like a short haired wig.

The Captain set up, underneath the Overpass. He angled four vehicles to block the north bound lanes, stretched another four across the south bound lanes facing the same way. Head lights all shining down the Hwy— all patiently waiting-- lights criss crossing, piercing the sky, brightening the night. Bright red roof lights flashing-- dancing off the overpass ceiling. Lighting up the scene like a thousand brothels. Captain strung three cars out on the grassy divide. Directing them to turn off their lights. Leaving a black hole in the middle of the blockade. Thinking if the fugitives tried slipping through the center-- believing they had a chance-- they'd be crushed.

The old proud Captain reviewed his troupes. Eleven big hulking OPP vehicles, plus his own-- out front in the lead-- meant twelve cars blocking the highway. It'd take a tank & even then I think we could hold em he thought to himself. All lights on, guns at the ready, all men set in their place. They were ready. A formidable force.

*****

'How much longer you figure we got to go, before we can hole up some-where.' Zit asked with a mouthful of chips & a cigarette dangling from his crusty lips.

'We gotta get past Barrie.' Sudsie said keeping his eyes straight ahead as he drank a coke.

'Where we going to sleep.' Zit was slouching like he was in PaPa's well used leather chair, MaMa's comforter on the back. He really was after all of this a total innocent without a clue.

'We'll just sleep in the car, tomorrow we'll go in buy a tent, make a hide out man,' Sudsie was getting tired explaining the plan over & over again to his friend. 'Look how many days Eddy spent in the bush.'

'But he got caught.' Zit whined.

'Only when he came out of the bush.' Sudsie smiled feeling smart.

!!!!!

Officer Purdy was updating the Captain on the radio telling him each time he passed a mile marker.

'Not far now, ' Purdy said into his mike. He could see the fugitives red tail lights clearly within view. Purdy was closing in. To say he was excited would be compromising.

'Roger that.' The Captain curtly replied replacing the mike in one motion back in its place. He picked up his bullhorn from the passenger seat & got his bulk out of the car. He turned & addressed his invisible men hidden in the light. Talking through a dull slight breeze being brought on by the night.

'Well men any minute now. Be prepared be alert. Shoot only if they don't stop. Have your guns on the ready.' All the officers—hidden from his view by the glare-- heard the message clearly. The evening air became tense as everyone breathed in, ready.

Captain put the bull horn down. He turned round his intensive stare into the distant darkness. Standing out in front of his car hands on hips the Captain breathed deep. He wouldn't hesitate to do what was needed to take these fugitives down-- fearing nothing.

He spied a pair of headlights, pin pricks in the dark. Moving closer.

&&&&&

'Give me one of those chocolate bars in the bag,' Sudsie said to Zit. He was leaning over from the wheel butting out his well spent cigarette in the ashtray. The radio was playing 'The Day the Music Died 'about the rock n roll singer who died, tragically, too young, in a plane crash. No comparison to our destined two? Of course, what is too young? Are we all not just victims to our own fate?

Zit saw it first. Sudsie was trying to open a Mars bar with his teeth & watching the road at the same time.

'What the fuck is that?' Zit said in a highly elevated emotional curious manner.

'Fuck?' Sudsie startled to see it come into view.

'What the hell!' they both said screaming in unison.

They were both staring in awe through the front window like at an outdoor picture show. It looked like fireworks display right in the middle of where they were headed. Red, green, white a kaleidoscope of colors bouncing off walls, roads & stars.

The Boys were coming closer & closer to a perceived apparition. A space ship in all its blinding glory lights flashing screaming. Ascended from some hidden dimension (to which our two fugitives were soon headed). Sitting stopped right in the middle of the road. The boys untutored imaginations running wild at the site.

'Fucking freaky man.' Sudsie & Zit mused out loud again together.

It took them so long just trying to figure out what the fuck it was that by the time they realized what it was it was way too late.

. . . .

'Fuck it's a road block,' Sudsie howled.

Captain now crouched down in sharpshooter stance. Which wasn't an easy pose to take considering his weight. 'Here they come boys,' he yelled like a command into the night. 'All eyes front,' he bellowed over his shoulder. Looking like some soldier fighting in the Boer war. This one's for the Queen as he kneels waiting for the ravaging hordes to come pouring over the mountaintop dressed in outrageous skins racing to their death. Captain had a bit of old school in his imagination.

Sudsie panicked. He turned the wheel sharply to his right sending the Comet hurtling over the six foot deep ditch that ran alongside the Hwy. They hit the far side hard & fast. The Comet going head over heels. Then starting to spin flipping like a seal in a farmer's field. A football bouncing in the night. Finally crashing violently to a stop.

Wheels down tires blown to smithereens. Crushed frame hanging like a belly on the ground. Innards dragging down like its having a baby. Gas tank painfully punctured dripping drips of gas like blood. Roof smashed in like a pumpkin. Front hood bent resembling a pretzel just hanging, dangling sharp bits of metal. Trunk open & tossing up & down like gasping for air. Doors squeezed in like an accordion sounding a silent dirge.

Sudsie & Zit had been tossed about like rag dolls in a dryer.

Zit was scrunched up dead like a crumpled tea towel in the backseat. A piece of metal stuck through his head, ear to ear. Sudsie was draped around the steering wheel like cloth. Lifeless & without form.

Officer Purdy had pulled over just in time to watch the show. What the fuck he thought as he pulled over & jumped from his Ford Plymouth, right off the assembly line, police car. Looking over the roof past his now flashing lights leaning on the top of the Plymouth. Watching in almost slow motion this car curl across the field. Turning his head he looked at the line of cops standing under the Overpass as if to ask are you seeing this too. He looked in disbelief back to the crash.

The Comet had stopped rolling, hisssssssssst of a smashed in rad-- smell of gas like bad breath or a stinky fart.

Fucked up.

There was the briefest of moments when the earth stopped spinning. Suns & stars & all those police watching, wondering what the hell just happened. All were suspended in time trying to take a collective breath All the officers looked at each other disbelievingly. And for the splittist of a second there was absolute silence among them-- before they sprung into action.

Even the old Captain who thought he'd seen everything couldn't believe his eyes for a second. Like a drive in movie he thought.

He sprung from his stance & rushed for the mike, 'I need an ambulance at the Bradford Overpass, right now.'

,,,,,,,,,,,,,,,,,,,,,,,,

By the time Detective Southern arrived on the scene the ambulance attendants were carting Sudsie away. The coroner coming for Zit hadn't yet arrived. The stocky one Southern noticed-- all wrapped up in blankets, bandages & oxygen on a cart. Still alive-- unfortunately-- Southern thought as he walked across the field to the crumpled Comet.

Empty bags of chips, chocolate bar rappers, blind bottles of coke spread astrew over the terrain. Southern swears he saw a construction boot without a foot. Pieces of glass reflecting back black. What a mess Southern sneered.

Car all mangled, how could anyone live through that Southern thought as he came upon the scene. Steam spraying up from the banged-up radiator. Lights staring glaring through the artificial mist. Still shining after all of that. Shimmering sparks of light-- like tears-- spotting a shocked evening night. Stench of leaking gas & burst rubber tires. Southern covering his nose.

Southern stuck his head inside what was left of a window. There was the spindly gangly one in a t-shirt he'd been after. That's the one he knew. The one who pulled the trigger. He was lying crumpled in the corner covered in blood like he was taking a shower. Dark dead eyes popped out of their sockets. Probably caused by that spike through his brain Southern thought. Definitely dead.

He started back across the field to his waiting patiently police car. To his sudden relief he felt a lot lighter. He picked up the pace anxious his fellow officers should hear that they've caught Whitey's killer.

'He's waiting in a field for a taxi to the morgue,' he'll tell em.

Whitey of course was most anxious of all. When that bullet went through his brain he knew he was dead. It made him immediately mad. That was his last thought. His spirit remained lingering. Knowing It could never exit to the next dimension until his colleagues caught the fuck who did this to him. Now he could move on, reluctantly of course. He'd miss his buddies.

'Hello Captain,' Southern said into the mike as he slipped back into his anxiously waiting undercover police car. If a car could pant that's exactly what it would be doing. It had been pushed to its limit to get here on time.

'Go ahead Southern,' Southern's Captain replied obviously a bit frayed. His night had been a busy one. He'd had to sit & listen as this whole thing unfolded.

'We got em. The one that killed Whitey is waiting in a field for a taxi to the morgue.' Southern paused for a breath. He hadn't realized till now how much this all meant. 'The other one's all banged up on the way to the hospital.'

A pause hung in the air.

' WE GOT EM BOYS ' the Captain sighed into the mike in absolute relief. His message was heard by all & all cheered.

And that's the end of the story.

The End

Heroes Lament

Part One

2006 (Fall)

There was an empty gum wrapper on the front floor. He was just switching off the van & noticed it by the passenger door.

Atticus must've dropped it when he was getting out. Harold didn't care. He had talked with Atticus about picking up after himself & not just discarding trash in the vehicle like it was an oversize trash can. For the fourteen-year-old it was in one ear & out the other. The last thing on a young boy's mind is getting rid of a gum wrapper.

Atticus was a games player. So many games so little time. His mind always one step ahead thinking about strategies in the next game he's going to play or poor decisions he made playing the last game. Gum wrappers took no precedence in his life.

Atticus was always glued to the latest technical device. Harold never knew which game was which. When he tried to show a fatherly interest, he was met with a grunt & a vacant stare. The inference was clear—don't bother me now I'm engaged in saving the world—now is not the time to interfere.

Harold smiled as he reached over & picked up the wrapper. Putting it into the already too full ashtray. Stuffing it down as ashes & cigarette butts started spilling out onto the van floor. Fuck it he said to the little man in his head.

It made him think he's been smoking too much. To emphasize the fact he coughed a little bit. His body letting him know it was fighting back.

He checked the backseat for further mess. Sure enough it was in serious duress. His youngest son Adrian was a slob. The ten-year-old had made the backseat into his own room. Potato chip bags, empty dishes, half-filled cans of pop, clothes thrown every which way. It looked like a hurricane had just passed through a garbage dump.

It seemed chaos just followed his boys around like a cloud. No matter how loud he objected they just didn't get it.

No time to clean it up now. He had to go. Time was running late. He had to get a move on. He didn't want to be late for the show.

Harold locked all the doors to the van. Taking solace in the lingering smell. Hopefully he'd be able to remember that smell—the smell of his sons.

It was a huge parking lot he was in. His anxiety level was full bore. It was a defense mechanism. If he wasn't on full alert, it could compromise his survival.

Doing W/E's wasn't the cakewalk the general public assumed it to be.

Sometimes he had thought it would have been easier just doing the time in one go. But he wouldn't have been able to keep the boys. So W/E's it was.

He looked across the full parking lot. He was still a long way to the main gate of the prison. The longest walk of his life. He always felt like dead man walking, like in a movie. He always picked an actor's walk as he passed across the parking lot, John Wayne's was his favorite.

Time was always a factor. He had to check in by 7 o'clock. If he was late they'd issue a warrant for his arrest. He picked up his pace, slipping & sliding across the concrete space on this cold damp autumn's eve. Sun long gone, chilly prairie wind blowing constantly across a vast vacant plain.

He'd talked the boy's mother into looking after them on the W/E's. That's how he sold it. He presented it like he was doing her a favor. She definitely didn't have to know he was doing time. If she found out she would try & use it against him. Try to get custody of his boys. That would never happen. He'd make sure of that.

She was a fuck up. Drugs, stripping, going through men like syrup. There was no way he would let her have his boys.

They'd agreed, long before his present situation had gone down, that she could have them—for a visit-- as long as she was sober. That was the agreement he had found-- he would have to do-- to avoid a custody battle.

He would have won in the end but he didn't have the money to pursue it. He was also not a swine & sincerely wanted the boys to know their mother. As long as they were able to avoid her stream of lovers.

So his doing W/E's in jail had fit comfortably in their—out of court-- arrangement.

The boys were really too young to understand what was going on. He didn't tell them about jail. He just let them think he was doing ok while they were visiting their mother. He didn't want them involved so they would have to lie & it would become a conspiracy. Easier just to cover up what was really going on with happy thoughts. Knowing it wasn't forever. Knowing what he had done to get himself into this mess was totally fucked up.

Atticus & Adrian were both way more involved in video games & making friends then being tied up in the mess's adults get themselves in.

Every Friday he'd have to play the happy Dad. Encouraging them to have fun with Mommy as he dropped them off in Red Deer. Then turn around & head back to Calgary. Down to the penitentiary. Psyching himself up doing it one W/E at a time.

Now it was almost done. His caseworker was working on him only doing six months instead of a year. If that panned out after this W/E he'd only have one more to go.

It still didn't mean that every minute inside wasn't a challenge. He still had to be on constant guard .

He came up to the chain link fence which signaled he was getting near.

It was an immense structure. Like approaching a midlevel castle. Razor sharp wire decorating the walls. Cold hard concrete painted in pathetic white.

He rang the bell. The guard at the gate let him in. He knew the routine.

'How you doing Ralph,' he said as the guard let him in through the heavy reinforced steel door.

'Christ Harold you must be almost done.' Ralph replied.

Ralph really wasn't that bad of a guy. The guard job wasn't his ideal job. He had failed the cops exam & with a baby on the way he had had to get something right away.

They seemed to always be needing guards. So, he signed up. That was ten years ago.

Harold watched Ralph do his paperwork through the cage.

'Almost done,' Harold said to himself.

Funny Harold thought when this had first started, he figured he'd never be done.

*****

The first W/E wasn't the hardest. He had anticipated they would get easier as they went along. But it never did. Each W/E was as hard or harder than the W/E before.

He had steeled himself for his sentence. Once the judge—almost apol-ogetically—explained he had to give him time Harold knew things would be fucked up. He vowed to himself to make it work. The law dictated he had to spend time behind bars. Screw it he thought I'm going to have to do it.

They—the lawyers, crown, judge—had to decide which way would be the best means for Harold to pay his debt. Harold was insisting he had no regret for what he'd done. But they had to impose some kind of punish-ment to meet the crime. So they let him do his time on W/E's.

Harold had been terrified at the thought. He was a movie buff. He'd seen all the stories about what goes on behind bars.

Even worse was Stephan King. Harold's imagination was fueled by King's work. Harold's mind exploded in possible Stephan King situa-tions. He imagined himself trapped in a horror story where he was being inflicted with great pain. Strapped to a gurney—bare ass out-- crying out the lord's name in vain.

So, he was prepared for the worst. But really how can you be ready to settle for life in jail.

That first W/E he'd spent the entire time in his cell on his bunk. Not even coming out to eat. His cell mate—who looked like a pre-evolutionary gorilla—mentioned to him he's going to have to come out eventually. If not the boys are gonna come & pull you out & no guards gonna save you.

The next W/E the first thing Harold noticed was that he had a differ-ent cell mate. This was-- he found out-- the routine. He would never know who he was going to be with when he walked through the cell door.

By his second W/E he was learning how to deal with his primeval fear. The most frightening thing was going to sleep.

He'd heard so many stories, mainly in the movies & on TV, of inmates being pulled from their bunks in the middle of the night & liberties being taken which are best left unsaid. Harold was terrified of being raped.

The anticipation of this kept his mind on fire. Which comprimised his need for sleep.

161

The first W/E had taught him that while laying in your bunk-- waiting in anticipation of being raped-- your thoughts went on & on like an out-of-control mind train. Every sound every movement was a threat. Your imagination your mortal enemy.

The key was to listen for the snoring. Once he heard his cellmate snoring, he knew he was relatively safe. How safe you can be in a jail full of endless criminals is always contentious. But he felt a bit of the anvil lifted off his chest.

This dab of relief did not bring him peace. The sounds of a jailhouse at night are hideous. What goes on in cells after dark is not for the weak of heart. It sounds like a zoo in a horror movie scene. Cages full of beasts, minds free to mingle in their own warped jungle.

The roars, the squawking, the screeching, the crying. The sounds for which there is no name. The sounds of the out of control insane. The sounds of human beings slowly dying. The sounds which drill through your head when you lie awake & shake in fear that something beyond your creation is near. That-- to a millionth degree-- will give you an idea of the sound of the penitentiary after the lights go down at night.

Harold would lie there wide awake. Listening to outrageous conversations with no rhyme or reason. Someone pleasing himself, have they no shame Harold would think. Someone being taken, raped, cries of rage, cries of pleading. Pleas for forgiveness to a God long lost-- in this den of heathens. The walls would start to squeeze in on him. Harold would just lay there, trying to shut the night away. To say it was absurd would be grasping for a word which didn't exist. Harold would wait, praying for the break of day.

Harold was starting to learn sleep wasn't an option. If he did nod off it was with one eye open. But it was never enough.

Harold did take his pre-evolutionary gorilla's advice the next W/E & ventured forth into the yard to join the general population Saturday afternoon. Trying desperately to show no fear.

Harold wasn't a tall man. On the other hand he wasn't small either. He was medium build & height. He could take care of himself in a fight if it came to that.

He was respectful & polite in the yard. He tried to keep to himself. When approached he'd make sure to keep his distance but not enough to imply he's scared or a snob. He'd stand strong, trying not to look whoever in the eye. Make sure that if ever asked a question he didn't respond too smart-- balanced with trying not to sound too dumb. Knowing it's important to not appear weak or some asshole will try to stick his cock up your bum.

Harold had been a good athlete at high school. An especially talented basketball player. So he gravitated to the pick-up game always being played on the basketball court set up in the yard.

He tried not to be too good. He didn't want to be seen as a hot shot. He toned down his game. He'd at least play the same as everyone else on the barren prairie concrete court.

The next mountain to climb was the mess hall.

First thing he noticed was the size. The mess hall was immense. He had done time in the army earlier in his life. He'd adjusted at the time to eating in a mess hall. But certainly nothing as large as this. What presented was thousands of men lining up & filling their jailhouse plates with heaping spoonful's' of mush.

Then heading to long banquet hall sized tables. Seated in long straight rows men of all, color & sizes. It seemed they were all staring at him. Grotesque hideous glares scaring Harold to death.

Terrified Harold waited in line. Having no idea what he'd find to eat. He edges closer pulled along-- like tied to an invisible string-- to the jailhouse buffet. Spread out before him like a steaming smelly misty mess. Metallic aroma mixed with stale potatoes & steaming sour. Better to just keep his eyes close to his chest.

He grabs a metal tray & waits his turn. The line moving ever so slowly. No reason to hurry. The cutlery all plastic of course. Don't want one of these animals stabbing someone else to death with the fork you just used to stuff your face. Or the knife you just used to cut your mashed potatoes. Or the spoon you needed to eat your meat.

Harold stood tall, hiding his fear behind a wall of desperation making like he does this every day, it's no big thing he had to believe. Yet inside his guts were just churning with knots of anxiety induced treason.

If ever there was a time to regret what he did to get himself into this mess it was now. Yet deep down from some ingrained sense of right—he knew he'd never forget what had brought him here—he knew that he never ever would regret decisions made.

So he picked up the plastic utensils & held up his metal tray as the man behind the glass counter with no teeth grinning like a full moon-- a tattoo of mother painted on his bare chest slaying some dark dragon-- dished out the slop & a splash of plop & away Harold walked into the din. Definitely not the buffet at the local Keg he thought suppressing a snicker.

He looked around for somewhere to sit. Knowing there was no way in hell he could eat this shit disguised as spaghetti with sauce. Looking at the platter he knew he just couldn't do it--his stomach was turning at the thought-- but he must look the part, try to fit in, be one of the boys. He took another look down at his tray & let out a silent moan as his bowels reached out to him—you gotta be insane—they rumbled.

One thing he was learning right off was that everyone stayed with their own kind. Here in the mess hall & out in the yard everyone kept up their guard, hanging with others who were of similar color. It was usually the color of their skin which helped each one fit in with the other. So that now instead of one they were many & had no need for fear if someone got in their face for some ridiculous thing or another.

In the mess hall, as well as the yard, you had a quilt of colors each section representing something unique. Each colored square staking their turf for their own protection. White, brown,yellow,black splattered about the venue each intent on staking out their turf. In the mess hall each table resembling a different nation. Everyone in sync with the color of their own. Each con bound to the creed essential to survival; mess with one of us you mess with us all.

Harold had trouble finding a place to sit down to eat. He knew he was being watched, so he tried to smile, a strained stretch to say the least. Plan was to keep to himself, eat as much as he could & then make a beeline back to his cell.

Harold was right. He was being watched with mixed curiosity & intrigue. His fellow cons were wondering about this relatively straight looking guy doing time on W/E's. What was he in for, where was he from, what's he doing here, is he a narc. All these thoughts went through the minds of the masses as they all looked up from their chow & watched Harold looking around for a place to sit.

In jail everyone makes it a point to know everyone else's business. It's a reality of human nature no matter what the situation you're in. You always want to know what the other guy is doing.

Harold ended up finding a spot at the end of a long table & was able to ignore his dinner companions as he jammed food into his mouth & hastily split like the anxiety prone individual he portrayed. Placing his nowhere near empty metal tray carefully back into the rack, meant just for that. Back in the solitude (for the moment) of his cell he curled up holding firm his knees letting the anxiety of the moment slide off him like water off a mallard.

By Harold's third W/E the cons had already started asking around, who is this guy. Harold for his part had learned-- all emotions aside-- this could be a boring ride. He learned this on his first W/E-- being in jail can be downright boring.

He started bringing in reading material. Harold was reading in his top bunk, a book he had brought in, 'Surfacing' by Margaret Atwood. He knew no one in the joint would want to borrow a book written by a lady & wasn't full of violence & sex.

It was early afternoon on one of those bright cold blue sky sunny days Alberta is famous for. There was just a hint of sunlight in Harold's cell. It was secondary light coming through the window high up in the hall of cages. Just enough streaking through the bars bouncing off the cell's concrete wall to remind Harold what he's missing. His cell mate laying in the bunk under him, got up & stretched. Then laying his hands on the railing of Harold's domain looked Harold straight in the eye & in a straightforward frightening way stated,

'So you think you're tough,'

Harold immediately turned his head away from his book & looked his roommate directly in the eye,

'No, not really,' Harold replied thinking this is it.

'Well keep your eyes open when you're in the yard.'

'Why, what have you heard,' Harold answered back, 'And why are you being so nice,' Harold said figuring for sure he was after his ass.

'Words out on why you're in & some of the guys don't think it's fair that they gotta stay in here while you're only doing W/E's.'

'Maybe they're right,' Harold replied & went back to his book being careful not to role on his side exposing his butt, just in case. One thing he was learning in here you just never knew the way a guy might swing.

*****

The next W/E at Saturday supper, Harold was terrified. He knew his presence by some was resented & that put a bullseye on his back.

Waiting in line for whatever noodle slop they were passing out for food that evening, he couldn't stop his knees from shaking. Every little sound pierced his heart. A dropped fork almost gave him a heart attack. The food slopping onto the tray, shoes shuffling on the concrete floor, the guards adjusting their guns in their holsters. The constant din his every thought sensitive like a fox to every sound & movement which could be a threat. No matter what he had to be ready to deal with whatever comes next.

I just gotta make it through tonight Harold thought. Stretching levels of stress like surfing waves flooding through him.

His hands were shaking as he placed his tray in front of the toothless cook who gave him an exaggerated knowing toothless grin. Smiling with his eyes he whispered to Harold,

'Have a good day my friend.'

Slivers of melted butter flowed up & down Harold's spine. A sensation of dust dissolving crashed in his head. This guy couldn't have scared Harold more if he had come at him with an axe. It's always the hidden innuendos which are the worst & this was placed with strategic intent Harold thought.

Harold was scared. What did the cook mean, what did he know. Was something already in the works which was going to cause Harold grief. Harold's imagination was flashing images of carnage through his brain. He knew if he didn't do something to stop his chaotic paranoia-- he would end up doing something completely insane.

Harold grabbed his slop laden tray & started to walk. Each breath taken with control. Each step as if walking on crystal. Each sound out of every convicts mouth talking about him, at least that's what he thought. He stood for a moment before starting to look for a place to sit. His mind in total pain unable to process the scene. It took on the feeling of standing on a rocky shore in the middle of a thousand seagulls-- the racket unreal-- as their squawking took over every inch of your sanity.

Harold's knees became weak his mind melting into survival mode. He figured he couldn't take it anymore. This chaos this unknown sensation this anticipation of what's to befall him. He made a decision. Not realizing all that was going on through his head was fueled by paranoid delusions which were not real. In actual reality non of the cons really cared about Harold they had other things more important to sort out. Yet Harold could no more of believed this then telling him he had to stop breathing to live.

Harold couldn't take it. He prepared to throw his tray on the floor & scream,

'Come & get me you fucks, I've had enough.'

At least this way Harold figured he'd get in a few licks before the whole mess hall piled on him & beat him to shit. Suddenly—just as he was raising his arms to smash his tray to the ground-- amidst the thrashing in his mind he heard a voice which wasn't in line with the cacophony of sounds piercing his ears.

167

'Hey part timer over here.'

Harold paused in mid action, looking around for that one safe sound. Looking through his maze of fear Harold saw standing down one of the many aisles a guy yelling & gesturing him over. It was his bunk mate from last week's cell. Harold cautiously made his way towards him. Feeling as though his every step was going to be his last. Like a cat in the wild every step could send a signal that could mean your end. Finally after a span which must have covered eternity Harold reached the offered seat. He sat down confused & sweating profusely.

Harold slowly said, to this one sane voice distracting him from the chaos which was filling his head,

'Hey,' Harold grunted, putting his face down & breathing deep.

Harold later would look back at this moment & credit it for saving his life. I was fuck'd he'd think, I was definitely paranoid like a druggie on meth. Definitely Ron saved my sanity. I probably would have ended up in the sanitorium if not for Ron's intervention.

His mess hall saviour—Ron-- was his cell mate who'd poured fire on his fear last week in the cell.

Ron reminded Harold of his name, 'Harold right,' which broke the ice.' I'm Ron remember.'

Harold obviously had no idea how to start a conversation. It turns out Ron was one of these guys who didn't talk much but when he spoke up people listened. Ron became a breath of fresh air-- in the stifling life of being in jail-- for Harold.

The next day on a dreary grey Sunday afternoon Harold & Ron hung out in the yard. Ron pushing Harold to talk about what's happening outside. In the real world.

Harold found out his new friend was just a regular guy. Sometimes Harold thought trying to get Ron to talk was like pulling teeth. He was doing long time but he didn't like to talk about it.

Harold couldn't help but notice that in the hall & in the yard no one messed with Ron. The other cons would move aside when Ron was walking offering a mumble greeting. Harold picked up on this quick. He also noticed that hanging out with Ron gave him cred. No one dared to challenge Harold on his part time time & who the fuck does he think he is status. Knowing that to mess with Harold meant you mess with Ron.

Now also clarification had finally been straightened out through the con gossip stream. The reason for Harold serving his time became clear to the general population & this gave Harold some of his own cred in the jailhouse community.

Over the next few months Harold & Ron became jailhouse friends. Harold's relationship with Ron gave him strength to pass the time preserving his sanity.

By the time Harold met Ron his life on the outside had fallen into a doable routine. The kids were with the Mom on the weekend & no one suspected a thing. Harold was having a little bit of a hard time responding when-- as he dropped the kids off his ex would say in all sincerity,

' Have a good weekend , don't do anything I wouldn't do,' she'd say smiling from the door of her apartment, kids long gone inside. She'd be thinking jealously he must have a girlfriend. She really didn't get it.

Harold calling back as he walked down the stairs,

'No problem, see ya Sunday night,' hiding his tears.

Everyone else in Harold's life knew enough to just not ask any questions. Harold had always been a rather secretive creature. Never divulging what was really going on in his life. So the rest of the family, mother, brother, father & friends had grown accustomed to just putting it off to Harold being Harold & let the answers to their curiosity-- slide.

Work was a different story. Harold was partner in a tire store, 'Tacky Treads'. He specialized in making specific tire treads for tires used by racing vehicles. This meant he was required at times to do weekend work if something happened to his racing treads during the race. Often he'd be standing at the finish line praying everything would be fine knowing his delicate treads couldn't go around one more time. He'd wait in anticipation having faith in his newest specialization tire tread with steel tracks knowing if one of them blows his business is cacked. Harold worked in a highly competitive field.

His partner & best friend Paul was the only person Harold trusted to tell about his situation. This however meant that if a call came in from a frantic race team Paul had to pick up the slack. Paul was cool to this but did insist that he'd expect extra pay for his inconvenience. It wasn't Paul's idea of a good time to drop everything he was doing on a weekend to get some racer back up to speed.

This of course cut into Harold's share of the profit. Jail time was definitely affecting his bottom line.

On the other hand he was saving money by not having the kids every weekend. Though he was giving money to the ex to cover at least their food costs. Any extra money she had went to wild men, dancing & drinking. Harold would explain to the boys that money was tight but soon if everything went the way he planned everything would be alright & soon they'd be back rolling in the clover. The boys would usually just look up from their game, smile & say ok.

∧∧∧∧∧

Harold was about half way through his penal obligation when the shit hit the fan. Was he a fuck up or was he a man; a hero. He was challenged to the depths of his being to have to come up with the truth of who he was.

Ron & him were sitting in the yard on concrete stairs, everything in prison was ceded for discomfort. Another grey bleak chilly Albertan afternoon. They were talking about a variety of things.

'One thing I've learned,' Harold said. 'Is that when it gets down to it everyone's just trying to get along in their own way,' Harold proceeded to take a long contemplating drag on his store-bought cigarette.

Ron was politely listening as he always did when Harold was talking. Harold was like a breath of fresh air in this moldy place. Ron looked forward to Harold coming W/E's. Even if they didn't share a cell Ron would always make sure every Friday night he'd track Harold down & they'd go out for a smoke before lights out.

Ron tried to understand what his friend was often saying. Ron was stubborn. It would take a lot of swaying before what he believed wasn't the way it was.

Harold continued, 'take a look at those jalapenos over there'. Ron turned his head in the direction looking at a group of Philippines' clustered. Speaking in conspirational tones thinking what cons whispered really mattered.

'They're standing round like they're in a garden. Look at those Ethiopians, from the way they're looking & standing around its like they've formed an African tribe. It's a survival technique used in a jungle.' Harold took a drag thinking about what he just said.

'We all gravitate to where we feel safe. Everyone has their place in the human race.' Harold looked over to see if Ron was listening to his profound observations.

Ron's mind was onto other things.

'Fuck it, I don't think I'll ever get out of here,' Ron said sadly to himself.

Harold was now watching the cons in their groups spread further throughout the yard.

He was thinking about the different stages in the human condition. The ones who walked tall & straight, others who slouched nose to the ground making their way around the yard scared of the least little noise. Its sad he thought that some guys come to that.

Harold got up from his step to stretch. His legs were cramping up. He noticed they were playing a pick up came of basketball over in the corner of the yard.

'I'm gonna go over & play some ball,' he said to Ron.

Harold failed to notice a heightened tension in the yard brought on by mind numbing boredom & the advent of winter.

'Be careful,' Ron cautioned. 'You got some cred but that can come back on you,' Ron was sensitive to the scene he knew there was something going down.

Harold knew his meaning. But he was prepared to throw caution to the wind for his need to just get moving. Try to run away from his own boredom.

Harold made his way across the yard trying to walk in a tough guy theatrical strut he'd been practicing at home. As he was passing by the African contingent a big black arm reached across & blocked Harold's way. It was the prehistoric hairy gorilla Harold had shared a cell with his first week.

'Where you think you're going, homeboy,' said a black baritone voice blatantly being challengely obnoxious.

'Gonna play some basketball,' Harold replied, looking at the big black man with his arm stuck across Harold's chest. Harold staring him right in the eye like a coiled cobra ready to strike.

'What's it to you,' Harold went on,

'Homeboy got himself some jam,' said another black voice leaning against a wall in the back.

The rest of the yard was starting to take notice. Groups were breaking up & making their way over to what might prove to be some afternoon entertainment. The big black antagonist let his arm drop & smiled an incredibly huge bright white toothy grin right through Harold.

Harold was caught like a moth in a spotlight. All eyes were looking at him. Harold was prepared in his heart not to back down. Was ne a man or was he a mouse.

If it came to a fight, which appeared quite likely, he'd be ready. He knew at that moment he'd be alright.

Harold was not necessarily a fighting man. He was actual quite passive out in the real world. Now though he was prepared to throw a punch if the situation warranted it. He had had some army training which actually prepared him for just such as was happening here. He hoped.

The lines were drawn. The situation was tense. The boys on the fringes started yelling encouragement to the big black man,

'Kick pretty boys ass,' was heard, 'cut up his face,' was the scary one that caught Harold's attention. Fuck Harold thought, what would he tell the boys if this guy cut up his face & made him look like a monster from a Stephen King movie.

Harold now looked down & sure enough big black man had what looked like a knife. Harold recalled the proper term in his fear. Ron had taught him—shiv-- is the name of this prominent jailhouse weapon which was positioning to slice Harold up. For some silly reason that was all Harold could focus on. SHIV. Perhaps he was relaxing his mind in anticipation of what was to come.

Just as Harold & his worst fear were squaring off. Harold resolving to himself this is it. The big black man making a move. Harold reacting taking up a defensive position.

Walking out from the shadows-- like Marshall Dillon saving the day-- Ron emerged. The crowd letting him through no questions asked. The big black man stepped down. The spectators walked away disappointed, no blood today.

Harold knew this was no time to act smart & push anything further than it already had gone.

'Think I'll pass on the basketball,' he said to Ron.

'Good choice,' Ron replied.

Ron & Harold turned & walked back & stood by their perch. Harold offering Ron a cigarette.

'Hey man,' Harold said. 'I knew you got cred, but that was impressive.'

Ron finished lighting his smoke, took a long drag & flicked the match into the concrete yard not looking round. Finally he said, 'everybody knows I got nothing to lose. Tell it to the warden he ain't ever letting me out.'

Harold was confused. But just let it go. They stood leaning on the railing of the concrete steps which led into the gym. Watching their ciga-rette smoke drift up into the grey. Even the smoke couldn't make it over the grey walls which confined them all.

Ron sat down on the steps. He was a man of reasonable height to see him on a downtown street racing for a bus would not be out of place. Ron's chiseled cheek bones almost sticking out they were so prominent. The high cheekbones & square face of a man whose family came to Canada a long time ago.

Harold looked down on this man who had just parted his way through a sea like Moses. Quite sure it wasn't the light of the lord leading him. A sea of violence. Enormous swells of hate crashing round like spittle frothing from the mouths of beasts.

'You know, that was quite an exhibition of respect. What the hell did you do to merit that,' Harold asked.

Ron looked up at Harold, 'Some pretty bad things ,' Ron replied & snapped his smoke somehow only using his thumb, sending it sailing half way cross the yard. 'Talking about it just ain't my way.'

'Look man,' Harold said. 'We've all done things we regret. Things that make us think--jesus christ what was I thinking-- sometimes its better to just talk about em.' Harold was being genuinely concerned.

'You sound like the cops.' Ron answered. 'Come on man we got you, that's what the cops said when they arrested me. Just admit you weren't aiming at our buddy & the judge won't give you life. Talk it out you'll feel a relief.'

Ron pensively turned his big oversize Canadian neck toward Harold, 'Maybe you're right,' he said. 'It ain't that I'm ashamed. Sorry for sure but ashamed I don't know. Life is what it is.'

'Look I'm not here as a volunteer.' Harold said. 'You know my story. Its wrapped itself around the grapevine many times. Tell me yours I'm curious now. You didn't stare down half of black Africa because of your pretty face.'

They laughed. Ron exposing a cracked front tooth.

'Well, if you really want to know. I shot a cop. That's why everyone knows I got nothing to lose. The guards been hard on me since I came in. Throw me in the hole I don't give a damn.'

'That'll do it,' Harold said,' I'm sure you didn't just wake one morning & decide, I'm gonna shoot myself a cop today, what's the story.'

'Here give me a smoke & I'll tell you' Ron gestured up with his big sausage fingers as Harold pulled his pack of store bought smokes out of his pocket handing one out to Ron. Ron took it & lit it striking a match off the underside of his, grey con issued all-purpose jeans.

'I used to have a construction business. Building houses. Well business went bad & I took a couple of bad loans & before you knew it I was down the rabbit hole. Wife, kids, cars & I was fucked.

'So, I robbed a bank. One of the pretty big titted tellers tripped the alarm while she was smiling at me & stuffing cash in the paper bag I'd shoved in her face. By the time I fled the scene the cops were just showing up as I ran through the door onto the street. I fired a random shot at the cop car, thinking it might hold em up for a bit. Fuck if it didn't hit a cop-- just a fucking fluke-- as he jumped out of his car. The bullet crashed right through the window on his door right into his heart. He was dead before he hit the ground they told me later.

'Well, I was fucked. They gave me life & the cops family swore they'd be at every parole hearing to make sure I never get out.' Ron looked at Harold, 'that enough for you?'

To Harold's absolute relief the horn sounded in the yard to tell everyone to get back to their cells. Time to tidy up for inspection before the evening meal.

Ron stood up & laughed, 'still want to be my friend,' Ron said with just a cautious hint of a grin.

'Fuck you,' Harold laughed back, slamming his fist into Ron's rock hard wall of a chest.

∧∧∧∧∧

Harold's time was going by like a snail delivering mail. You waiting for an answer to that letter you sent, forever ago, that's never coming.

As time goes he'd faired quite well Harold thought as he was sitting down to eat what he hoped to be his last supper in the can. He'd heard from his lawyer & there was an excellent chance this would be his final W/E. But Harold had found out by now that you never trust for anything to happen until it does.

Ron was trying to show he had an interest in what was happening to Harold. Harold was insisting on turning the conversation around back to Ron. Telling Ron a guy's gotta be Samson strong to get along & how they'll stay in touch.

Ron had grown fond of Harold. It had made him look forward to the weekend. It made him think of high school. When every weekend was something to look forward to. At one time in his life he'd bin just fine, he thought. He'd been the cock of the block, the man back then. Girls loved him, all the guys were his friends, wanting to be with him whenever they could.

He'd just thrown it all away & he knew it. It brought him pain to remember how much he blew it. He'd started to slide at university. When money put him in blinkers. It was all he could see in front of him. Everything became about money. Dropping out to pursue his own business. That didn't take long to go wrong. Him pushing hard. Knowing better, stretching what he believed, just to hear that cash register ring.

What had it got him? Serving 25 to life a guest of the federal government. A death on his conscious to live with for the rest of his life. He was sincerely sorry-- he wasn't a gangster. Nothing mattered he was fuck'd. All he needed was to somehow just stay alive. But for what?

Ron listened to Harold's plans about staying in touch with a skeptical ear. He looked up from his thoughts putting his plastic utensils down. Finally fed up, he'd heard enough.

'You know man what you're saying don't mean shit,' Ron said & stood up from the mess hall table, leaving half his meal on the metal tray. It looked like he hadn't even finished his mashed potato salad & usually that was the only part of the meal worth eating.

'Just fuck yourself then,' Harold yelled after him as Ron made his way out of the mess hall. Small tears dropping from Ron's soft steely eyes dampening his rock-hard cheek. Back to his cell, his only reality.

Fuck it Ron thought. What the fuck am I doing, how have I become this pathetic excuse for a man. Ron left the hall without looking back.

Harold looked around, still sitting in front of his own unfinished meal. He took a forkful of mashed potato salad looking around to gain a sense if anyone else in the hall was interested in what was going on between Ron & him. No one seemed to be paying attention. Everyone keeping their head down minding their own business. It's the only way to be, when the only hope in front of you is your memory.

*****

As it turned out Harold never saw Ron again. That last Sunday lunch was Harold's last one inside. The next day Harold got a call at work. His caseworker was on the line,

'Harold how ya doing,' he said.

'I'm just fine,' Harold replied, a little taken back by the friendly tone.

'Good news, they went for the sentence suspension, your time doing W/E's are over. You don't have to go back to the Pen.'

Harold was half expecting the news but it was never real until it was actually said.

'That's great,' Harold said, a littler stunned. But in his heart he still felt he should've never had to serve any time anyway. He was still steeled to his resolve that no matter what they threw at him he'd be ok just to spite them.

'All you got now is to report to me for another six months & then hopefully it'll be over.' The caseworker sounded quite upbeat on the phone. No matter what the job it's always feels good to be the bearer of good news.

'I'll see you Wednesday at 4 pm,' the caseworker said.

'Sounds good,' said Harold, relieved, 'Hey thanks for all your help.'

'Just don't miss any appointments,' the caseworker hung up the phone.

Harold had done six months of W/E's.

Harold phoned the boy's mother right away & told her he was taking the boys to the mountains next weekend. She was fine with that the last six months of having the boys every weekend had cramped her party lifestyle. When she had originally agreed during the custody hearing to having the boys on a regular basis it was more to please her parents then her want for the boys.

She had been happy with Harold just dropping the boys off at the odd time. But her mother had insisted on a custody hearing, which had forced them to a gentleman's agreement, which had been going fine. Gramma wanted to make sure her grandchildren didn't grow up without a Grammas love. This last six months had been weird with Harold dropping the boys off so regularly, she had thought. Before he'd either been a little late or forgot, it was all cool. She just figured over the last six months Harold had found a women & was getting laid or whatever. She really didn't care all she knew it made her mother happy to see the boys.

She was curious but not displeased at Harold's call. She celebrated silently when she put down the phone. More then anything she was relieved. Time to party.

This regular weekend responsibility was more then enough to challenge her motherly instincts. Which at best were minimal. The boys were a handful & if truth be told she'd relied on her parents to carry the major part of the load. Dropping them off at her parents as much as possible so she could meet her social obligations of drinking & getting high. Telling the boys to keep their mouth shut. Trying too hard at playing the charade was wearing her out. Harold & her had worked it out a long time ago regarding the boys after the second one was born. She just couldn't do it & she ran away. Harold stepped up & became a father. He recognized realistically her priorities.

Harold left a message at the front desk of the jail to give to Ron letting him know his time was up. He never heard whether Ron ever got it. Harold went back after a couple of weeks out but they told him at the front gate Ron had been transferred to Prince Albert. Harold wrote but never got anything back.

Part Two

2004 (early spring two years before)

Harold knew something was terribly wrong.

Atticus wasn't home & it was almost midnight. He hadn't been home since breakfast the day before. Atticus was twelve & was starting to spread his wings a little too much. Harold knew he was hanging around some unsavory older boys. Atticus wasn't stupid but he needed to be liked & was always after some sorta self-gratification. This had led him into trouble & putting himself in unsafe situations.

Harold had already bin down once to the cop station to drag him home. Being very thankful to the police for not charging him with break & enter after a couple of the older boys had talked Atticus into squeezing through the dog door of a house because he was so small--even for his age--& letting them in the front door. They were just leaving with the liquor when the cops drove up—being alerted by the silent alarm-- & arrested them all.

Harold was trying hard to come to terms with Atticus. Telling him he had to be careful. He can't be believing everything that he's told. Use your head Harold said. In one ear out the other was the impression Atticus brought to the discussion. Harold just couldn't tell if he was getting through. Atticus would always nod his head in feigned understanding. Really Atticus just wanted to go down to his room & play ' War Soldiers '. He was almost at level 9 he only needed 8 more kills to get to the really good part of the game.

To make matters worse there was evidently a pervert on the loose in the neighborhood. Harold had overheard two mothers talking while he was waiting in line at the grocery store a month before. He had stopped in on his way home from work to buy frozen pizzas for dinner, always peperoni the boys needed their meat. As he was waiting in line to pay he listened in on the women's conversation who were two up in the line where he was patiently, standing waiting. Four frozen pepperoni pizzas in his arms. Standing bored his ears perked up for entertainment.

'I know at that new house they built two streets over the blinds are always closed & there are young kids always going in & out,' the soccer mom standing directly in front of Harold said like a piece of gossip.

'Well maybe it's just they have a big family,' sarcastically replied the overweight middle-aged women first in line with a shopping cart overflowing with goods. Vegetables, soup, eggs & packets of meat. Boxes of cereal, jugs of milk, ten two litre bottles of pepsi & enough potatoes chips & cheezies to sink a battleship.

'No,' soccer mom pertly replied. 'I don't think that's it. No one has ever seen a mother. Just a big husky middle aged man who's out & in all day,' Harold standing behind her checking out her tush. She was actually quite attractive. Soccer mom was looking on as the fat overweight middle-aged women wearing a bright flowered Muumuu standing in front of her-- with the cart full of food-- obviously wasn't going to let her through. Soccer mom's shapely attractive hands holding only soda water & spaghetti sauce.

'How do you know these things to be true'

Said the overweight mother curtly—flipping her short curly blonde hair-- as she started emptying her overloaded cart meticulously onto the check out counter. Harold couldn't believe that amount of pepsi, chips & cheezies even existed. Does she wash in pepsi he thought. Just as Harold was deeply immersed in imaging that fat ass coming out of that pepsi filled bath tub-- it suddenly waggled like a fish & flopped around. Now Harold was looking at this flappy slappy woman straight in the face. Over the pretty soccer mom's shoulder. He was trying not to look down soccer mom's blouse at the time. The fat overweight mother wasn't even aware of her rudeness in regards to grocery line till etiquette. She was totally all ears in this rumor moungst the neighborhood. Even though she had a houseful of kids & a loving husband she was very lonely. She caught Harold watching her through her squinty piggy eyes. She gave Harold a cute coquettish smile. She quickly turned, possibly embarrassed by her brazenness & got back to the task at hand. With her round like a ball features. Peering eyes hidden like faraway stars on the blackest of nights. She thought always that she was in charge.

' I was walking by that house last night,' Soccer Mom with long straight black hair said as she stood waiting still trying to be polite in spite. Her arms starting to ache with the weight of the soda. Fat Overweight with tree stumps for legs—peeking out from under the Muumuu tent she was wearing-- not even close to an apology for her behavior. Turning to the Soccer Mom as the cashier was busy ringing up her bill which was clinking in at a rapid pace.

'I always go for a walk after dinner it helps my digestion & keeps down my weight,' Soccer Mom went on. Harold commenting in his head it sure looks like it's working.

'I was passing by when I saw this man getting out of his van & a boy sitting in the front seat waiting. The boy couldn't have been older than 14. He waited in this van-- with a picture of a plumber on the side-- while the man went into the house & came out seconds later with something in his hand. Looked like he was carrying a wallet & then they drove off.'

'Well, that doesn't tell me anything,' Fat Overweight-- with her cart still half full-- aggressively replied. 'He could be a coach or something like that,' she said with a touch of scorn. Harold noticed her tits as she spoke flopping causing floral waves throughout the brightly flowered Muumuu. Oh my god he thought she's not wearing a bra.

'It just didn't feel right,' said the Soccer Mom who was becoming concerned about how she looked. She was sensing Harold's attention. She had no cause for concern. Standing there in nice tight slacks, waist length leather jacket over top a crisp white blouse Harold was having no problem with her appearance. She needn't have worried.

'Excuse me ladies,' said the overworked cute cashier interrupting the chat to get on with it. 'Are you gonna pay for your groceries or are you just gonna talk.' The cashier challenged in a serious teen age voice.

'Well excuse me,' Fat Overweight curtly replied getting back to emptying her almost empty cart with an exaggerated piggish expression. Starting to place the rest of the pepsi, chips & cheezies onto the checkout counter.

Working faster now with a hint of disdain for this lowly cashier interrupting her conversation.

This ended the gossip giving Harold grave reason to ponder. Though it also brought Harold some cause for concern of his own confidence. Maybe he should chatt up Soccer Mom. Maybe they could go for a walk together. You never know where something might lead. But alas as he rationalized, he was too tired to engage. Soccer Mom checked out so fast-- once Fat Overweight left-- that really, she was gone by the time Harold finally got to put the frozen pizzas down which were freezing his fingers..

A month later we find Harold reflecting on this bit of knowledge worrying about his son. Who wasn't home.

Harold sitting alone at his kitchen table. He lived in a nice neighborhood in south Calgary. Place full of pickup trucks & boats in the driveway of the split level, two story or ranchers recently built. He was worrying about where Atticus is at. Time well past from when he is due home. Atticus lived so much in his own mind that he often forgot to mention something important. When Harold would bring it to his attention it was in one ear & out the other in light year speed. Harold was thinking he must be over at a friends & he had just forgot to tell. Even that he should be home by now. He's still only twelve.

Atticus had been behaving well since the incident with the police until the last couple of days. He'd been staying relatively close to home. But Harold had noticed a few days ago he was starting to slide. When Harold asked him how he was doing. He was evasive & avoided eye contact. Harold knew in his fatherly gut Atticus was smoking weed & that could be trouble.

It was getting near midnight. Adrian was long since to bed. Harold decided to call the police. He couldn't get this picture out of his head of Atticus lost somewhere out there & no one looking for him. Every father's nightmare.

The police were no help,

'How long's he been missing?' the constable asked.

'He's been gone since he left for school yesterday morning,' Harold said.

'So he's not been home for a day & a half,' the constable replied almost distracted.

'Look I'm really worried,' Harold spoke sharply he didn't like the attitude.

'All right then I'll let the boys know to be on the lookout for a 12-year-old boy whose missed his dinner & his Dad wants us to do his work for him.'

'Fuck you,' Harold was furious at the policeman's nonchalance.

'Listen sir there's nothing we can do. Phone us back if he hasn't shown up by tomorrow morning,' the constable said & hung up the phone & went back to finishing up his crossword puzzle. He was looking for a six letter word that rhymed with cupid.

Harold realized that he wasn't going to get any help from the cops. He was going to have to take matters into his own hands.

He came up with a plan to try & track his boy down. Harold was totally aware the city can be a particularly evil place for a young boy with an innocent face.

Harold took to his computer. He had searched porn before. He knew there were some obscene images on the screen which were very illegal. He knew perverted men living lonely perverted lives longed for perverted pictures of young innocent things-- boys & girls-- to fantasize into their reality. Little boys whose bodies were in demand in a world which made Harold sick to think that it is really real. He steeled himself to his task & finally he had reached the nether world of the dark web. Searching for any clues to see if any of these sick people were living in his city. He finally found himself deep enough in this mind-numbing scene that ads were coming up for young boys who were available to touch for a price. These sick sites had pictures of boys positioned alluringly reaching out as if they needed you. Trying to get you to contact them-- money should be no object for the thrill they will deliver. Harold couldn't help but feel relief as Atticus picture didn't appear. However some of the ads appeared to be local, Harold could tell as they portrayed the young boys wearing cowboy hats & chaps.

Harold sat back, the time was two thirty, he remembered the conversation he overheard at the grocery store about the fat man with a van who seemed to be inappropriately entertaining young boys at his house. At least that was the concerned illusion the caring mothers were implying.

Fuck it he thought. Harold phoned his women friend, who wanted more from their relationship but Harold wasn't ready yet to make a commitment. He knew it was late but he needed help if he was going to cruise the neighborhood looking for Atticus. He couldn't just sit back & do nothing. His lady friend who would do anything for Harold, agreed to look after Adrian while Harold hunted for Atticus.

Adrian didn't even really wake up as Harold put him in his van & dropped him off at the-- wanna be Harold's woman's-- place. Good luck she longingly cried out to Harold from her front door holding onto a sleepy Adrian's hand.

To say Harold was determined would be an understatement. To say he was a father on a mission to save his boy-- with the focus of a superman-- would be more in line with his intent.

It didn't take long for Harold to spot the van. A picture of a cartoon plumber-- hands grasping a plunger -- painted on the side. It was in the area where the ladies in the grocery store line up had inferred. Just a couple of blocks over from the grocery store sitting in a driveway outside of a nice split level suburban home. Streetlights highlighting a black night gave Harold his view. Harold could tell the home was newer. It was built in the more modern style. Big wide driveway, fancy iron decorative rail leading to the front door. Even though it was the middle of the night Harold could see the yard was well groomed without a fence which was the style for this upbeat suburban neighborhood. To any discerning eye the house presented as just like any other. A house harboring a man & a wife & a couple of kids. With the plumbing truck waiting patiently in the driveway for the man of the house to get up in the morning & go to work. Living the suburban dream or was it accommodating a suburban nightmare.

Harold's fatherly intuition sensed something was wrong. So he parked the van just far enough down the street—settled snugly to the curb-- &

settled back to watch. Van idling just in case. It took all his patience &
control to not just burst in & scream what the hell's going on. But he knew
to do that would mean he would be the one who could be led away by
the police.

One thing he certainly noticed. The lights were on in the house.
Someone was up. Porchlight like a moon making bright the front porch.
Casting shadows.

After Harold's third cigarette something started to happen. Two young
boys a few years older than Atticus walked by his van & up the steps to
the house going in without knocking. Harold watched them walk by like
a trained observer. Noting their gate—more a shuffle. the style of their
clothes, floppy everything. Their foot wear, running shoes & Kodak's. Hats
on backward of course. They were both carrying cartons of beer & wearing
big jackets with lots of pockets. A couple of punks. Acting much too old
for their age.

Harold knew the right thing to do was phone his concerns in to the
police. Which he did. The police balked, Harold sensed, not taking him
seriously. Snickering into the phone saying they'll get right on it. They
took the address before sitting back & finishing their coffee. The dispatcher
radioing out to patrol that if they are in the vicinity to check it out. It certainly doesn't sound urgent he insinuated. The conversation in the station
going back to talking about the Flames chances in the upcoming season.

So, Harold bit his tongue & waited. But not for long.

That would be an important point that was made during the investigation.

Harold had waited long enough. Those boys were older than Atticus
but not by much. They certainly weren't old enough to be drinking. He
could justify any action he was prepared to take saying he was concerned a
criminal act was taking place inside the split-level house. Citizens right to
show concern & anyway he had a right. He was looking for his boy.

Harold pulled the van up across the driveway leading to the onerous
split level house. Blocking any getaway attempt by whatever's inside.
Leaving the van idling Harold opened his door & got slowly out. The
streetlight drew a dreary halo around the vacant street. Luminating the way

as Harold approached slowly walking up the black asphalt. The porchlight spreading a dull yellow eerie glow over the scene as Harold approached the house. The plumbing van was parked halfway up the driveway. Harold found himself looking into the black cartoon eyes of the plumber with the plunger decorating the side. Harold took some time to take a look through the front windows. It was all totally black the window on the side was shaded over he took note. He was a bit relieved. In a corner of his head he half expected to see Atticus gagged & tied on the back floor. But no, he pressed his face tight right against the glass & the van was totally empty. Which was a bit unusual Harold thought. If he's a plumbing service where's his tools. Harold's suspicion & spidey sense started kicking into high gear.

Harold was calm. He wanted to present as being in control. His mind was flashing on sets of scenarios screaming a million miles a second bouncing round in his head.

Harold headed for the porch stairs taking him up to the door. Four concrete steps. It was late enough-- early enough you make the choice-- that the feint tweet of an early bird waking up stretching its wings started to sing. Harold heard it & tensed like a cat.

Harold got closer to the stairs. Decorative wrought iron railing across the top of the porch. Straight black wrought iron hand rails down each side of the steps. Harold slowly stepping up one step then another, balancing himself with his hand on the railing. Feeling an early morning dew on his fingers. Harold started hearing feint sounds of music the closer he got to the house. He leaped up the last step now standing on the porch stoop, silent. Harold moved closer to the standard suburban door & pressed his ear against the door just below the peep hole-- which was standard security install in this particular suburban development. The music & merriment became obvious, mixed with the odd yelp & laughter that sounded like a party going on.

I've gotta get in their Harold thought. He knew he was on the right track. As he listened longer he was sure he heard Atticus. That high pitched squeal Atticus did when he was shooting down the enemy in one of his games.

Harold knocked hesitantly, lightly, on the door. His heart raging in his throat. His anticipation of what was about to happen—had-- to be in his boy's favor. He didn't want to risk the chance of anything happening to his boy in a moment of desperation. So Harold decided to approach with caution & keep his head in a rational based frame of mind.

To Harold's surprise the door opened slightly at his touch. Those punks must've left it open. Butterflies for minds he thought. The door slid awk-wardly—opening farther-- Harold's pushing with his fingers.

This was another important thing to remember when it came up during the investigation. The door was open.

Harold cautiously stepped inside the house the white wooden door now almost completely open. At the last split second a hinge squeaked a fatal squeak. Making just enough noise for it to be heard. Harold closed the door quietly behind, avoiding ever so carefully the squeak again. The smell of marijuana filtering like a funnel up a tunnel from whatever was going on down the stairs inside below. The upstairs silhouetted black through a single dull almost green solitary light on the ceiling. Harold hesitated on the landing-- silently listening.

&&&&&

The ears of the fat man in cowboy hat & chaps in the basement perked like a wolf in the woods. He had heard the squeak.

Harold stood listening to the tunes & sounds of teenagers loud now. Nonsensical chatter about things which didn't matter. The sounds of tings & tongs & guns blasting & cries of joy from the boys playing the games & screams of winning. Head bashing metal music playing loud snarling up from the basement.

Harold found himself on the landing of a split-level house alone. Stairs going up, stairs going down. Piles of shoes all around. He was sure one of the pairs was Atticus's. Black hand rails leading up to what was obviously a sparsely furnished living room, black rails heading down to what was obviously the family room in the basement.

Harold was now in the house, door closed silently. He knew illegal entry into another person's house was highly against the law. He knew enough about the law to know what he was doing was insane. But nothing was going to stop him from finding his boy. Nothing else mattered except to find out if his boy was down below.

The upstairs presented as empty, no sound from above. The wall of light coming up from the basement lit up where Harold was standing. Harold had to put his hand over his eyes as he gazed through what presented through a dirty mist into the basement down the stairs. Harold's eyes started to focus while the rest of his body tensed in anticipation. Of what he did not know. But he was getting a pretty good idea of what he's walking into. He was catching his breath to try & calm a thudding heart. Deciding how he was going to make his descent. He focused on his breathing as his mind steeled to what was in store.

When to his alarm;

Coming charging up the stairs like an out-of-control locomotive in full throttle-- holding above its head what looked like a baseball bat— an apparition appeared.

It was obvious to Harold it was after him.

As it grew closer Harold realized it was a man much bigger than he would've thought. A man with a large sized girth & a cowboy hat. All Harold could immediately think was wow what a fat cowboy.

Harold thought he was fuck'd. He was in this guys house & this guy had caught him like a deer in the headlights.

In this western town killing a man for break & enter was well within a person's right. Especially if that man was standing on your landing looking for his boy itching for a FIGHT.

To Harold it was a no brainer. The law could go to hell is what he thought. What had it done for him. He was here all alone where were the cops.

It was now or never. This big fat cowboy with his frilly unbuttoned shirt & a jelly for a belly, flopping down over tight white chaps was charging up the stairs in his cowboy boots. Big cowboy hat on his head, as he got closer Harold noticed the name PETER written across the front.

He was an enraged hippo remarkably fleet for its bulk, approaching-- within baseball bat swinging range-- our Harold at a remarkable pace.

Harold steeled himself to action. With no hesitation Harold slipped under the swing of the bat as it came down just missing Harold's head, glancing off his shoulder. Harold immediately reacted unleashing an anvil punch smashing the fat fuck square in the face. Blood sprayed from its nose like water from a fire hydrant. Stopping the pudgy apparition dead in its tracks. Propelling it back down the stairs head over heels. As Harold watched in horror, he heard the fat man's neck snap.

All music & smell took a backseat as the massive pervert had tumbled & flopped like a ragged whale doll to the bottom of the stairs. The sound of the crack was so loud it made everything else serene. Fat bloated eyes ending up staring dead into space. Head all crooked like it was put on backwards.

A blank stare focused on an unknown spot that only the dead can see. Body splattered on its back with its neck obviously of no use. Head lolling about like a fat flag flapping in the breeze. Cowboy hat knocked recklessly aside PETER splattered in red.

Harold didn't waste any time. He scrambled down the stairs stepping over the lifeless blob. At one step near the bottom, he pushed the still quivering mass aside with his boot. Reigning in the urge to give it a violent boot to the bloody head just to give it one last degradation to satisfy Harold's furious need for anger & revenge.

Harold kicked away the bat still clutched in the dead man's lifeless fingers. He kicked it away out of reflex, knowing full well that it had swung its last swing. It rolled off into an open closet full of electronic equipment. This reaction was to prove an unfortunate point. When all this behavior was being investigated the bat in the closet was a concern. The crown alleged it had been there, in the closet, all the time. The crown implying that Harold was lying. It made it difficult for Harold to prove the fat man had evil intent, with the crown saying the fat man had no weapon at the time of the attack.

Harold was now at the bottom of the stairs. Releasing himself from the wooden hand- rail he'd been clutching. The rail had provided a solid wooden foundation feel so he wouldn't stumble or fall & bang his own head into the wall. His legs were going a little mellow. His knees were definitely wonky.

He took a solid stand & looked around to see if there were any more fat pricks he could lay a beating on. Harold noticed right off all appeared so loud it was quiet. The smell of marijuana filling the room like a fine perfume. The music blaring, TV screen on the far south wall reflecting the faceless glare of 6 or 7 teenagers sitting around a typical-- second generation from the farm-- suburban rec room. Linoleum floor, wainscoted wooden paneled walls. Bright lights overhead. Great big couch bordered by big cushy chairs all with kids in some sort of teenage sprawl. Glass fireplace on the west wall flicking flames just enough to flare the room. Giving an eerie dimension.

Harold couldn't remember if he'd ever seen a TV screen that huge before. It was surrounded like a semi circle by the kids sitting slouching as only teenagers can. Each looking remarkably comfortably at home. The flames from the fireplace reflecting deep in the images on the screen. The game the young boys were all playing & watching was spectacular with gore. Harold couldn't help but notice it was like he had entered an enemy's underground lair. Some of the kids had handles in their hand's others waiting for a chance to show what they can do.

Picture posters on all the walls. Portraits of pretty girls. Some dressed up in dark white skimpy bikinis. Beautiful faces framed in curls, straight black hair, some long & blonde. Others with breasts & bums sticking out alluringly. Visible underneath polka dot lingerie.

A few posters with men posing. Men with rock hard chests, crammed hips into skimpy briefs, sweat glistening on sculpted torsos.

On the north end of the room stood a bar. A mirror ball in the ceiling sparkling the space. Twinkling highlighting the cowboy wall paper. Images of cowboys in full flight filled the wall. On a background of a wide-open bright blue sky, steers & bucking horses, wild men in chaps & cowboy hats raising the roof at another rodeo. The wall almost in motion, coming to life with each sparkle shooting out from the glistening Disco Ball.. Behind the bar was lined with shelves of liquor. Thick wide wood oak counter top. Harold was quick to notice the speakers built into the bar. He was a bit of a stereo buff. They sounded nice in the wood he thought.

Finally, sitting on top of the bar-- like a raptor predator-- Harold saw all the camera & video equipment. All pointed in the direction towards a small open dance floor. A space in front of the bar posed for the cameras. The floor was covered with a few mattress's & pillows & cushions strewn about in strategic positions. For the enhancement of the camera angle no doubt. Sexual toys scattered about like a mess.

Harold hoped he hadn't been too late.

All the boys by now had looked round. Distracted from their game by the loud thud of the perverted cowboy's head meeting the basement floor. They were all looking at Harold now. Eyes in various stages of astonishment. Harold recalled the music playing at the time was mind bashing metal hip hop. He remembered thinking he wasn't a big fan of that particular musical genre.

There was Atticus-- part of the crowd on the couch. His innocent face flushed with confusion. The last thing he expected to see was his Dad in this place.

Atticus sprang to his feet. His game box falling askew from his lap onto the white shag carpet. His face flushed with relief. Atticus roared over to his Dad & threw himself into Harold's outstretched arms. Atticus fleeing that feeling of fear of anxiety prone desperation. Flying fast out of danger. A place where just a flash second ago his life was out of control.

Harold turned & put Atticus on his back & caried his boy piggy back up the stairs. Taking precaution to shield Atticus' eyes. Harold wanted to save Atticus seeing the dead bloated blob of a perverted mess sprawled at the bottom of the stairs.

———

Atticus had been playing games. Listening to music with his new friends. He was smoking pot. Having the odd shot of booze. That old guy had been offering him anything he wanted anything to keep the party going.

Eventually though something just didn't feel right.

It had all started innocently enough Atticus piling into the van at the behest of his new friends. All laughing & joking, smoking a joint. Atticus feeling part of the cool crowd as they said come on, we're all going back to Peter's house. The fat old man in a cowboy hat driving, looked around big friendly smile on his face. Atticus reacted naturally as a twelve-year-old boy who was up for anything would do. Back at the house the party started. Atticus felt the stray hand crossing his bum during the errant play fighting. Which seemed to always end up with the old guy clutching his cowboy crotch. The old guy always in charge. Telling the other boys to be nice to the new boy because he's kinda shy. Atticus smiling his innocent grin. His face looking like a Michelangelo cherub full of innocence & youth.

The first night Atticus ended up passing out on the couch. Right in the middle of playing 'War Lords'. The others were there carrying on, some slumped over the couch's edge. Sprawled unconscious from to much inebriants. Atticus was too young to know about passing out. Too young to know this made him innocently vulnerable.

The next day when he woke up he asked the old guy, who called himself Peter, if he could use the phone to call his Dad. Tell him he's ok & sorry he didn't tell him where he was.

Peter said don't worry about it. He had called his father for him. Atticus had given him the number last night.

'You probably don't remember you were so into your game.' Peter said. 'I called your Dad last night & explained that you were over here with me. You were fine just playing some videos. I said it was late & would you mind if Atticus stayed the night. Your Dad gave his ok so you don't have to worry about a thing,' Peter explained.

It never dawned on Atticus Peter was lying. Peter was an adult, adults don't have any reason for lieing Atticus thought. Atticus didn't question what Peter said he'd done. Atticus was too young to notice the malice in Peter's voice & the malicious intent in Peter's pudgy demeanor.

That next day Peter said Atticus didn't have to go to school. Which was ok to Atticus, he hated school. Peter said they could just stay at his house & play. He even made everyone a nice breakfast of scrambled eggs, bacon & toast, ice cream & cake. Enough for everyone.

Atticus was at first glad. But after awhile he wanted to go home. He went upstairs to tell Peter. Peter turned on him like a monster from one of Atticus's videos. Telling Atticus in the firmest of monster voices to go back downstairs & play.

'I'll tell you when you can go home,' Peter said. Peters' eyes turning green & his head exploding in anticipation. Atticus noticed this transformation in Peter & turned his head in fear. Scrambling back downstairs to play more video games with his friends.

Atticus was scared for awhile but soon his fears were redirected into playing games listening to music, smoking pot with his new friends. Who were now talking of letting Atticus into their gang but he had to be cool. Keep your mouth shut, don't tell anyone about Peter & this place. Not even my Dad & brother Atticus asked. Especially not them the gang replied. Atticus didn't like the idea of keeping secrets from his family.

As the day wore on the fun started to fade. Atticus started to get bored & lonely for his family. There was chips & dip, all the pop a kid could drink & watching movies he'd never seen before. Movies with girls doing weird things with men who were older then his Dad. Atticus started to feel uneasy as the day wore on. When day became night & Peter ordered pizza for dinner Atticus was starting to feel there was something not quite right about what was happening.

Something was wrong. Atticus felt a twinge in his heart a feeling that usually came just before something bad was going to happen. Like just before the monster showed itself in the movie & all the teenage boys & girls were hiding in the closet waiting for some impending disaster. Atticus' heart was trying to tell his brain, what he was doing was nowhere near smart.

But what could he do? He couldn't leave. Peter made sure of that. Telling the older boys to keep an eye on him make sure he doesn't sneak away. Atticus was being groomed with weed & booze. As the night wore on Peter was picking his spot. He knew with Atticus' angelic face & smooth pearl skin & what Peter anticipated to be a hairless-- peach fuzz at best-- crotch, Atticus had the very real potential to make Peter a lot of money in videos & older men seeking perverted sexual release. Peter himself was attracted to Atticus & was waiting in eager anticipation for just the right moment to get him on one of his mattress'.

Of course, Harold killing Peter put a stop to all of that.

When Atticus heard the commotion & turned his head away from his game seeing his father brought on a tidal wave of relief. It was crazy. Where did his Dad come from, Atticus couldn't believe his eyes.

Eeeeeeeeeeeeeeee

Atticus didn't know was that with his Dad to the rescue he was saved from a life of confusion. From having to live a tormented life of flashbacks & irrational behavior. Of feelings which just weren't natural. Missing living a normal life. A future filled with horrible guilt. Memories of horrible crimes perpetrated on your innocence. Atticus was saved from the dread of depravity Peter had in store for him. Peter's propensity was to perpetrate, probing, Atticus's sensitive teen age brain-- objective—destroy.

Peter was born with a silver spoon. Rich & well fed. He'd always been Fat Peter the Perverted Cowboy. Living a deviant life, making his own rules. A truly evil despicable person. A blight of puss, polluting the plight of humanity.

Harold saved Atticus from all of Peter's criminal intent. Like a good Dad should. He knew what would be in store if he didn't save Atticus in time. Saving Atticus from being assaulted in sins of the flesh. Avoiding his son the outright pain ascending-- like a hot poker-- into the young boy's head. This perverted behavior alters the course of a young boys mind & affects the rest of his life . Harold knew that because it had happened to him. He didn't really like to think about it & hadn't ever mentioned it to anyone. Harold knew that if Atticus was sexually assaulted it would shorten his life. Atticus was an innocent soul. One they would have called in previous years as a gifted child or possibly autistic. That's why Harold always tried to keep a special eye on Atticus. He knew he was too innocent to grow up. The world was still an adventure for Atticus. Every move-ment every smile cause for celebration in Atticus' world. Harold knew that others with evil intent were watching too. He couldn't prove anything of course. Harold always lived with a touch of suspicion. But he'd always had a feeling that Atticus could be just a bit too friendly & naïve. Harold-- who was a man of the world-- liked to see things for what they really are. He knew that there was a good possibility that one day he'd have to come after Atticus.

Atticus had always been difficult to discipline. Making like he didn't hear when you tried to scold him. Thinking he's smart, growing up way past his age. The thing is Atticus has a smile that melts butter when he smiles. I dare anyone to say no to that smile. Atticus has the smile of a puppy dog licking your face. If anything bad happened to Atticus, Harold would regret it for the rest of his life. It would destroy a true innocent spirit.

This thought had flashed through Harold's mind as he watched the fat fuck roll up like a balloon ball & tumble like humpty dumpty rolling down the stairs. A creature not even human how could you do these things to young innocent boys. Watching its body explode into what Harold hoped was its first vision of hell.

*****

When Atticus saw Harold he was so happy he started to cry. Somewhere deep inside of him-- it made no rhyme or reason-- he just knew Dad arrived just in time.

He threw his arms around Harold's neck. Harold reached down & picked Atticus up like the little boy he was. Holding him like the loving son he is, pinning him to his chest. Harold took a split-second look around peering over Atticus' head. He saw scared eyes & confusion. He saw a bunch of teenagers who thought they were caught doing something wrong. Harold knew that's what teenage boys were like. Thinking they're always in some kind of trouble. They had no care that what the pervert at the bottom of the stairs demanded-- in return for free weed & booze, all the games you could play & all the movies you could watch, all the while listening to your favorite music-- was that you had to suck his cock.

Harold decided in a moment he couldn't save them all right now. He had at least killed the perpetrator he thought. His sole intention had to be focused on Atticus. He turned abruptly throwing Atticus on his back & leaped back up the stairs two at a time. Stepping around the sprawled body of a pervert draped dead over the stairs.

He had to hope Atticus had not seen the death stare of the perverted fat & bloated cowboy corpse. It was really gross Harold thought as he took a last look. He could only hope-- looking down at the bulging black eyes full of blood-- this Peter—won't be confronting his namesake in the immediate future. If there was justice, his fat demented spirit, should be spending eternity puking in hell.

With Atticus fixed firmly on his back Harold reached the landing. Harold caught his breath reached down & turned the front doorknob of the door he had just a flash of time ago silently shut. Flinging the door open he found himself standing staring into a Wally's World of headlights.

Oooooooooooooooo

Harold had left the van running by the curb. In his haste to save his boy he had forgot to turn out the lights. Helen Daimler from two doors down noticed the idling van with it's lights on as she looked out her front curtains sipping her morning coffee. She was wondering what in the world was that rumbling noise on the street. She stepped out her front door to investigate & must've heard the commotion going on in Peter's house. That was enough for her, investigation over it's time to phone the police. Helen rushed indoor picking up the phone on the wall in her kitchen, making sure she placed her coffee on the kitchen table careful not to spill a drop & called 911.

The constable on the end of the line perked up his ears when Helen rang off the address where she suspected trouble. The number & the street rang a bell. He checked his records & indeed their it was. A call had come in an hour prior with a concern about the exact same address. He got on the radio & put out the call to see if anyone had followed up on his prior request to see if any of his cars had passed by this address.

All the police in the donut shop heard the radio blasting & immediately put down their coffee & crammed the last jelly donut in their mouth & guiltily sprang into action. They were all getting around to following the dispatcher's request from before but had gotten distracted by their early morning needs. Police have to go to the bathroom & eat just like everyone else. So they knew they had been a bit negligent in following up the dispatchers request to check out what was going on at the address of the house he had given over the air before.

Now they were all motivated & full. Inspired they all jumped in their police cars & drove as a train to 744 Tally Ho Lane.

Needless to say Helen Daimler was impressed with the response to her request for assistance.

Harold couldn't help but notice the cops had finally arrived when he opened the front door stepping out onto the porch. He looked out on an impressive display of light highlighting the dwindling night. Harold thought they had been responding to his call for assistance. When in reality it was Helen Daimler who had inspired this overwhelming reaction.

Harold couldn't help but think that if he'd waited for the cops to arrive-- like a good little citizen-- their would've bin a good chance his

boy, wouldn't have survived what that pervert Peter had in store for him--
or worse. All who got involved over the next few years agreed it was good
thing for Atticus, Harold arrived when he did.

Now the cops-- just arrived -- did not know what to expect. So they
expected that perhaps this may be a marital dispute. Marital abuse was
always the worst. So they parked their six cars in an aggressive position.
All headlights, circling the van, highlighting the house. Rooftops flashing yellow, white & red sparkling the grey. All waiting at their wheels
in anticipation.

Then in the click of an eye the front door to the house flew open.
The cops sprang from their cars reaching for their guns. Standing steady
weapons ready.

Harold thought he was hit by a wall of white decorated like a Christmas
tree. All bright in yellow, white, green & red. He thought what the fuck.
Behind their flashing cop car roofs the cops were all taking cover flinging open their cop car doors using them for cover all crouching for self-
preservation. Waiting, peering just enough through their car door window.
Making sure if given an inch this guy-- who they don't know from Adam--
might be taking a shot at you. Waiting with excessive anticipation to just
what was going to come out of this nice split level suburban home. Trying
to keep down the jelly burp bubbling in your tummy.

!!!!!

The distant eastern sky seemed to be waking up. It appeared it didn't
want to miss the scene as the sun anxiously scrambled up, trying to catch
the action.

Harold paused on the front door step. Shading his eyes from the head-
light glare almost forgetting Atticus on his back. Piggy back like a mother
carrying its child in a back pack.

The cops paused behind their cars & looked at each other with their
eyes asking each other what do we do now. Harold tried to stop. To catch

his breath & evaluate the situation but he couldn't he was in too much in shock.

Harold started to walk towards the nearest twinkling light. He was in serious distress & gasping for breath. The cop behind the door of the closest flashing car stood up raising himself slowly. The unsaid decision as to who would do what was decided. That cop started shouting questions at Harold. But Harold couldn't respond, he was beyond conversation. Harold mumbled some unintelligible sound & walked right past the cop & sat on the curb. Atticus still holding tight like a wall of snow.

The cops took this as an indicator that something was askew. There was something going on inside the house which required police intervention. It hit them all at once. The order was shared to start moving in. All cops stepped cautiously outside of the cop car doors protection. Nervous nellies they all were but none would say such to one another. Most of them had realized by now that being nervous was just part of the job.

They stormed the house, leaving Harold who-- by this time-- was trying to wrestle Atticus to the ground, his back was aching something terrible. He wasn't having much success as Atticus was clinging to him like a baby bird to its nest when mama bird is trying to teach it how to fly.

The cops moved like a human wave of motion. All extremely on the alert for, what they may come across, inside.

As the cops started to proceed through the door in a practiced precision manner their forward progress, became impeded. Eventually coming to an immediate halt. The teenagers from down below had started to straggle out. With each one wondering by looking like a zombie. The cops grabbed each teenage spaced-out form as they came & flew them face first to the ground. Checking them for weapons. Once the cops were satisfied they were just dealing with a bunch of spaced-out kids they figured something had to be done for these zombie creatures. These kids look likely to just wonder off into the ascending daybreak. Never to be seen again, some of the confused cops mentioned, concerned. Lost in the Canola fields forever one of them commented. It was decided to detain them. One of the members asked if anyone had any blankets in their trunk. A couple of guys indeed had blankets left over from the Calgary Police Company picnic last July. So they hauled out the blankets & gave one to each kid then shoved them into a locked back seat of their cop cars. Each child to the last of them immediately curled up into a fetus ball.

Meanwhile Harold was settling on the curb. Atticus at his side clinging to Dad's arm like a koala. Harold couldn't stop shaking but no one offered them a blanket.

The cops had to refocus & resume their onslaught into the interior of this split level house-- that's presenting as a pretty crazy situation. Crashing through the front door the first ones immediately see the blob lieing dead at the bottom of the stairs. 'Any one in here,' the bravest of them yelled. Guns drawn ready to shoot the head off a parakeet if it chirped. Only the music filtered up from down below. The teen agers must've turned off their game before going upstairs. It's just a wonder how a teen age boys mind thinks. Carnage all around yet what's important is to turn off the game because you might wear down the batteries. The cops heard the feint thud of hip hop in the basement all else was silent. By this time a few of the cops had crowded through the door. All standing on the landing, looking down the stairs-- taking their look at something they'll never forget. More out of curiosity then apprehension. Now that any danger seemed to be nonexistent, one of them told his colleagues in the back they better call this one in.

The cops proceeded to search the house. But not for long. It was pretty evident they better leave this one to homicide. Yet after a cursory survey, making sure there were no more dead people. They couldn't help but notice the matts & camera equipment in the basement. A couple of them were actually camera buffs. They knew all the best equipment & both agreed whoever lived here had some pretty fine stuff. They'll have to ask homicide if they can sit in on the evidence film showing. They'll bring the popcorn & coffee.

No one touched the body. Boy was he fat could be heard whispered amongst them. All were relieved they wouldn't be the ones who would have to carry that. No one had found any guns. Except a shotgun & two pistols in what looked like this fat man's cowboy boudoir. His bed was right out of a Liberace home movie. Mirrors on all walls & ceiling. Western sculptures of cowboys on horses, rocky mountain views in pictures. The guns were locked up in a nice glass hand carved pinewood case. Heavy lock on the glass. It was actually quite nice some of the gun enthusiasts remarked. They all gathered back on the inside in the middle of the split level some standing on the stairs some on the landing. All the cops had had their share of discretely looking around.

Meanwhile Harold was outside standing up stretching his legs. Atticus clinging to his arm like a baby gorilla. Harold's mind was slowly coming back but it still wasn't clear. He had to piece together his memory like a drunk trying to recall what he did last night.

Then all the cops burst out of the house the same way they went in. Exploding out of the front door as one. Harold knew something was up. They all had on their serious faces & their controlled cop walk & their guns were back out of their holsters & pointed at him.

Inside standing on the landing the decision had been made. Someone killed this guy.

'Did you see that fat deadman's face,' said one, looking down the stairs.

'It didn't get that way from the fall,' emphasized another.

All the cops, especially the experienced ones who'd seen it all agreed. That fat guys face looks like it was hit by a two by four.

The team all tensed hesitating opening the door before going back outside. Had that guy walking by done this. They all agreed this was a potentially dangerous situation. The decision was made they'd take Harold down, though at that time they didn't know his name was Harold.

Harold stood still not really knowing what to do. The cops all looked so intent, all eyes focused on him. He decided it was best to just stand still & let them do what they will. The dawn was taking its time to emerge. The sun though anxious to see what's going down still had to follow protocol & rise sunrise slow. A last grey cloud of night was also blurring its vision.

The musky mist of dawn presented a challenge to the cops. Objects could appear which just weren't there.

The cops en masse drew closer to Harold's statuesque pose, each one squinting to help make their vision clearer. All guns at the ready.

'He's got a shot gun,' one cried out mistaking Atticus as a weapon of destruction. This one cop was prone to panic & always saw the worst in every situation.

They all hit the ground as one. Now this was a very uncomfortable thing to do as the early morning dawn had just deposited its dew & all officers went flat on the grass for coverage. This resulted in them all getting quite wet. Their nice clean white shirts & creased cop pants soaking up grass sweat like a sponge. Then one noticed as he was spitting out damp grass from his mouth,

'That's not a gun it's a kid.'

When they all got back up it looked like they had all gone swimming.

They all looked on in disbelief. Indeed Harold was not carrying a weapon but had what looked like a big lizard clinging to his arm.

They all must've missed seeing the kid when they all ran past Harold in their impatience to rush the split level. In what felt like an eternity ago. But was really only a few minutes ago. Everything was happening quite quickly.

'Drop the child,' the chorus of cops cried out in unison. Guns remaining raised poised at Harold.

Well for this command to take effect Harold knew it would take a lot more than just asking Atticus to let go. Harold said softly to Atticus,

'Please son just let go.' Atticus's head hidden deep in Harold's shoulder.

But Atticus was having none of that.

Harold certainly wasn't prepared to push the issue.

It was a standoff.

Atticus wasn't budging.

After a few tense seconds one of the cops—who was a little younger-- showing a lot of sense told everyone to put their guns away & stand down. Which they all did at once milling about resembling a guerilla force in their grass covered uniforms. All checking their guns back in the holster.

One cop, an older man who had experience in dealing with critical situations took charge. He walked in an appropriate authoritarian manner directly into Harold's space. Atticus looked up & turned his head away on a swivel—like a Linda Blair-- he wanted nothing to do with anyone but his Dad.

'Hell of a mess in there,' the old cop said. Looking for any reaction at all from this guy who's dressed like me when I go out to get milk, & here he is holding this terrified child.

Sun broke through the grey. Slicing a piece of light on the eastern horizon. Finally it was peeking in on the action in a universal kinda way.

It was shining directly behind the cop right into Harold's eyes. That cop wasn't so dumb. Harold couldn't see a thing. Blinded by the light.

If Harold could, he'd see a reasonable cop asking for a rational explanation.

But he couldn't. All he saw was a figure exuding some sort of authority coming his way. Like a monster emerging from a shadow.

To tell you the truth a monster was in line with how Harold was thinking. The way this night is, he thought, it's got to be happening in another dimension. It can't be real. Did I really just kill that man. If I did that means this apparition coming my way could be anything. Harold was scared.

'Excuse me sir are you alright,' the cop asked showing confused concern. Reaching out a hand in a compassionate gesture.

Harold saw something coming out of the corner of his eye towards his shoulder. He totally overreacted.

Harold was seeing it all in slow motion. Like an animal cornered protecting its young. He reacted like a lion readying himself to attack. Atticus clinging to his neck like a flag hanging down his back.

The old cop who'd seen it a few times before caught Harold's reaction immediately. It's incredible, in an instant, a man can become a beast in a coin toss. The first time he had seen that stance was down a dark alley downtown years ago, it had cost him two teeth & a concussion.

'Whoa man,' the old cop backed off-- as if his fingers had hovered over an orange oven element-- sortta softly quickly pulling back his hand & taking a step in retreat.

'Just stay here,' he said to Harold as he walked cautiously away, eyes never leaving Harold's vision.

The old cop eventually turned back to the cop crowd who were all eagerly alertly waiting. All congregated around the one cop car. The one without any kids. The kids by now were all asleep under their blankets in their respective back seat bedrooms.

When all saw everything seemed sane, they let out a collective breath & started to relax a bit. Now time to try & put what they'd just seen inside the house into perspective in their heads. To break the instant silence, one started talking about the last episode of 'Cheers,' that Norm was hilarious he said & they all laughed liked they had other things on their mind. It was a good distraction from the horrible image mulling in their minds.

'I need one of you guys to watch this guy. I gotta phone homicide,' the old cop yelled. They all looked at each other like gamblers around a card table knowing someone has to make a move. No one wanted to go over & watch this guy. But when all looks were finished it ended up Ray the Rookie taking the job.

Harold relaxed. Something inside of him was saying you won this one. The animal instinct settling into an emotional mess. He & Atticus sat back down on the curb & waited. Atticus strangling his neck like a baby bear.

The dawn was promising to be irrelevant. A dark cloud had entered the fray & the sun was growing more irritated by the minute. It had arisen with such promise of being an observer to the action happening down below & the irritable clouds had proceeded to congregate blocking its view. As Harold sat waiting for the next wave of intrusion into his actions the sun fought like a trouper slashing its way through an African jungle trying to get a better view at the action.

Atticus had loosened his clutch on Harold's neck just a tad. Enough to say to his Dad, in a sad voice,

'Daddy I'm sorry.'

204

'Its ok son,' Harold said taking Atticus' arms gently from around his neck & helping Atticus to sit down on the curb beside him.

There they sat in silence. Each knowing what the other was thinking.

YYYYY

. . . The cops were getting their orders. The cars with the kids in them were told to leave.

'Get those kids back to the station & get a hold of their parents.' The cops Captain ordered,' We're gonna need an adult around,' the Captain explained, 'when we start asking them about what happened inside that house.' The Captain took a second, 'it'd be a good idea if we got those kids something to eat. As a matter of fact we could all use some breakfast.'

So before they dispersed back to the station they all agreed that they'd stop at the MacDonalds & get take out to for all to eat back at the station. Macdonald's all around, they radioed back to the Captain.

At the last moment one of them, Clem, spoke up. 'Well we all don't have to go to MacDonalds why don't you all just give me your orders & I'll pick up something for everyone.' Clem was the cop whose belly stretched his police shirt so the buttons strained to stay done & the top of his pants concealed a mystery buckle underneath a wave of flab. This way Clem figured he could get himself double. Get all the cops & kids their order to eat at the cop station & something for him to eat along the way. All this action & intrigue had made him ferociously hungry. Sounds alright to me the rest of the cops replied relieved & all chipped in their share. Enough for a large quantity of egg McMuffins, hash browns & coffee all around. They all hopped in their cop cars & took off. Clem the only one going the other way to MacDonalds. Leaving Ray the Rookie & the old cop who was in charge to wait for homicide to arrive on the scene.

It wasn't long, maybe only a couple of minutes. Time to Harold at this stage was very vague. A plain dark big Plymouth car was seen by Harold heading towards them on the street. Trying to be discrete going slowly as if checking house numbers. Coming through the dawn like an ominous presence. No bells or whistles or flashing lights, but everything about it said cop. Harold just knew it was the homicide detectives arriving upon the scene. The dawn waking becoming brighter the sun rising higher the Plymouth moving with purpose closer & closer. Driving deliberately, the streaking early morning rays, highlighting its approach.

Harold watched them pull up & stop alongside the old cop who was waiting for them in the middle of the silent suburban street. The only sound Harold's still running van, which everyone in the commotion had apparently forgot to turn off. It was idling anxiously like a purring pissed off kitten. The undercover Plymouth pulled over to the curb on the other side of the road from Harold. Harold watched them get out of their car, motion practiced, each step precision. Nothing rushed. Both detectives took a tersary glance Harold's way. Atticus crunched up beside Harold like a sponge, asleep. Each detective stretching standing taking command in their heads of the situation. Though one did need to reach back & turn off Plymouth. They waved a greeting at Ray the Rookie who was watching their every move trying to learn how a homicide detective approaches a crime. After the briefest of pauses taking stock-- breathing deep that fresh dawn air—the detectives turned to talk with the old cop.

Harold saw the old cop pointing him out. They all looked over at Harold with concentrated stares. This made Harold take notice & he started to stand up. But first he had to wake up Atticus who was now sprawling like a blanket asleep across his lap.

'Come on son, wake up,' Harold gave Atticus a gentle shake.

Atticus like a child stepping out of a dream replied,

'Dad can we just go home now,'

'Not yet,' Harold said quietly talking softly as if to one whose dying.

The detectives & cops weren't in any rush. That was obvious. By this time Ray the Rookie was having trouble prioritizing his allegiance. He knew his job was to watch Harold. But he really wanted to hear what was being said. So he nonchalantly, but with purpose, tried to position himself so that he could hear the detectives talking. While at the same time trying to stay close enough to the prisoner so that if this guy did take off-- he Ray the rookie would still be close enough to catch him.

Ray the Rookie really didn't have to worry. Harold had no intention of going anywhere. But Ray the Rookie didn't know that. He couldn't read minds-- that's what they taught him in training.

'You got a dead man at the bottom of the stairs in there,' Ray over heard the old cop say. 'He looks like he took quite a beating.'

'Has anyone talked to this guy over here,' asked the tall homicide detective who was wearing a fedora hat. He looked like he had just walked off a movie set. Every inch of clothing every movement of his face were meticulously tailored to a prewritten script.

The other guy-- a short fat guy wearing a big cowboy hat, one of those guys who always looks disheveled-- was taking notes. He was the definition of pudgy. Rolls of fudgy fat slitting his eyes & overflowing his belt. Blue jeans tight just under a canopy of gut. Covering up what could faintly be seen of a fancy rodeo buckle. Pity the poor horse that guy sits on thought Ray the Rookie.

'Now just so I've got this straight there was a bunch of kids who ran out of the house when you opened the door?' The Fat Cowboy detective asked for clarification cause the old cops story wasn't very clear. The old cop had mentioned the kids in passing. Did the kids kill the dude inside the split level house, Fat Cowboy detective thought why not.

The Detectives questions are throwing the old cop into duress. Two questions at once after what he's just seen. People forget the cops aren't overly impressed with dead bodies anymore then you or I. The old cop had seen a few. He knew sometimes when it kicked in it threw his mind out of whack. The old cop took a breath & got his thoughts back.

'No the guy over there wasn't in great shape,' the old cop said, addressing the first concern. Turning to face the detective wearing the fedora. 'He just walked out of the house & sat down over there.'

'Was he injured?' Fedora Hat detective asked.

'No not like that. He was walking fine, talking gibberish. It just didn't seem to be the right time to ask him questions.' The old cop was getting his composure back.

'There were five teenagers who were placed in cars & are on their way to the station.' The old cop replied to the Fat Cowboy detective's inquiry in a professional filing a report manner.

'Anymore kids in the house?' Fedora Hat asked.

'No, we did a very thorough search,' the old cop said but quickly retracted. Knowing these guys just flip out if they think one of the lowly patrolmen might have touched something at a murder scene. Once a few years ago, a man & a woman were lying dead on their bed--murder-sui-cide—the old cop first on the scene. He watched in silence, as a homicide detective lost it on a rookie patrolman for stubbing out a candle on the bedside table.

'Didn't touch or turn a thing-- masta,' the old cop submissively replied with a big smile. The two detectives laughed. A good laugh never hurt at a murder scene.

Harold was watching & waiting on the curb. He couldn't hear what they were saying like Ray, but he was getting the gist of what was happen-ing or so he thought. Though the laughter threw him off a bit.

Fedora Hat & the Fat Cowboy detective moved off a little down the street & talked to each other. It didn't take long for them to get back to the old cop. By this time Ray the Rookie had almost forgot about Harold. He was intense on learning what the homicide detectives were going to do next. This was Ray the Rookie's first homicide & he was taking it in like watching a movie in his mother's basement all alone.

The old cop was wishing this was just all over so he could go back to the station & lay down. But he knew he was stuck here unless he could get one of the guys back at the station to relieve him. He'd have to wait & see what the hot shots wanted done. They always needed lowly patrol-man to do something absolutely trivial he thought, like interviewing a dog or standing guard while they went into someone's house & took a shit.

This unfortunately put the thought of having to piss in his groin. Fuck he thought.

Fedora Hat looking over at Harold said to his partner Fat Cowboy detective, 'I'm going to go talk to the human statue standing over there,' pointing at Harold.

The Fat Cowboy detective followed up, 'I'm going in to eyeball the dead guy.' Each had their preferences as to what they liked to do. Fedora Hat was the sociable one he liked talking to people. Fat Cowboy detective just liked looking at dead bodies.

'I'll shut that van off on my way,' Fat Cowboy Detective offered.

'Be careful,' Fedora Hat mentioned to him cautiously. 'It's evidence.'

Fedora Hat turning back looking directly at the old cop giving him his orders,

'We want Ray the Rookie in the house with my partner. We want you sir,' he said smiling to the old cop,' to phone the station & call in some relief. You look beat.' The old cop silently expressed his appreciation.

The old cop became animated, 'Right on it sir,' he replied with a mock salute..

The old cop motioned Ray the Rookie over to give him his assignment. Ray came rushing over like a puppy being called by his master.

The Fat Cowboy detective took off for the house. Ray the Rookie right behind him like a horny hound. Fat Cowboy detective stopping at the irritated van & slowly reached his arm through the open driver's window & turned the key on the steering wheel to off. You could almost hear a sigh of relief from the van engine. Ray the Rookie watching taking mental notes. I shoulda thought of that Ray thought. Making a mental note.

Fedora Hat made his way towards Harold. By this time the sun had finally broken through the cloud. It was watching like a warrior who's triumphantly made it to the top of the hill. Now looking clearly down onto what was to happen next. Unfortunately for Harold said sun's blaze was directly into his eyes again. He had to squint like a prune to watch the detective approach.

Atticus by this time standing. Hiding behind Harold, clutching Harold's stylish leather jacket. Atticus hands red with blood from clutching Harold's sleaves. Which still displayed the scarlet remains of some of the pervert's brain.

Fedora Hat approached Harold compassionately. Fedora had been around; he'd seen it all. This was looking to be one of those murder in suburbia scenarios. If it was even murder, he thought. Don't jump to conclusions. That's the first rule in being a good detective.

'Good evening, sir, my name is Detective Fancy,' Fedora Hat said.

Harold stood silent. Atticus right at that moment started tugging on his jacket. 'What is it son?' Harold asked looking down into a scrunched-up face.

'I gotta to go pee,' Atticus squeaked.

' Ok, can you just hold on for a minute,' Harold said to Fedora Hat, ' the boy needs to pee.'

Harold didn't wait for an answer but hustled Atticus onto a nice close-cropped lawn with some big lilac bushes. Not yet in bloom, it wasn't warm enough yet for spring flowers. Ground still damp from winters snow. Harold directed Atticus to go behind the bush & do his thing, he'll wait here on the edge of the lawn. Harold failed to realize the lights of this chosen house were on. The man of the house was looking out his front bay window curious as to what was happening on his front lawn. Only to be met by the sight of this young boy pulling out his wang & doing his business on his shapely lilac bush.

'Hey what's going on out there,' he shouted pounding on his bay window. The banging on the window scared Atticus & when he turned to look the pee went all down his pants & he started to cry. Harold stepped up & gave the man in the window a wave that everything was fine don't get your nuts in a knot. The man screamed, ' who the fuck are you,' through the window. Harold couldn't hear him of course & could only read his lips. He certainly understood the mouthed version of fuck. This ticked Harold off so he turned to the window & flipped the guy the bird.

Fedora Hat had been watching all of this clearly. He was a bit put off because he was used to being in charge of the situation. This one hadn't even started yet & it felt like it was getting out of control.

Fedora Hat walked up on the grass & flashed his badge at the irate homeowner. Spying him through the bay window on the front of the two story-- garage attached-- suburban home. The homeowner sneered back at the badge & silently mouthed-- realizing yelling at the bay window was falling on deaf ears. So he framed his words very succinctly at the detective. Like he was talking to someone deaf.

'Fuck you too,' the homeowner clearly silently said. His mouth churning like a horse eating an apple. He pulled tight his robe & strode back to his spotless kitchen to make the mornings coffee.

Fedora Hat couldn't have cared less. Coming up to Harold (though he didn't know Harold's name yet) just as Atticus was zipping up his pants.

'Come on man,' gestured Fedora Hat & Harold followed him back to the street. Atticus holding his hand, still all sticky from pee, Harold who is a bit of a clean freak cringed a bit at the touch. He should'a got the boy to wipe his hands with the lilac leaves. Something to teach him next time we go camping he thought as he followed the homicide detective back to the street.

Its odd what the mind thinks about in period of crisis.

They made their way over to the unmarked Plymouth. Fedora Hat in front Harold shuffling behind. Atticus practicing sliding on the slick dew covering the street. Fedora Hat reached into the car & pulled out a pad & pencil. Turning to Harold he got down to work,

'Name? '

'Harold,'

'Well Harold nice to meet you. I'm Detective Fancy from homicide.' Fedora Hat purposely repeating his name. Trying to make Harold feel at ease.

They both stuck out their equally brute beefy hands (Harold's a touch sticky). Each eagerly grabbed. Man to Man. Harold looking cautiously beyond Fedora Hat's gaze. Fedora Hat trying to pin Harold with his eyes.

'Who is this little guy,' Fedora Hat said, bending down to address Atticus as he wiped his hand discretely on his fancy creased slacks. Atticus had by this time purposely slid across the dew right into Harold's back. Now holding Harold in a half hug. Hidden as much as curiosity would dare.

'This is Atticus,' Harold said softly, sternly, showing the homicide detective very clearly don't mess with him.

'Well Atticus I am Detective Fancy. Nice to meet you,' Fedora Hat almost losing his fedora hat as he bent down further to shake Atticus' hand. Which never really happened. Atticus wasn't touching anyone other than his Dad.

'So I gotta ask. What went on in there,' Fedora Hat asked rising, pointing at the split level house right in front of them, 'Do you know anything about it?'

At that precise milli second all clouds dissipated the sun exploded. Looking like lights on a film set. All of a sudden everything just changed color. Sun now sat in the glory seat. Knowing this story was approaching a climatic conclusion.

Harold leaned back against the police car & asked the cop if he had a cigarette. Which Fedora Hat of course had. He always carried a pack with him it helped relax the suspect. Fedora Hat wasn't beyond having the odd cigarette himself. Especially when he was out with one of his lady friends burning up the dance floor to the revised rendition of the Glenn Miller band.

He pulled the pack of smokes out of his top pocket & offered one to Harold. Following it up with a light from his flip top lighter. He didn't take one for himself, not the time he thought.

Harold took a drag holding it in his hand, the one that wasn't sticky with Atticus' urine. For the first time that night Harold felt a cold chill, even though his leather jacket was lined. Atticus' grip now firm on Harold's tingling fingers.

Come on urged the sun I don't have all day.

'A guy came at me with a baseball bat & I knocked him down the stairs. I went in got my boy...' Harold said interrupted, for at that moment

Cowboy Hat detective came back into the scene. With a big gangly Ray the Rookie following him like a lover.

'Harold, this is Detective Drab; Drab meet Harold,' Fedora Hat introduced Harold to Fat Cowboy detective, ignoring Ray the Rookie. This wasn't a social gathering.

Fat Cowboy detective wasn't really interested in Harold. He was reviewing his pictures on his phone & his notes.

'So, here's what we got,' The Fat Cowboy detective started up speaking, ignoring Harold.

'One dead body at the bottom of the stairs. I'm no coroner but I'd say broken neck.'

Fat Cowboy detective showed Fedora Hat the picture on his phone.

'Is that the guy you hit,' Fedora Hat asking Harold, showing Harold the picture.

'Might be,' Harold replied. Harold could sense something was going sideways. He didn't really know what he expected. Somewhere deep inside of him he just figured he'd done nothing wrong & they'd just let him & Atticus go home. Back to their life.

'Did you see any bat,' Fedora Hat asked the Fat Cowboy detective.

'No didn't see any bat, 'the Fat Cowboy detective checked his notes, ' No no bat.'

Fat Cowboy detective turned to Ray the Rookie almost knocking off his cowboy hat Ray was standing so close to him.

' Did you see any bat,? Fat Cowboy detective asked.

Ray almost feinted. They were including him in the investigation.

' No sir,' Ray replied trying to infer he does this every day.

Fedora Hat looked at Harold & said,

'I gotta arrest you.'

Ray the Rookie, was standing alert eager for action, steadied himself for a reaction.

The sun was done watching. It's always nice to start the day with an action drama.

———

Fedora Hat approached Harold handcuffs out.

'Hold on,' said Harold. ' I didn't do nothing but save my boy,' Harold stood proud like a handsome man with wide shoulders.

'Not according to the law,' the Fat Cowboy detective replied in a snarky manner.

After that it became a mass of confusion which changed Harold's life for the next two years.

The Detectives passed on the handcuffs & moved to put Harold into the backseat of the unmarked Plymouth. Harold insisted Atticus must come with him. Atticus was clutching Harold's hand hard, Harold could almost feel his fingers cracking. Just another thing for Harold to deal with, a couple of cracked fingers.

'Atticus please ease off you're breaking my hand,' he winced.

'Dad what's happening,' Atticus cried tears swelling up in his eyes he knew something was going wrong. He couldn't deal with anything anymore. Atticus wasn't stupid. He knew he had fucked up royally. If only he had listened when his Dad had told him to not get into any man's van. No matter what. But he fucked up. His need to be included overrode any concerns his Dad might have had. He was a lonely young boy. Desperate for attention. His mother had left him his Dad always at work, his younger brother always interested in sports he had nothing ever to do. He got into that van as an act of rebellion against his lonely life. He had no idea what strife was in store as a result of his actions. He thought life was a blank page, he just wanted something to write.

Harold bent down & lifted Atticus into the back seat, he wasn't going to wait for permission. Fedora Hat holding the door open, putting his cuffs aside for the time being. The Fat Cowboy detective going round to his passengers' side door. All he could think of was how he was going to write up his report.

Harold settled down in the vinyl caged back seat & Fedora Hat closed the door on him. The first time of many to come Harold would be put in a cage. Fedora Hat got in the drivers side. Taking off his hat & placing it in a pre ordained place between him & Fat Cowboy, whose hat was already in its special spot hanging on a nail just underneath the shotgun rack.

'I gotta make arrangements for my boy,' Harold said.

'We can do that back at the station,' the Fat Cowboy detective replied. This wasn't a taxi ride he thought.

The Plymouth drove off into the morning sun. Leaving Ray the Rookie standing alone in the middle of the street.

^^^^^

The ride to the station didn't take long. There was time enough for Harold to make a plan of what had to be done. He wasn't stupid he knew he was in for something he hadn't planned. He thought, if I knew they were going to say I murdered that pervert would I have hesitated. His answer of course no, it really wouldn't have made a difference.

At the station Harold arranged for his women friend—who wanted desperately to be more a part of Harold's life-- to come down to the station & pick up Atticus. He spent the time waiting with Atticus in the front room of the police station sitting on those hard wooden benches meant to be uncomfortable on purpose. The detectives were giving him space to do what he had to do. It was plain to everyone they were going to lock Harold up. At least overnight.

Atticus by this time was learning to shut up. He knew events were transpiring which he just completely did not understand. His Dad was telling him he had to be strong. Be strong for what Atticus thought as he watched Dad's friend—dressed as though she just stepped out of a glamour mag-- come in through the police station door. Harold didn't even notice how odd it was for her to be dressed so nice at six o'clock in the morning.

'Adrian's asleep on the back seat in the car,' she whispered sensuously in Harold's ear, touching him tenderly on his shoulder. Dragging her lips down his cheek. Stopping, giving Harold a peck on the edge of his mouth, which was more of a kiss. They really weren't a thing but she was wanting more.

She went over to Atticus & said a few soft comforting words into Atticus's anxious ear. Atticus reluctantly got off the bench, gave Dad a hug & took Harold's wanna be girlfriends hand & walked out the police station door.

Harold watched her march off with Atticus holding her hand. Her hips swaying her hair tossed back. Nice looking legs Harold thought. Maybe I should hit it.

'I appreciate what you're doing,' Harold sincerely yelled, with a hint of flirt. Atticus turned & smiled happy safe thanks to you Dad. Harold's wanna be girlfriend seductively wriggled her rump.

Harold spent that day & night in jail. He was so exhausted any bed will do he rationalized.

The following morning was arranged for Harold's interrogation.

During that twenty-four hours the cops had been busy. Everyone was high on CSI figuring this one out. Some of it just wasn't making sense. CSI went over the house with a rake. They found a billion finger prints & gross sticky samples on the mattress' in the basement. Cupboards full of Vodka & Rum in the kitchen, Tequila & schnaps behind the bar in the basement. One-ounce bags of weed placed like sprinkles throughout the house.

They confiscated all the camera equipment & a massive amount of video tape & pictures. Most were found in the closet off to the side of the stairs in the basement; cords & electrical equipment, stands & boxes of film. It was here rolled behind some boxes they found a bat.

While Harold was sleeping--dreaming of big hairy men shoving pipes up his ass—the cops & detectives watched the videos & reviewed the pictures. Eating popcorn & drinking coffee supplied by the curious camera fanatic patrolmen. The detectives as a team-- Fedora Hat the manager & Fat Cowboy detective the coach-- presented their case to the crown early the next morning. Just enough time for the crown to review & come up with some of his own questions. It was scheduled they'd meet with Harold at 11.

Harold was woken for breakfast & then once done he just went back to sleep. The guard would make sure he made his interrogation. The one thing everyone forgets is by the time you're arrested & thrown in jail you're fucking exhausted from the circumstances which got you there. It takes a lot of energy to kill a man. Harold wasn't thrown in the drunk tank he was given his own cell, three meals & a bed. He had slept like the dead.

By the time Harold got called again at 11 he was fresh like he was on a vacation. The crown & detectives were waiting in the designated interrogation room. The mood was overwhelmingly sympathetic. Fedora Hat thought they should give Harold a medal, The Fat Cowboy detective thought they should give Harold the keys to the city. However, there did linger some valid concerns which the crown insisted must be impressed upon.

Harold was directed into the interrogation room. Fedora Hat, standing leaning casually on the wall in the corner, offered Harold a cigarette which Harold graciously accepted. Fat Cowboy detective, sitting at the typical interrogation room table, his poor chair leaning back, his cowboy clad boots resting on the table, hat tilted back. He leaned in looking up directly into Harold's face. Scrunching his flab in the exertion. Offering Harold a light from his—horse engrained on the side—flip top silver lighter to fire up Harold's ceremonial smoke. Harold bent down & took the light. Standing back straight enjoying the drag. Fat Cowboy detective showing a marked respect, a radical departure in his attitude from the day before.

The crown was sitting at the head of the table, papers & pictures spread out within reach. He was an old overweight hard drinking cowboy lawyer a couple of years away from retiring. He was looking forward to making a living breeding horses. His family pioneered this land. He was as comfortable in his ways as a cat having a nap on your lap. His bulk --encased in a well-tailored suit-- flopping over the edge of the chair like a swell, big thick fingers filled with rings. He had a couple of questions he had to ask.

He wasn't prepared to just let this one slide. He had been in control for so long he never considered other.

He directed Harold to please sit. Which Harold anxiously did facing right across the table from the Cowboy Crown. He was asked if he wanted a lawyer by the Cowboy Crown & Harold replied he didn't see the need for one.

Cowboy Crown jumped right in. He knew Harold wasn't stupid he'd read the report. Best leave the meet & greet by the wayside.

"Why did you not just phone the police if you were worried,'

'I did & they never showed,'

'Couldn't you have waited?'

Harold was taking this the wrong way & it was getting him mad. His arms were stretched out on the table his fingers were clenched. He just stared at this Cowboy Crown & said nothing.

'How did you get into the house?' Cowboy Crown carried on. Not missing a beat.

'The door was open & I just walked in,' Harold replied.

Fedora & Fat were picking their teeth with private toothpicks. They'd both had bacon for breakfast & their morning constitutional had gone well. Fat looked up from his seat at the table lighting up a smoke. Toothpicks put back in pockets, Fedora, still standing, pulling a packet of smokes from his inside jacket pocket, now deciding he wanted a smoke too.

'Yesterday you said, & I quote, 'he came at me with a bat,' how do we know that,' the Cowboy Crown asked Harold.

Fat was puffing up smoke now. Fedora stood just fuming. They all knew CSI had discovered a bat. It was found away in the closet easily within reach of the scene. They couldn't prove it had been in the dead perverts' hands at the time of the assault unfortunately. They only had Harold's word to confirm that. The prints on the bat—CSI—processed proved irrelevant they couldn't be proved recent.

'He came at me with a bat. He was fuck'd up,' Harold replied his fingers starting to tighten.

218

Harold had to take a breath He needed to know if they had seen the movies. He had one question for them. A question he dreaded. But he had to ask, before this went any farther. Cowboy Crown would just have to wait.

' Did you guys watch the movies,' Harold directed his eyes back to the detectives.

They all knew what Harold meant & which way this was going.

Fedora Hat said yea we watched all the videos & viewed all the pictures.

'If I had my way we'd give you a parade.' Fedora Hat concluded.

Harold appreciated the sentiment but that wasn't what he was looking for.

'Was my boy in any of them,' Harold knew the answer to this question could affect the rest of his life.

'Fortunately, your boy wasn't in any videos or pictures we gathered at the scene,' Cowboy Crown replied, a serious tone in his voice trying to get the focus back on him. He went on to say, 'this unfortunately doesn't help your position that your boy was in danger.' Harold looked at him curiously.

'So, you're telling me because I killed this guy before he got to abuse my boy it was a bad thing,' Harold said straight at Cowboy Crown. He was furious yet elated at the same time. He had really saved his boy from years of trauma. Inside Harold was jubilant.

'Look we all acknowledge this guy was a scumbag of the highest merit. We'll give you that.' Cowboy Crown clarified, 'But someone was killed here & the law is clear. Someone has to be held accountable.' Cowboy Crown concluded. It didn't matter fuck what they thought he was the one who had to decide whether Harold was a danger to the community. He packed up his papers got out of his chair like a pregnant whale & left the room.

'Fuck you,' Harold yelled at his back.

Harold was let loose early that afternoon. A judge had followed Cowboy Crown's recommendation of release on own recognizance with terms. Check in once a week with a court appointed probation officer & get a lawyer.

Over the next two years the crown did everything it could to try &
avoid the fact that though Harold's actions could be interpreted as justifi-
able (cause for celebration said most working the case). The reality was
that Harold had killed the fat pervert in the fat pervert's own house. The
law demanded persecution. The actual fact of the matter was not really the
murder. It was a matter of was this fat pervert guy just protecting his own
property was the point in law that needed to be addressed. Had Harold
the right to do what he did. Harold's vigilante behavior must be dissuaded.
Cowboy Crown had a duty to deter such behavior or it would run rampant
in this western town. The law said Harold was an intruder & had to be
held accountable.

The matter of the bat had to be addressed. Harold had said this guy was
coming at him with a bat. They had found a bat in a closet on the basement
floor. Any good lawyer could use this evidence on Harold's behalf claiming
self-defense. It could raise a reasonable doubt if the charge was murder.

Harold for all he was worth had no idea how it got there. Harold, in all
the excitement, couldn't remember kicking the bat out of the dead man's
hand when he was looking for his son. He was in a fury, in a hurry just to
get Atticus & get the hell out of there.

Harold got himself a lawyer from legal aid. The lawyer was out of his
league. But all he had to do was sit & listen. No one wanted to throw the
book at Harold. Cowboy Crown finally settled on a charge of aggravated
assault causing death.

———

Harold just wanted to get this over with. Finally he was in front of a judge.
A stern looking fella with dark eyebrows which almost made him look a
little neanderthal. The immense sloping forehead didn't detract from his
neanderthal appearance. The stubby overly hairy arms sticking out from
the robe looked more suited to eating mammoth ribs around the fire then
striking a gavel.

Cowboy Crown presented his case. The judge was a stickler for the law. The law was the only thing between civility & chaos. He also admonished that the law-- to be effective-- must be reflective of community realities. Can't hang a man for stealing a loaf of bread anymore.

Then it was Harold's turn.

The judge heard with an open mind Harold's story. How he had rest-lessly waited for as long as he could in his van. How he walked through an unlocked door, into another man's house & struck a man in the face who was coming up the stairs at him with a bat. With obvious intent to cause Harold harm. The judge heard Harold was after his boy who he was sure was being held against his will in this guy's house. He heard how hard it was for Harold to wait after he had phoned the cops. How he had grown too impatient to just do nothing. Then there was the issue of the bat. There was nothing to prove the dead man had it in his hand when Harold punched him in the face sending him flying down the stairs breaking his neck.

'What do you think happened with the bat,' the judge asked Harold.

Harold took a moment to answer,

'I don't know, everything was happening pretty fast.' Harold sincerely couldn't remember.

The judge listened to what Harold said. Harold's lawyer a thin academic who just practiced law to please his mother-- what he had really wanted to do with his life was be a writer-- spoke elegantly on Harold's behalf.

In the end the judge accepted Harold's position regarding the cir-cumstances surrounding the death of the perverted cowboy as being in Harold's favor. However, their remained the issue that it was all about the trespassing for which there was much legal precedent to convict.

Harold killed a man in that man's own house after going in as an intruder.

'The law is unequivable. You must pay a price.' The judge said firmly (almost trying to convince himself) looking down at his notes.

The court then decided to take a break to try & figure out a penalty. Everyone was in sorta agreement about the bat. They all agreed Harold wasn't lieing. It remained a mystery how it got in the closet.

'I think he just unconsciously kicked it aside in the heat of the moment,' Fat Cowboy detective said.

They were all standing outside the judges chamber having a smoke. Judges, detectives & lawyers. Fedora having a slim cigar, Judge on his pipe. Cowboy Crown having one of his unfiltered cigarettes. Fat leaning on the courthouse wall flipping his fancy lighter. The two court secretaries standing appealingly off to the side-- looking like they were in an old movie, smoke delicately dripping from their extended fingers-- talking about that one of them has to leave by 5 at the latest because she's got the kids tonight. Harold's lawyer trying to look worldly but he instinctively felt all he needed to do was just keep his mouth shut. This was going their way.

'I think we can all agree on that,' said the judge through a puffy cloud of smoke.

The judge went on to say ' he has to do some time, he did kill a man while trespassing, what's fair?'

Fedora spoke up, frowning, he hated this side of the job. 'They should give him the Governor Generals Award' he said to no one in particular.

They all laughed. Except the girls. They didn't get it.

Cowboy Crown picked up on that theme.' Yea a real hero,' he said. 'Everyone standing here knows exactly what we'd be looking at if Harold hadn't gone in there & killed that son of a bitch.' Cowboy Crown turning his head apologized to those of the fairer sex for his language.

All concerned nodded like big puppets on a thin string everything has to be done gently.

Cowboy Crown, The Judge & Harold's lawyer stayed behind as the detectives & secretaries stubbed out their smokes in the iron ashtray set out for just that purpose. Making their way back to the courtroom. The secretaries flapping their arms like chickens trying to get warm. Everyone else had three-piece suits, vests & robes. The secretaries only had on short sleeve shirts with stylish tight skirt attire.

Harold was waiting patiently inside. Sitting behind the desk for the defense. He wanted a smoke but his lawyer had made it quite clear for him to wait at the table. Harold was trying to go over in his head if he had everything appropriately in place if they sent him directly to jail. He had to make sure the boys would be looked after. Money was going to be an issue. His friend who wanted to be his girlfriend had said she would discretely take them immediately without Harold really having to tell the boy's mother what's going on. The least the mother knew the better. But the wannabe girlfriend would need money, only fair. Harold knew if he let her look after the boys, he was going to owe her big. There goes his freedom he thought.

Harold also knew that if he was sent away for a period of time the boy's mother couldn't be trusted to provide the kind of care the boys needed. She could maybe handle weekends but anything more would be stretching it. Also Harold knew the boy's Grandmother was just waiting in the wings to pounce.

The courtroom was pretty well empty Harold thought looking back over his shoulder. A couple of guys in the back who looked more like they just slipped in for a snack. It's amazing how focused you are Harold sensed. You don't even feel the gallery at your back & all of them watching you. You're the star of their show. At least you would be if anyone was here, Harold chuckled to himself.

The sheriff in the court was looking at his phone. He didn't smoke but Harold didn't know that. Harold thought the Sherriff stayed back to keep an eye on him. Even the secretaries left, Harold noticed. Harold was sure one of them was flirting with him-- she's got a like on for The Harold-- he joked to himself, a little gallows humor he smirked. He was going over the financial figures in his head when the outside door opened. The court feebly started filtering back in. The secretaries always first, then Fedora & Fat followed dragging behind the tight skirt samba, like hounds. People are always funny if you just see them as human Harold thought. They just want what everybody else is looking for; peace of mind. Harold's lawyer, cowboy crown. the Judge—ominously arrived—taking their respective places in this legal facade.

'Everybody please rise,' the sheriff said looking over at Harold giving him a thumb's up. He knew by the walk of the judge they were going to try & make this as fair as they could. He was relieved. In his world they made statues for what Harold did.

All was quiet. Harold's life flashed before his eyes in an instant. He saw the boys in their cribs. He felt the texture of their diapers on his dry hands, he smelt their scent when he pulled them out of their bath. He saw them at Christmas their wonder over the mystery of Santa coming to their house. He saw their faces clear as a bell in front of his.

The judge put on his reading spectacles & took a pause for effect & clarity. Harold was given a nudge by his lawyer & they both stood up.

'I'm sorry son,' The Judge said. 'You killed a man in his own house. The law is unequivable you must pay. I find you guilty of aggravated assault causing death.'

The judge took off his specs looking Harold eye to eye. Harold holding his gaze man to man.

'I'm sentencing you to one year in jail, to be reviewed in six months.'

Harold said fuck under his breath. Right up to this exact moment he really held out hope he might get off.

Harold's lawyer immediately addressed the court,'Your honor are you prepared to honor our deal.'

'Yes indeed,' the Judge said. 'Son.' He sadly said looking directly at Harold, 'in order for you to continue raising your boys you can serve your sentence on weekends. Believe me son this brings me no joy. I must respect the precedent. The law is clear you've been found guilty of killing a man while trespassing on his property. Society insists for this you must pay a price. Or else there could be chaos. Even though most of us sitting here in this courtroom would probably of done the same as you if confronted with similar circumstances.'

The judge paused & sat back in his elegant leather covered chair & stared at a spot on the wall covered with a picture of the Queen in all her regal robes. Oh lady he thought this is really obscene. This father, like an avenging angel, saves his son from hideous torment & the only thing I can do is put the heroic soul in jail.

The judge sat back up straight,

'Is there anything, Son, you would like to say?'

Harold still standing squared his shoulders. His face took on a saintly sheen. His voice took on a grand godly tone,

'The law is an ass,' Harold said & sat back down in his chair.

The End

The Ballad of Stephen Truscott

Introduction

He had given her an innocent ride home on the handlebars of his bike after school. It was a beautiful sunny day. Seamless blue sky stretching on forever, over endless fields of hay. They laughed, giggled, were happy. Delighting in the freedom of youth. Innocent, not a care in the world. Gliding on gravel, laughing at the bumpy ride. Stephan Truscott was an athletic active fourteen-year-old boy. Lynn Harper was an innocent, sparkling, full of life twelve-year-old girl with golden brown hair.

In Clinton Ontario—a farming town just south of the Clinton Royal Canadian Air Force Base—later that same night, Lynn's body was found dead in a field-- raped & murdered. They arrested Stephan within 48 hours of finding Lynn. Stephan pleaded innocence to deaf ears as they led him away,

'She got into a Belaire with a chrome grill. I saw it when I waved goodbye.' Stephan said.

Three months later Stephan was sentenced to hang. Stephan Truscott was charged, convicted & sentenced to death for the murder of Lynn Harper when he was fourteen years old.

The year was 1959. The trial was in Goderich Ontario. A small Canadian town northwest of Toronto on the shores of beautiful Lake Huron. A lake well known for its gorgeous sunsets & its raging storms. Clinton was too small to have it's own courthouse. but that didn't stop the Clinton mob from being in attendance in Goderich when the judge read out the sentence. The verdict quickly read said—dead.

Stephan waited from September 1959 to January 1960 in the Huron County jail-- under sentence of death.

Stephan's sentence was eventually reprieved to life in prison. He was transferred to Kingston Penitentiary—for assessments. He was now fifteen.

From Kingston he went to Guelph where there was a juvenile detention centre & then, at sixteen, transferred to Collin's Bay Penitentiary just north of Toronto.

In 1967 Stephan's case was reviewed & his guilt reaffirmed. Stephan remained in Collin's Bay until paroled in 1969. Parole terminated by the National Parole Board in 1974.

Eventually Stephen won back his honor. In 2007 the Supreme Court of Ontario found Stephen innocent but still a suspect-- in the never solved case-- of the rape & murder, of Lynn Harper.

Canada abolished the death penalty in 1976. In large part due to Stephen's ordeal. Lynn's rape & murder—a tragic black molasses mist, which still shrouds the memory of truth.

Prologue

My innocence
the courts
    did eventually
        declare.
For me, it
brought
an end.

For that which had started
so innocently
    & ended
        with the death
            of my friend.
    This,
my story is being told
    for only one reason,
        to never forget Lynn Harper.
            Whose angelic spirit
                never
                    got the chance,
                to grow old.

Jim White

The Ballad of Stephen Truscott

It was September 1959, the guilty verdict from Justice Ferguson was read, it hit like a slow bullet straight into my head.

My mind became numb, my fear became real, it all came down to the mob's obsession to feed their revenge.
Truly honestly 'Why won't anyone believe me; I just didn't do it.'

My eyes sunk back in, shoulders slumped to the chair, tears wouldn't come down,
        I drowned awash in a dry despair.

+++++

I was four plus ten, when I was awakened in my bed. Harry ' Hank ' Sauer of the OPP shaking my head,
    To no avail twas no dream. Roughly stirred, handcuffs put immediately on hands behind my back.
    My frantic pleading in fear, futile to steeled ears.
    They threw me in the back of a police car & told me to shut up. My friend was dead & they said I did it.
    I couldn't understand what I was hearing. I sat stapled to the seat.

Why were they doing this to me, why is 'Doris 'my Mom screaming. Little did I know I was being taken to be tarred & feathered & simmered at the stake.

Events had happened for reasons beyond Stephan's imagination after he left Lynn.

Not the least was local revulsion inspiring a maniacal mob, intent on revenge.

Stephan was the target of the slobbering masses, who wouldn't stop until their lips were seared with bloody molasses.

So Stephan sat steaming in The Huron County Jail. Rosy red blood dripping from the nails of the satisfied self-righteous.

Lynn's body was soon buried, flooded with tears.

All of Clinton was at the funeral, except for Stephen.

———

The summer day had been one of those super ones, deep blue sky flowing on forever, an exploding sun. Me & Lynn were kids on our way home from school, never in our wildest dreams did we know life would be so cruel, so fleeting.

We were young, barely yet teens, time was not yet something we knew of.

How could this eternal pain have become so insane from something, so innocent-- so beautiful.

What Is death to a teen of tender years, life is supposed to stretch on for forever, joy & wonder.

*****

A tale of fools unfolded not suited to rationale ears. Unfortunately for Stephen, it cost him his freedom & Lynn's attacker never caught.

*****

Here I sit in their police car-- in a cold hardened way-- OPP Hank telling me again my friend is dead, & I am responsible. What in the world is he talking about?

They weren't going to let me go, I soon realized as they carted me off to jail, I had to steel myself to my reality.

All pretense of innocence was lost. In the court room they were intent on my conviction. No matter what the cost.

it was just all so unreal. I lost all perspective, becoming an aging angel watching down from above, at this display of rage.

It wasn't about Lynn any more it had become about me & that was so wrong.

Pain crying out in fear what what what were they doing.

I left this earthly space as I sat watching the guilty verdict on display.

Not wanting any part of this lynching. My mind becoming a woolen mist, my innocent presence dissolved. I was no longer part of this place, my body transcending this mortal existence my resolve devoid of mortal resistance.

For to remain part of this earthly domain was just too insane.

I heard in disbelief when the sentence was read, condemning my body to exit the human race.

To be hung by the neck till dead was my reality.

=====

But that's where they got It all wrong, as their bullet exploded my mindit touched a force, a hereto hidden source from somewhere deep within.

Awakening a spirit, it struck like a spark in a bucket of oil.

Later that night I gazed through window bars into the empty night, waiting to be hung. What does that even mean to a boy of fourteen.

I determined-- I was not to go passively by-- I would rage rage rage at this farcical injustice which was now intent on taking my life. I would strike like a Thor shattering their ignorance.

Lynn wherever you are I will fight to bring you peace.

And me back my life.

It was at this time that I-- Stephen Truscott-- was forced to become a man.

While the rest of those my age were fretting about the latest hairdo rage,

I languished four months in my cell waiting to die. I thought a lot about Lynn.

I found my need to stay alive was severe, for if I let up for but a second, I would be dead.

As Stephen's battle to avoid the noose took on a desperate mood, his peers were listening to Elvis & learning how to cut loose.

Stephen was not to feel innocent teenage dreams.

Stephen's lot was to fight for his life, angst & despair filled Stephen's fourteen-year-old reality.

Fighting the mob which was determined to see him hung.

Finally—after four months-- Stephen's sentence was commuted to life in prison, thanks a lot he thought, it sounds worse than the noose.

The Federal Government had stepped in & reigned in the mob from taking Stephen's life.

For the next ten years Stephen spent behind bars not a day went by when Stephen didn't think-- in some way-- of Lynn.

Jim White

^^^^^

Time wore on like it didn't even exist.

As his school chums were dancing the twist. Stephen was not even aware. That such things exist.

As his old friends were grooving to the new sixties scene all young Stephen could do was to try & confront a world intent on the obscene.

It was 1964.

The Beatles were coming to Toronto you read in the paper. Every teen age girl in Clinton would be going crazy. The Beatles were playing at Maple Leaf Gardens, two shows. Every Dad would be desperate for tickets for their teen-age daughter.

You'd have been no different.

You would have arranged to get four tickets through work. There would have been a list of favors & promises -- that would take you to your post-retirement days-- to make good on. Your golden brown-haired sixteen-year-old daughter & three of her very best friends would've been going to see the Beatles on Dad.

You'd drive them in. They'd phone when the concert was over. You'd go back & pick them up.

Driving in it'd seem every Dad living in Clinton had the same idea. Traffic would be insane along Highway 401. The scene dropping them off at the Gardens would be absolute chaos. Horns honking, lights flashing, teenagers everywhere. You'd get as close to the front as you could. Telling your sparkling full of life daughter to be careful & be safe, as you pulled up to the curb. Her friends & her in a frenzy. Feeding off the energy. Completely out of their minds with excitement.

'Ok here we are,' you'd say, them scrambling from the car.

'Thanks Dad, love you,' she'd say back.

234

'Don't forget to phone & I'll come & get ya,' you'd reply as she & her friends filtered into the crowd.

My baby, she'd drift off as in a dream, you'd well up in tears watching.

The phone call'd come around 11. Away you'd go. Back in. Finally finding them waiting right where you told them to be. They'd be totally exhausted-- like Chuvalo after he fought Ali-- at this very same Gardens in 63.

By the time you hit the highway they'd all be fast asleep. Oh the dreams they'd have had. You'd wake them all up when you got home & get them into the house. Them all going into the kitchen & getting themselves a snack. Getting their second wind & away they'd go up to your daughters' room & play Beatles records. Singing Beatle songs into the night. No matter to you, your day would be done. It was a day you would have cherished.

It would have been so beautiful.

=====

In the age of peace & love Stephan's tortured soul, cried out from a nine foot cell for some sanity from above.

Outside the world was changing at a hectic pace,

Behind bars Stephen's daily routine remained forever, tediously in one solitary place.

———

Some nights as the darkness sets in. Through the cracks in the wall I can smell the stars, & think of normal teenage things. Clothes, music, girls & cars as I drift off to sleep.

Images of dancing at a high school prom, scoring the winning goal, kissing a girl a vacant space in my dreams.

Abruptly awakened I'm brought back to the reality of my cell. Awoken by the sounds, of farting snoring whimpering cons, making sleep another forlorn task in this den of inequity.

Consciousness raises its ugly head full of horns & fangs.

I always awake afraid. Dreading my day. A free man caged.

Sucking in the foul fecal air, steeling myself as I stand to prepare for another day in the pen,

Thinking of Lynn, our two fates bound together for eternity like Venus to Mars.

*****

The year was 1966. The Clinton High School prom was being held at Castle Loma in Toronto. An historic edifice heralding the glory days of northern Ontario mining. A true castle --built in the 1920's-- very elegant, very fancy. 'A true reflection of Glasgow Castle back ome,' said the fabulously rich Scot who built it. A true prom fantasy land.

*****

You were in a dream. Your dress was gorgeous. Of course. Strapless, elegant, silk. Your golden-brown hair was in ringlets.

Your date was your football player boyfriend Steve-- whose family lived on the base. You'd been seeing Steve for about three years now. Your love life was still in its development stages. He pressured, but you wanted to wait until you were married or at least until it was on your own terms.

That night Steve picked you up in his father's old cream-colored Belair, with a chrome grill. The standard issue vehicle for officers at the base. Special night, special car.

Steve coming to the door. Your Dad letting him in, shaking his hand. Mom calling up & you coming down the stairs. You were a sparkling vision floating on air.

Your Dad took pictures, corsage on your wrist, Mom doing her best to hold back the tears.

Dad stoic. 'You two have a good time now,' he'd say. You went over & gave your Dad a long hard thank- you, teary-eyed hug.

Your Mom couldn't hold back & threw her arms around both you & your Father. You were a family once again.

'You're so beautiful,' Mom whispering in your ear, her eyes dripping tears.

Your Dad went over & grabbed Steve's hand, who had been politely, patiently waiting watching.

'You look after my little girl,' Dad'd say looking Steve straight in the eye. Quickly turning away, so Stephen wouldn't notice the tear on his cheek.

On the walk to the car, Steve would gush over how beautiful you looked. He was sincerely blown away. You were so full of life.

Your first stop was a pre-prom house party. All the cool kids were there. You had a sip of wine, Steve had a beer. You listened to The Beachboys, Beatles & The Rolling Stones on an incredible stereo system.

On the drive in to Castle Loma Steve talked endlessly about football, friends, red lights & how he was going to join the air force. Which made you feel close.

Castle Loma was lit up like Buckingham Palace at Christmas. You entered as the princess you were. You danced -- like Cinderella at the ball -- to the rock & roll sounds of The Ugly Ducklings.

By the end of the night, you were dancing softly on stars. Your feet tip toeing across venus pirouetting on mars.

There was an after party. You found yourself in a beautiful home, drinking coffee with liqueur. You were a queen holding court. Laughing, smiling, happy.

Steve would be in the kitchen having beers with the boys.

Time to go,

'You ok to drive,' you would ask.

'No problem', Steve would reply & smile. You giving him a quick little kiss.

You & Steve parked out front of your house, lingering longer than usual. You did a lot of smooching, letting him get to second base. You surprised yourself at how pleasant his fingers felt on your bare breasts.

As you straighten your dress, Steve opens the car door & walks you up to your porch. After a prolonged kiss—under a porchlit moon-- he retreats & you wave goodbye at the Belair. You turn-- in a mist-- seamlessly entering your house.

Dad would still be up. Watching the test pattern on the TV.

You'd bound over & flop down on the couch beside him. Falling asleep in his lap, him stroking your golden-brown hair.

In 1967 Stephen went to court again, only to be told they still thought he killed Lynn.

Stephan languished in his lonely cell, time sliding by till 1969.

Trapped in a strangling spell trying to transcend his eternal living hell.

Stephan lamenting a passing youth. What could have been a spirited time worthlessly spent.

I was caught up in a world which was caught up in me. I was well past revenge.

They all along trying to convince themselves that I was the one who murdered Lynn.

I survived.

My rage at the injustice, my courage to fight, saw me through.

I reinvented my life & lived.

&&&&&

Stephan's freedom the courts eventually did proclaim.

But those years which he spent melting in a cell will forever be in vain.

Nothing can ever take what was forever lost, back again.

&&&&&

Stephen is sitting on a swing. He's on his porch. He's of course much older now. It's dark. All the lights are out in his house. The family all gone to bed. The stars are out. Glistening a painted black canvas. Stephen staring deep looking for something. A special sparkle makes itself known. A twinkle of a smile wrinkles Stephan's gaze. A spark starts to descend. Softly settling on Stephen's swing. Snuggling up close as an ethereal mist. Stephen turns from his gaze & they hold hands. The spirit of Lynn settles in for the night. They finally share what was so tragically taken away.

Epilogue

We mourn the lost lives of innocent youth
Stephen's acquittal brought some relief.
But not until he had spent a lifetime fighting a perverted octopussing grip.
Lynn's angelic spirit never got the chance to dance. Never got justice.

CPSIA information can be obtained
at www.ICGtesting.com
Printed in the USA
BVHW040517171222
654185BV00002B/7